CROSSED IN LOVE

As Gabriel sat on the berth across from her in the small cabin, Yvette reminded herself he was just another Yankee.

"What's wrong?" Gabe asked her, concern furrowing his forehead.

She must think of him a Yankee, she admonished herself. Not as Gabriel Davis or as another young man wounded by this war.

"I am counting up the thousand reasons I should hate you," Yvette admitted.

She knew she ought to hurry him away. The hour had grown late, and propriety bespoke one danger if he lingered, her situation quite another. His gaze rose to meet hers, and then he glanced down in wonder at her hand, which she had placed atop his.

Yvette leaned forward, only half-realizing what she offered, only half-guessing that this blond Northerner would lean forward as well. Would raise his hands to grasp her arms gently. Would touch his lips so warmly against hers.

She felt as if a candle had kissed her. Its heat seared her without burning, singed her without pain. Never had she imagined any kiss could feel like this. His hand rose to stroke her hair, to cup her cheek as though she were something precious. She felt her mouth opening to him. She felt how easily, how eagerly, the rest of her would follow. . . .

PRAISE FOR *AGAINST THE ODDS*

"Gwyneth Atlee has done a masterful job of telling a very compelling story . . . of the Sultana's final journey as its backdrop . . . [and] leaving the reader satisfied with a tale well told. This is a must read for anyone who loves a good story."

—Jerry O. Potter,
author of
The Sultana Tragedy

AGAINST THE ODDS

Gwyneth Atlee

ZEBRA BOOKS
KENSINGTON PUBLISHING CORP.

http://www.zebrabooks.com

To my parents, William and Lois Swartz,
and to the memory of those who never made it
home that April

ACKNOWLEDGMENTS

Writing a historical novel based on an actual event requires a great deal of assistance from experts in the area. I would like to thank the many members of the Association of Sultana Descendants and Friends who shared their knowledge and the stories of their ancestors. Specifically, I'd like to thank Jerry O. Potter, author of the excellent history *The Sultana Tragedy* for his enthusiastic support and assistance; Gene Salecker, author of *Disaster on the Mississippi,* another outstanding volume; and Michael Johnson, Pam Newhouse, Ken Riggins, Joe W. Smith, and Helen Chandler.

Thanks also to John Dougan of the Memphis and Shelby County Library for his help in gathering research materials and to John and Kathy Haase for the Memphis hospitality. Kathleen Y'Barbo was also very helpful in researching the Creole culture of New Orleans and by faithfully reading the manuscript. Jack E. Custer of the *Egregious Steamboat Journal* was also of assistance.

I'd like to acknowledge my editor, Tomasita Ortiz, and my agent, Meredith Bernstein, for their encouragement and support of this project.

Thanks also, as always, to my husband, Mike, and son, Andrew, for offering their enthusiasm as well as a lot of quiet time in which to write.

Finally, I'd like to say thanks to the members of the Northwest Houston Chapter of RWA, Guida Jackson, Bill Laufer, and the Friday Nighters. But most especially, I could never do without my fabulous critique partners, the Midwives: Bobbi Sissel, Wanda Dionne, Betty Joffrion, and Linda Helman.

Prologue

April 28, 1865
Memphis, Tennessee

As he rested on the narrow hospital cot, Gabe could hear the whispered speculation about the impending investigation into who was to blame. But he barely listened, for he had little interest in the rumors of a Confederate bomb planted near the boilers or in the whispers about bribes passed between Union army officials and the *Sultana*'s captain.

Some part of him realized that perhaps he ought to care whether the steamboat had carried too much weight or had been pushed to an excessive speed, whether the destruction was intentional or the result of gross stupidity. But that part of his mind felt separated, as if it had been walled off behind something lead-gray and impenetrable. None of it really mattered now.

Only the people mattered: the soldiers catapulted from their sleep into the flooded Mississippi, the panicked passengers clutching and then overwhelming the same sinking wooden plank, a woman shrieking frantically as five crewmen—her own husband among them—abandoned her in a small boat used to sound the channels.

Yes, the people mattered, and certain people mattered to him even more. One woman and three men. A tiny fraction of the hundreds, perhaps even thousands, aboard the overcrowded vessel. But so was a heartbeat a tiny portion of what made up a man. Tiny but so crucial, something that he couldn't live without.

He covered his eyes with bandaged hands, as if that action might blot out the pain of all that he had seen. But darkness afforded him no mercy, for memory is made up of far more than a man sees. As he lay beneath a crisp white hospital sheet, his body trembled with the smells of what had happened, the acrid odors of burning wood and coal, the sickly, meatlike stench of roasting flesh. And even more insufferable were the sounds that rose up like specters from a thousand moonlit graves: the muttered prayers and curses, the wrenching pleas and screams—all nearly drowned out by the almost deafening explosion, by the thunder on the river, in the waning days of war.

Chapter One

America has no north, no south, no east, no west. The sun rises over the hills and sets over the mountains, the compass just points up and down, and we can laugh now at the absurd notion of there being a north and a south. We are one and undivided.

—Sam Watkins,
First Tennessee Infantry, CSA

Four days earlier
Monday, April 24, 1865
Vicksburg, Mississippi

Yvette hurried through the streets of Vicksburg. Nothing about the wounded town encouraged one to linger, from the buildings scarred by Union shells to the faces that remembered the pride of holding out against the long siege and the shame of their ultimate surrender. Unlike her New Orleans, which painted on its bravest face, the citizens of Vicksburg wore their pain for all to see. She saw in it the defiant stiffness of the backs of women as they shopped and in the sullen expressions of men as they paused to mutter among themselves.

Had her errand not been so urgent, she would have remained hidden aboard her stateroom on the steamboat, as she had the past two days. She wasn't at all certain she had not been followed, and if that devil Captain Russell approached her here, she would not know where to run. Her discomfort turned to distaste as a horde of shabby-looking men shuffled past the sidewalk toward the wharf. Bedraggled men and boys who wore the cursed Union blue.

Her distaste became horror when she heard the sergeant's order.

"Make for the *Sultana,* boys. She's the one to take you home!"

The *Sultana!* The same steamboat she had used to flee her New Orleans home. And though she'd left it long enough to risk a quick trip to the telegraph office, it was the very steamer she had no choice but to reboard.

Two old men not far from her stood talking, and she couldn't help but overhear their words.

"Them's those pris'ners goin' back North. Pris'ners of war, sent here from Andersonville, Cahaba, and the like. And good riddance to 'em, I say." The man jabbed the air with a walking stick as if it were a saber. Beneath his thick white brows, his eyes glittered with hate. "If we'd shot every Yank we'd caught, we woulda won this war."

"Looks to me like we *was* killin' these—the slow way. You ever seen the likes of that?" The second man's white beard stopped wagging as he gestured toward the soldiers.

This time, Yvette saw beyond the hateful uniforms, noted the shockingly thin limbs and sunken cheeks. Slow horror rose like gorge as she realized that the South—her own people—had starved them. She'd been so righteous in her fury over the North's invasion of her homeland, its occupation of her city, that she'd never given credence to the reports of Confederate sins.

And surely, this was sinful. . . . She turned her gaze from the pathetic wretches, but not before she felt the waves of hatred and suspicion emanating from those men, which was shared by the people around her on the street and threatened to erupt at any moment into jeers or even violence.

She wished in vain she might forget the ticket she held for the *Sultana* and that these last two weeks had ever happened. She ached to flee this tense scene and take the first steamboat heading southward—and home. New Orleans thrashed restlessly in her memory with the voices of her noisy family, the dancing of her fingers on her piano's keyboard to accompany defiant lyrics, the delicious scents of jasmine blooming in the courtyard, of café au lait and bread pudding. All of them together formed a mélange so sweetly painful she could cry. But New Orleans was as lost to her as poor Marie—and her own good name.

Turning her thoughts from home, Yvette once more focused on the hostile glares of the Union soldiers, and the idea occurred to her that these men blamed her—and all Southerners—not only for their hardships but for the murder of their president as well.

Our president, she reminded herself. Lee had weeks ago surrendered, and the last few bands of Confederate stragglers were stacking up their weapons. Lincoln had been their president as well.

But now he presided over no one but the dead.

Of course, Yvette realized that the mob of Yankee soldiers wouldn't see her as the actual assassin, but in the wake of Lincoln's murder, all Southerners were suspect. And if they ever learned of the charges against her—especially if they learned it involved the death of one of their own officers—it would be all too easy to imagine their summoning the strength of outrage to string her up—even in the shadow of the steamboat meant to take them home.

"Remember Old Abe! The damned Rebs killed him, too!" they would cry. "Hang every murderer among 'em!"

Yvette shuddered, and her knees grew weak as she pictured the noose, the very same one she had fled shortly after her arrest.

She crossed herself in an attempt to banish the horrifying image. But the gesture did nothing to ease her foreboding until the prisoners' footsteps faded as they passed.

She wished she did not have to follow, that instead her steps could take her somewhere other than downhill, in the direction of the broad brown Mississippi. Before Marie, she would have felt relief at the sight of the familiar river. But today it seemed swollen with menace even more than spring floodwaters. It pressed impatiently against the levee, as if in eagerness to wash away the taint of war.

Still carrying the delicate burden of her hand-basket, Yvette crossed a gangway that led onto the wharf boat, a floating platform used to load passengers onto waiting steamboats. As she glimpsed the muddy water beneath the wooden span, she reminded herself that it would also flow past home.

I'd jump in and swim there for a Hard Times token and a cup of good New Orleans brew. But no one offered either. Instead, she approached the mass of waiting Yankee soldiers, wishing she could become invisible for long enough to blend with the few female passengers aboard, then disappear into her stateroom.

If she had more money, she'd demand a change of boats. However, for the first time in her life, she was forced to endure the shameful necessity of counting every penny. She'd have to make the best of it. There simply was no other choice.

Steeling herself, she drew closer to a knot of soldiers near the line's end. She needed information, and there was no one else to ask.

"Excuse me." Her heart pounded as she spoke. Surely these men had been captured all over the South months before. Surely none would recognize her from New Orleans. Even so, she fought to control the quaver in her voice. "Would you know where the ticketed passengers are boarding?"

She wondered if they recognized New Orleans in her speech, if they would pelt her with crude remarks—or worse. But she needn't have worried. The moment the ragged men noticed her, those who wore caps snatched them from their heads. Those who didn't made little bows, though some of the thinner ones moved stiffly, like skeleton men whose bones might tumble into pieces with the effort.

"Pretty gal like you can have my spot in line any-time," one offered with a grin. His eyes glittered brightly, but several missing teeth spoiled the effect.

"Mine—or no man's!" challenged a man whose neck jutted from the collar of a dark blue shirt many sizes too large for his starved body.

Several others hooted laughter or their own claims at his boast. From somewhere nearby a coarse whistle heated Yvette's face with embarrassment. She was dreadfully sure that rosy patches now splotched both cheeks and the pale flesh exposed at her neckline. Pulling her ivory shawl higher, she tried to screen at least some of her thrice-accursed blush from view.

A broad-shouldered young sergeant she'd seen ear-lier strode forward. Healthy and well muscled, he looked immense compared to the former prisoners.

"Paying passengers to the front of the line."

His voice sounded crisp and officious, reminding Yvette of the hated Union soldiers who had so long occupied New Orleans, especially the one who had destroyed her life.

When she stepped away from the line, he grasped her arm and dropped his voice. "You'll need to find another boat, miss. These boys have been locked up a long time. I'm afraid they may prove too rowdy for your taste."

She jerked her arm away from his too-familiar touch and glared into his flat brown eyes. Ignoring the mew-ing that came from her handbasket, she pulled a slip of paper from her reticule. "This ticket says *Sultana,* and I mean to reboard her."

* * *

Gabe couldn't shake the feeling that something meant to keep him in the South. Maybe since Lincoln had been murdered, the Confederates would take heart and try to drag them all back to their hellish prisons. In that case, they could leave his body here, because now that he'd tasted freedom, he'd make them shoot him before he returned to that stinking cesspit in Andersonville.

Or maybe it would be a sniper's bullet that kept him from Ohio. Probably it was too late for the Confederacy to resurrect an army, but still there were scattered soldiers who refused to admit defeat. The Union guards escorting the prisoners home had been posted not only to keep order but to watch the wooded shorelines for telltale rifle barrels, maybe even cannon.

More than likely, though, it wouldn't be the Rebels who left him dead here in the South. It would be the men of his own company, once they realized their last attempt to kill him had somehow fallen short. Just barely, anyway, Gabe remembered, thinking of the ambush his former comrades had sent him into.

"Got no use for a goddamn coward." Their judgment was a heavy stone cast into a pool of darkness, the ringlike ripples of it spreading ever outward, still troubling Gabe's waters despite the passing months.

He'd never imagined that some from his old unit had been captured, never dreamed that while he'd languished in Georgia, they'd been imprisoned in Cahaba in Alabama. When he'd spotted them in the release camp at Vicksburg, his heart had nearly thumped its way clear of his chest. He'd managed to avoid them, but here, aboard the steamboat, it would be much harder.

So hard to silence his protest. Hard but necessary. They'd no more listen now than ever.

In line on the wharf boat, he tried to keep his back to everyone at once. To distract himself from the threat at hand, he started Food Talk with his Andersonville friends.

"My first meal home's gonna be sweet peas with new potatoes and a beefsteak thicker than your hand. With onions piled on top. So many onions, you can barely see the plate."

He felt the ritual begin to work its familiar magic and the tension start to ebb out of his body. Left over from the darkest days of their starvation, the Food Talk fed their spirits, though it could do nothing to ease their bodies' ever-present hunger.

Gabe wondered if years after Appomattox, Food Talk's power would stay with them, faint compensation for the memories of Andersonville. When he looked at his three friends, he saw those bitter months in their gauntness and fatigue, in the oozing sores that had scabbed over and promised lasting scars. And then there were the deeper scars, the ones that did not show.

"Too early yet for sweet peas," Jacob Fuller told him, already reverting to thinking like a farmer, though he'd spent recent years shoeing horses for the cavalry. "And I'm more partial to chicken. Mama'll fix two fat hens, and I aim to eat them both."

"Not if I don't beat you to 'em," Zeke swore. Though he had to lean against his brother for support, some of the pain in his eyes dimmed with the familiar game. "And I mean to wash them down with a whole day's milking."

"Bacon." Captain Seth adjusted the cracked spectacles he always wore. Behind them, his gaze turned toward the line to board the steamer. Several men ahead of them were pushing for a spot. Some of them had looked half-dead a few days earlier, but the orders to board the boat home had revived their fighting spirit. Though none of them were Seth's responsibility, he'd take charge if the need arose.

Captain Seth, though only thirty, had been a professor before the war. Mathematics and logic at some little private college that Gabe had never heard of. But Seth's education had stuck with him in the calm way he invoked order out of chaos, in how he appealed to a man's sense.

"Bacon for my breakfast," Seth continued, watching as guards restored the peace, "with some thick chops for a snack, more eggs than a frog spawns, and biscuits—"

"Without your day's meat ration squirmin' in them. No more worm castles for us!" Gabriel interrupted, and every man within earshot cheered the end of infested, teeth-dulling army hardtack, though a month ago, all of them would have fought for the chance to eat it. Some who hadn't heard Gabe still joined in the cheering out of high spirits at the thought of going home.

Before Andersonville, Gabriel would never have considered interrupting an officer, even for a jest. But in the past six months, he had learned that to Capt. Seth Harris, rank meant less than the brotherhood that the four men formed to survive.

In spite of his friend's rank, Gabe had admitted what he'd done to Seth and Seth alone. Gabe frowned, remembering how hard it had been to relate the events of six months earlier, even after all the men had shared. Deliberately, he withheld the details out of fear that Seth would think he was attempting to excuse his cowardice.

But as always, his trust in Seth had been well placed. Without a word of reproach, the captain had told Gabe, "Better stay with us, then. There's no sense in making it this far, only to get killed by a bunch of Ohio hotheads. You can use Hale's name for the roles so you can sit with us. God knows, the poor devil won't be needing it again."

Weakened by a bout of typhoid in the camp, Lucas Hale had perished on the difficult rail journey from Georgia to Mississippi. His was only one of the bodies left behind for burial whenever the train stopped, a chain of dead Union men laid like new track across the shattered South.

Gabe had hesitated to use a dead man's name, but in the end, he'd had to agree with Seth's logic. Borrowing Hale's identity seemed a small price to pay for getting home in one piece.

The line inched forward, as slow as every other step of their release. As they moved toward the steamboat, Gabe wondered once more if the reception he'd so long imagined would in any way resemble the homecoming he'd receive or if his father had already learned of his disgrace.

Maybe that was part of why he sensed that something meant to keep him in the South. Maybe some part of him knew better than to return home.

Best not to think on it now. Better, instead, to dream about that steak. When he concentrated, he could almost smell the steaming onions and taste the mouthwatering juices, could almost—

"What the hell's the holdup?" Jacob Fuller demanded. Jacob's impatience made him supremely unsuited for the ranks of the U.S. Army. But as far as Uncle Sam had been concerned, his skill with horses outweighed his temperament. He adjusted an ill-fitting kepi cap atop his dark brown curls and shifted his thin frame to ease the burden of his brother.

Captain Seth moved to help keep Zeke on his feet. Gabriel would take a turn next, for Zeke could barely walk with his ankle so swollen. Gabe wondered once again if his friend would eventually lose the leg—or even die.

No, it wasn't to be imagined. Not after all that they'd endured. Zeke would heal with the tender care and good food he'd get back home in Indiana. His brother, Jacob, would see to it with the same stubbornness that he applied to every other challenge.

Without warning, the sight of the two brothers together jerked Gabe back, the way it often did of late, to an image of his own younger brother in the moments before he'd plunged through the river ice. Matthew had been laughing then, for he'd just surprised Gabe with a well-aimed snowball. He'd been laughing in his final moments. That had to count for something.

Hoots and whistles dragged Gabe back to the present. Someone yelled a crude remark before Seth ordered him to pipe down. Gabriel craned his neck to see what all the commotion was about.

And that was when he saw her, the most beautiful young woman he had ever set eyes on. She looked almost impossibly small and delicate compared to the huge man beside her. A bonnet hid much of her hair, but still the sunshine gleamed across the blackness of those spots that were exposed. *Like the glossy feathers of a raven's wing,* he thought. Though she'd drawn her wrap high out of modesty, he noticed the swell of a full bosom and the narrow waist below it. Lower still, the violet dress flared slightly, as if she had eschewed the huge hoops many ladies favored.

When she turned in his direction, he saw how the violet brought out the green that flecked her light brown eyes. Some called that color hazel, he remembered.

Jacob's elbow jabbed at his ribs. "You're gonna catch a fly, Gabe. Better close that mouth now 'fore she reckons bein' a prisoner of war's turned you into a drooler."

Ignoring his friend, Gabe stared as she pulled away from the guard who strode beside her.

"My ticket says *Sultana,* and I mean to reboard her." Her voice sounded stubborn, defiant—and deeply Southern.

Gabe's stomach turned, hearing that hateful accent coming from those pretty, bow-shaped lips. Lips that would no doubt sing the praises of the men who'd packed them into that tiny prison camp and watched them starve like dogs, that would relieve the bruised feelings of some young man who'd just laid down his arms.

"I'm only thinking of your safety and comfort," the sergeant told her. "A delicate young woman should not be exposed to such—"

She cut him off as he reached for her arm once more. "I'll thank you to keep your hands to yourself, sir."

She not only made the last word sound like *suh;* she said it like a swear word.

This section of the crowded wharf boat, noisy but

a moment before, fell quiet as men strained to hear
the altercation. The day had been long and tiring
enough that they welcomed any chance of a diversion,
especially one featuring a pretty girl.

Beside him, Gabe heard Zeke chuckle at the boldness of her tone. Abused as they'd been by the Confederates, the former prisoners wouldn't normally stand
for hearing a Southern woman dish up contempt.
But the sergeant had spent the afternoon making
enemies, ordering the men to "march sharp"
through the streets of Vicksburg. Before they'd left
the camp, he'd spent what seemed like hours strutting
up and down their line with much impatient huffing.
He'd taken special pleasure, for some reason, in
harassing the injured men to stay on their feet so as
not to "hold up" the immobile line.

If Gabe hadn't been so eager to avoid drawing
attention to himself, he might have knocked down
the pretentious bastard half an hour ago. He hoped
this young shrew gave him the tongue-lashing of his
life.

"And as for your advice," the woman continued,
glaring up at the sergeant, "I'm certain these young
men are far more interested in returning home than
in disturbing a lady passenger."

The sergeant made as if to reach for her again,
but the young woman turned her back on him and
continued walking toward the gangway.

"Got no use for a goddamn coward." The words rang
in Gabe's ears, pushing him the way it always did,
beyond the good sense of Captain Seth's collegiate
logic.

Recklessly, Gabe stepped out of line into the sergeant's path as the man tried to hurry after her. The guard plowed into him.

Thin and weak from his incarceration, Gabe fell with a grunt, banging an elbow hard against the wooden pier.

"Watch where you're going, idiot!" the guard demanded. Clearly annoyed, he yanked Gabe roughly to his feet.

Rubbing at his throbbing arm, Gabe made sure he blocked the man's progress. His right hand had already formed a fist.

The young woman turned at the sound, then hesitated.

"Are you all right?" she asked Gabe.

Those beautiful green-flecked eyes unnerved him, enough so his right hand unconsciously relaxed. Her smooth, unblemished skin, with its glow of good health, contrasted so completely with the faces of prisoners exposed for long months to the elements that he could not take his eyes from her. Yet within moments, he felt his own face heat with shame for what he'd done—was *doing*—siding with the enemy against a fellow Union soldier.

But like the boy who'd caused him so much grief, she refused to fit into the narrow mold his mind constructed to cast the Rebel foe. No matter how he tried, he saw nothing past his strong attraction to her.

When finally he found his tongue, he spoke to the sergeant. "Let her come aboard. She'll be safe. My—my friends and I will see to it."

Gabe offered her a weak smile, for he felt too agitated by this fresh evidence of his disloyalty to speak directly to her.

The sergeant's laughter mocked him. "You will,

will you? Well, since she's ignored my good advice, then your pitiful offer may be the best she can do."

He marched away, his stiff shoulders and swift stride marking his profound irritation. Gabriel supposed he'd made another enemy.

The young woman leveled her devastating gaze on him once more. "You never answered me. Were you hurt when that brute knocked you over?"

She cared what he felt. How long had it been since he'd last heard concern in a woman's voice, seen it in her eyes? Could it be possible a Southern woman might see him as anything other than a marauder?

She smiled politely, but those hazel eyes looked wary, warning him she felt as ambivalent as did he.

"Quiet, aren't you?" she asked. When he failed to respond, she raised one dark brow. "Well, congratulations, then. You're the first Yankee I've met who wasn't eager to confer his opinions as if they were gifts from on high. For that, sir, I am ever in your debt."

Her eyes glittered brightly with intelligence—and something bitter, too. His boyish fantasies dissolved into a haze of caution.

She masked her expression with good manners and dropped him a belated curtsy. "And I also must thank you for troubling yourself to speak up for a stranger. And for stepping out in front of that man, if I'm to judge."

At last, he found his tongue. "No, miss. Thank *you* for that. I've been looking forward to the chance to trouble him for the past hour."

The bright notes of her laughter hung sparkling in the warm spring air. "I hope you'll be thanking me still when the bruises start to form."

The basket on her arm shifted, and Gabe could swear he heard it meow.

"Lafitte's impatient for his milk," she explained. "I'd best go see if I can find some."

She patted his hand with her gloved fingers. "It was a pleasure, Mr. . . . ?"

Mister. Not soldier, not private, not damned Yank. Since the war's end, heaven was opening to him a little at a time. He basked in the sound of that civilian title, the same way he'd reveled in the humble luxuries of a filling meal and a uniform devoid of vermin.

"Gabriel Davis," he finished, too warmed by the glow to lie. Surprising himself, he ducked his head and added, "at your service, Miss . . . ?"

At her hesitation, he cursed himself. In thanking him, she'd offered only the barest of civility. Did he really think that interfering with the sergeant was an act so noble she'd forget he was the enemy, not to mention a young soldier? Before his embarrassment overwhelmed him, she answered.

"Miss Eve Alexander." Her gaze slid away from him, as if she hoped that would end this awkward conversation.

The high-pitched mewing grew more plaintive. To Gabe, it sounded like a kitten. He hoped she didn't open up the lid. Kittens might be cute enough, but he never could get past the fact they all turned into cats.

She peered behind her, as if she suspected the sergeant—or someone more unpleasant—might come back. Something near the line's end made her dark brows draw together and erased the last hint of her smile.

"I must be going, Mr. Davis." Without waiting for

a reply, she turned toward the *Sultana* and hurried up the gangway leading from the wharf boat to the steamer.

"Good-bye, Miss Alexander," Gabe called after her.

"Romance blossoms . . ." Zeke batted his eyelashes and affected a swoon against Seth, who still supported him.

". . . and then is nipped as if by a cruel frost," his brother continued. Jacob grinned. "Just as well, Gabe. What's some Southern woman gonna see in you but a calf-eyed, half-starved Yankee—"

"American," Gabriel corrected. "I'm not in the least interested, but if I were, I'd tell you she's not a Rebel any more than I'm a Yankee now. We're both Americans. Our side just won a war to prove it."

Seth snorted and slowly shook his head. "Tell that to Mary Lincoln, Gabe. Tell that to John Wilkes Booth."

After a brief trip to the main deck to fetch a bit of food and some milk for her kitten, Yvette hurried toward her stateroom. She paused for one last moment to watch the late afternoon light dance on the living water. An image came to her: Marie, hair waving in its currents, limbs as loose as her long tresses, flesh as pallid as the moon. Yvette's stomach plummeted in response.

Turning away from both the river and the unexpected jolt of grief, she stepped inside and secured the door of her cramped but well-appointed stateroom.

Reclining on the lower berth, she whispered, *"Dieu merci!"* With Marie's fate fresh on her mind, death had become both real and threatening. But behind this door, at least for the moment, she felt the beast at bay.

She never should have gone ashore in the first place. If she'd kept to the sanctuary of her stateroom, no one would have seen her. She'd taken a terrible risk, drawing attention to herself among all those Yankee soldiers. The whole accursed lot would remember the rare sight of an unescorted young woman, even if she were as unfashionable as a 'gator's snout without her bell-shaped crinoline. Arguing with that petty tyrant of a sergeant had only made her more conspicuous, but unfortunately, it could not have been avoided. She had to hurry northward, and her ticket said *Sultana*. She had no intention of explaining to that Yankee that she had little money left to change her plans.

Another impatient mew reminded her to unlatch Lafitte's wicker prison. The black-and-white kitten nearly exploded from the handbasket, then vaulted from the lower berth to a single chair and onto the empty washbasin. When he careened into the water pitcher, Yvette leapt up and grabbed it just in time to prevent it from falling.

It had been a mistake to take him out of the stateroom, she belatedly realized. She'd had the foolish notion to find a sunny patch of grass to let him play for a few minutes, but nothing about Vicksburg had encouraged her to linger.

As the kitten tumbled toward the floor to begin another circuit, Yvette scooped him up into her arms. Moving to the chair, she settled him on her lap.

"You'll have to make do, the same as I must, little scoundrel." As she scolded him, she scratched his white chin with a finger, and he erupted into such loud purring that she forgot her fears and laughed.

She could sympathize with his relief at being freed. For the last few days, this stateroom had felt exactly like a handbasket to her. She'd had to switch from her beautiful hoop skirt to a more practical silhouette just to maneuver her way past the narrow set of bunks.

That was one reason she'd risked leaving the *Sultana,* but not the only one. The delay in their departure had allowed her time to send a telegram to alert Uncle André in St. Louis that she was on her way, seeking assistance. She closed her eyes and tried to focus on her father's brother, a prosperous attorney she hadn't seen since she was nine or ten. She pictured a dark-haired, balding man, but the features of his face refused to focus. When she concentrated, she had an impression of deep and generous laughter. She prayed that she remembered right.

Heaven help her if she was wrong about her uncle or if her message had told him too little to be of help. Or worse yet, if it said too much, in the horrifying event that it was intercepted. She'd worked on it for hours, packing what she hoped was hidden meaning into every syllable. But if anyone could decipher desperation, it would be her brilliant uncle. His letters alone proved him a master of nuance. And having left New Orleans so many years before over some quarrel with Grandmère Régine, who ruled over her descendants like a tyrant queen, Uncle André would not care how the rest of the family had shunned her—or so Yvette most desperately hoped.

She risked everything on the chance that he would once more ignore *Grandmère,* who had cursed her bitterly. That he would help her clear her name and lay the charge of murder where it belonged instead, at Capt. Darien Russell's feet.

Yvette put the kitten on the floor beside the saucer of milk she'd begged off the cook. With the haughty daintiness of a debutante, Lafitte dipped in one white paw, then tasted before deciding it was fresh enough to suit his palate.

Yvette picked at the plate of food she'd brought with her. But the bread turned to tasteless sawdust in her mouth, so difficult to swallow that she soon gave up the task. Instead, she worried that she had truly spotted Captain Russell near the end of the line of prisoners. She wrapped her arms around herself and shuddered at the thought of facing him now, before Uncle André could protect her. At the thought of looking at his hands, which had choked the life out of Marie.

"No," she whispered to herself. She couldn't face him. She struggled to convince herself that the bearded man had been only another soldier, like that presumptuous sergeant. Just another Yankee who imagined he had the God-given right to order her about. One was little better than the next, and all of them so infernally smug in their victory. Every last one of them so . . .

Perhaps not. There *had* been that shy young soldier from among the prisoners. His dark blond hair had been neatly barbered and his whiskers freshly shaved, as if a civilian volunteer had wished to blunt his family's shock at seeing him return so thin. She recalled the pale blue of his eyes, which still looked as innocent as any farm boy's despite the horrors that they must have witnessed these past few years. She smiled at the memory of how he groped for words. *Maman* would have condemned her with the suggestion that she chattered more than enough to suit them both.

What was she imagining? He'd been a kind man, handsome even, but he was still a Yankee. For all she knew, he was the one who'd shot off Pierre's right arm. Remembering her eldest brother, she felt traitorous for thinking well of anyone who'd ever worn the Union blue.

As she'd learned from harsh experience, she must never for a moment let her guard down. Desperation had driven her to hide among her enemies, who would catch her if she couldn't curb her wayward tongue and kill her if they only knew the charges Captain Russell had contrived.

No matter what happened, she mustn't ever suppose any Yankee soldier was her friend. No matter how he'd stood up for her. No matter how compelling his thin face.

Pushing aside the unsettling thoughts, Yvette took out her rosary and began to chip away at the almost hopeless task of absolution for her sins.

Chapter Two

If one army drank the joy of victory, and the other the bitter draught of defeat, it was a joy moderated by the recollection of the cost at which it had been purchased, and a defeat mollified by the consciousness of many triumphs.
—*New York Times*, 1865

Capt. Darien Russell could barely look at the photograph of Marie without remembering his hands on her delicate white throat, without picturing the livid bruises they'd left there. He liked his ugliest memory of the most beautiful of women tamped down deep, a dead seed pressed into barren soil. So he kept his eyes averted as he showed the small portrait to the soldiers and wished again that he had one of Yvette instead.

He recalled the sisters' differences too well. Most importantly, Marie revered him. She never would have considered making him an object of ridicule. They also differed physically. Whereas Marie had been refined and elegant, her youngest sibling had the fiery eyes of a tigress set in an angel's face. Smaller and infinitely more vocal, Yvette resembled the graceful Marie only in coloring and in the long, thick lashes that provoked so many admiring glances.

That resemblance was enough, however, for the third man he asked recalled a pretty, black-haired young woman boarding the steamboat minutes before. If he'd had any doubts at all as to the passenger's identity, the man dispelled them when he laughed about the way she had dressed down the sergeant trying to keep order among the men crowding on board.

The little hellcat already had men laughing at another Union soldier whose only crime was helping to keep order. The sergeant should be grateful she hadn't brought with her a piano, her weapon of choice.

Yvette had never known the meaning of the word comportment. Darien well remembered how Marie had fretted over the girl's future in society. Their father's family background and his standing as a well-to-do coffee broker assured all of the Augerons invitations wherever better families gathered in the Crescent City. But it would take more than money to blunt the cutting edges of Yvette's razor wit. Marie had been tight-lipped about the cause of the girl's disgrace, but Darien had finally coaxed from her some nonsense about a stingingly acerbic little ditty she'd sung at a society soiree.

"Surely, such youthful mischief is not sufficient cause for social death," he'd told Marie. He'd been foolish enough at that time to imagine the girl harmless.

"Oh, I'm certain that the song might have been eventually forgiven if not for the unfortunate verse concerning Madame LaFarge's predilection for the *services* of handsome young gardeners." Marie's dark gaze flicked away, as if she found the subject too distasteful for discussion.

She continued, anger coloring her words. "It's bad enough Yvette is so extreme in her opinions, but Papa wouldn't force her to apologize. He's always spoiled her no matter how *Maman* feared for her character. Papa may have smoothed things over this time, but she's learned so little from it. If she does not begin conducting herself as a lady, no one in polite society will have a thing to do with her."

Darien wondered how they'd react if they learned that the proper Marie was keeping company with him, a Union officer—worse yet, an aide to both General Banks and, before him, the hated Butler, who had made such bitter enemies when he occupied New Orleans. At Marie's insistence, they'd been extremely careful. She'd been fond of saying that Lucifer might have regained heaven if he'd been more discreet.

Apparently, despite the fact that her meddling had cost Marie her life, Yvette hadn't yet learned the lesson of discretion. No matter. Darien meant to bridle the girl's tongue once and for all. Even if he had to steal aboard this crowded steamer, the vicious little hellion was going to share her sister's fate.

"I think you're gaining back some weight," Gabriel lied. If anything, Zeke felt even lighter. Or perhaps, with his returning strength, the younger Fuller brother was less a burden to Gabe's arms.

"In two months' time, I aim to get so fat I'll bust my buttons." Zeke tried to grin, but pain contorted his expression. His cut and swollen ankle, when they'd checked this morning, had darkened ominously. But Zeke refused to let either his brother or his friends call for a doctor out of fear he'd be left behind in the hated South. Like the rest of them, he told himself that time spent home would erase all traces of their incarceration.

Sadness washed over Gabe on a dark tide of misgivings. Zeke's bones felt so close to the surface that his shoulder blades ground into Gabe's supporting arm.

Gabe forced himself to agree with his friend's boast and tried to make himself believe in the future Zeke imagined. Zeke grown fat and healthy, married to some apple-cheeked farm girl. Zeke, in later years, father to a slew of children with the same green eyes, the same mop of unruly, straight brown hair. Maybe he'd be a prosperous businessman, organizing horse races at some Indiana fairgrounds with the same good humor with which he'd set up louse races for the entertainment of his fellow prisoners. It could be . . . because it *must*. Surely, a just God would see that Zeke deserved that much. Surely he'd fought hard and suffered plenty for one life. All of them had except, perhaps, for him, Gabe thought.

Zeke was already the thinnest and weakest among their group the day they had departed Andersonville. Even so, he'd been in high spirits when they'd left the Georgia prison camp. They all had, certain that the worst was now behind them. None had been prepared for the harrowing journey from Georgia to the Mississippi River. The tracks, torn up during the fighting, had been in such poor repair that the train derailed three times along one short stretch in Alabama. On the last occasion, their crowded railcar had overturned. Several men broke limbs made fragile by starvation, but at first it seemed that none of their group had been hurt. Only later, when he could not walk the final stretch to Union-held Vicksburg, would Zeke at last admit his injury.

Gabe didn't blame him. After all they'd been through together, he'd rather haul Zeke's half-starved body clear to Indiana than leave him behind to recover in Alabama or Mississippi. The war might be over, but Seth was right. Confederate resentment hadn't died. No telling what sort of "tender care" an injured Yankee might receive.

"Let's grab a spot right here before the best ones are all taken," Seth suggested, raising his voice to carry over the sounds of clanging metal.

Gabriel guessed that he was thinking of the difficulty of getting Zeke up the main stairs, where many of the other Indiana cavalrymen were heading. Also, this central section near the boilers would be warm at night, something that would especially benefit the injured man.

But Zeke shook his head.

"That banging might sound like a symphony to a farrier," he began, referring to Jacob's career shoeing horses, "but that racket will drive the rest of us insane."

Jacob rounded a corner and shouted a question Gabe couldn't hear. In a few moments, he returned.

"They're working on a boiler," he told the others.

"Might be pounding on it a couple hours more. I say we should go up with the others."

Zeke nodded. "Let's go on up, Jake. If we have to be stuck in one spot for three or four days, I want to sit where I can watch the South get farther distant and God's country come into view."

When he put it that way, all of them agreed. Jacob moved to his brother's left and helped Gabe carry him upstairs. Halfway there, they had to rest.

Gabe noticed the strained expression on Jacob's face. "What's wrong?"

"Must have been those extra rations I swiped when you boys weren't lookin'. I'm getting too brawny for my big brother to carry anymore," Zeke joked, making a bare swell of a muscle with his thin right arm.

Jacob shook his head and grinned. "Hell, Zeke, I've been carryin' you your whole sorry life. I'm not about to start complaining now. It's only that—"

"What?" Gabe urged. Despite his jest, Jacob's face looked grim.

"Come have a look yourself."

"What's the trouble?" Seth asked.

Jacob shook his head. "I'm not sure I like the looks of this. Probably nothing, though. How about if Gabe and I go check? Zeke needs to get off his feet, though."

"All right," Captain Seth said, but he didn't look too happy. Knowing Seth, he probably wasn't certain they'd stay out of trouble without his preaching good sense in their ears. "But come and get me if you need me. Zeke and I will find a spot for us up top."

Seth took over the task of supporting Zeke, and Gabe followed Jacob. As they passed several soldiers wearing the insignia of an Ohio infantry unit, Gabe scanned the area, hoping to God he wouldn't be spotted by anyone who knew him. The Ohio contingent of prisoners must be settling on this deck. Whatever Jacob wanted, Gabe prayed it would be quick.

The pair returned to where two men were hammering a patch onto a boiler. One man paused in his pounding to look up at Jacob.

"Something troubling you, soldier?"

"Just interested," Jacob told him, but Gabriel read concern in his friend's expression.

Gabriel glanced at the boiler, then looked back over his shoulder.

"Don't worry," the mechanic told Jacob. "We'll have this patched and get you home in good time. Didn't you see the elk's antlers on the staging? The *Sultana* broke the record last year—New Orleans to Cairo in four days and seven hours. She's a fast one, and no mistake."

The boiler mechanic returned to his banging.

As they left, Jacob said, "I'm more worried about getting home in one piece than making any records. They're slapping a patch over a bulge in one of the boilers. If I didn't know they were civilians, I'd think it was a typical shoddy army job. I don't like it at all. Makes a weak spot in the metal."

Gabriel nodded. He'd worked around metal enough to see the sense of what Jacob was saying, but every moment they spent on this deck begged a confrontation. Though he'd enjoy a chance to explain his reasons for running six months earlier, he knew his former comrades would no more listen now than they had the day he'd been drummed out. Only this time, instead of sending him into an enemy ambush, they'd likely beat him senseless, maybe even cut his throat.

And maybe they'd be right. After all, he hadn't learned his lesson in spite of nearly paying with his life. If he faced that boy again today, he'd do exactly what he'd done before. He knew it to his bones.

"Come on, Jake," Gabe urged, unwilling to tell his friend the real reason for his hurry. "These fellas work on boilers all the time. Surely they have inspectors lined up to check the work before we go."

Jacob hesitated, running a hand through his newly cropped brown curls. His natural impatience won out, and he nodded. Then the two worked their way upstairs, to the hurricane deck.

Gabriel could have sworn he saw, out of the corner of his eye, a hand lifted in his direction.

"Hey, Davis!" The words were faint but unmistakable.

Gabe quickened his steps and hoped that Jacob hadn't heard. They bypassed the cabin level and hurried up top, to the hurricane deck.

"It's getting mighty thick," Jacob said, gesturing to the soldiers who were crowding into every available spot. "Looks like they mean to pack us in like hogs."

It was a wonder Gabe could hear the way his heart was hammering. He hoped his voice would not betray his nervousness. "You'd think they'd split us up and put some on that other steamboat."

He nodded toward the *Pauline Carroll*, which was tied nearby. The big steamer appeared nearly empty.

"You aren't still trying to figure out the way the army big bugs think? There's only two reasons they do anything: bribery or lunacy. Tryin' to figure out which one'll only give you headaches," Jacob told him. "Look, there's Seth and Zeke, back toward the stern. Let's see if we can get to 'em without stepping on too many of these fellows."

But Gabriel already felt as if someone had trodden on his thumping heart. He'd been noticed, recognized. He scanned the crowd on the hurricane deck, hoping like hell that there was no one else.

When he saw someone he knew, nausea rushed at him until he realized it was only Mac Mahoney, from Andersonville. Shame heated Gabe's face. Had his guilt made him so jumpy that he flinched upon hearing another former inmate's voice two decks below?

At last they reached their two friends, who'd staked out a narrow stretch of deck in front of a wheel housing.

"So, brother, did you make 'em quit their banging, or did you just show 'em how it's done?" Zeke asked Jacob.

Jacob grinned. "I thought I might fix those boilers myself, but the fools suggested I stick to pounding little brothers."

Gabe couldn't help but smile at their banter, but he felt a measure of pain, too. He'd been with Zeke and Jacob for months, but in the past few days, seeing the two brothers together resurrected Matthew's ghost. Why now and not before? Was it prompted by his fear of being caught by members of his old unit? Or maybe with their journey home, Ohio was once more growing real inside his mind instead of a vague, unattainable idea, like freedom.

Well, he was free now, thank God, and soon he would be home. He'd have to face the fact that a grave was all that he would see of his younger brother, that the only Davis male to greet him would be Father.

His father. A memory rushed up at him, like a hungry fish rising to the bait. His mother weeping as his father jabbed the air with his pipe to emphasize his words.

"No son of mine is going to shirk his duty."

"But you said I'm more useful working on artillery design," Gabe argued. A part of him did want to go with his friends, to join in the grand adventure of the war. But Mama's tears, her whispered pleas, had stayed him. That and the satisfaction of working in his father's factory to build the weapons that would help the Union win the day.

Flint Maxwell Davis made a ring of his pipe smoke and sent it floating toward the ceiling. In a moment it dissolved into a sweet, ashen fragrance, like the ones that came before it.

"I can do without you, Gabe."

That was God's truth if he'd ever heard it. It always had been, ever since his father realized that Matthew shared so many of his interests, which Gabe found somewhat alarming. But Father had gleefully taught his younger son the workings of a dozen games of chance and encouraged him to breed bloodthirsty roosters for illegal cockfights. More and more, Flint Davis ignored his eldest, whose interest in sketching trees and animals he proclaimed unmanly. When Matthew drowned, Gabe could all but hear resentment buzzing in his father's skull.

Even so, hearing him admit what Gabe had long sensed stunned him. He remembered a wave of nausea rising, like one of Father's damned smoke rings.

"This draft notice cannot, *will* not, be ignored," Father insisted.

"Don't ignore it, then. Pay a substitute," Mama

told his father. Though she didn't give it voice, her terror hung in the air, fear that she would outlive yet another son. "It isn't as if we can't spare three hundred dollars. You've said yourself how well the business is doing."

"Like hell I'll pay a substitute!" his father roared. "And have everyone saying that Flint Davis, the man who built a fortune in artillery, was too cowardly to send his own son off to war? Or thought his money made him too grand? I've told you before, I'm not one of those damned blue bloods who thinks that a few dollars set me above the rest!"

"Plenty of families we know have kept their boys at home! There are men who need that money just as much as we need Gabe," she pleaded.

"No. *We* don't need him; *you* do. You need Gabe tucked under your wing so he won't die like *him.*"

The tears filling Mama's eyes spilled over. In the three years since his brother's death, as if by consensus, his parents never spoke his name. When forced to refer to Matthew, they said only *him.* As if by pretending Matthew had never existed they could assuage the pain of losing Father's favorite.

His mother straightened her spine and glared into his father's eyes. "Mr. Davis, you know very well you're only using this draft notice as an excuse! You mean to *punish* Gabriel!"

She didn't have to say for what. Though no one asked the questions, they hung heavily among the surviving family members. His sisters stared them at him. His mother wept them into lacy handkerchiefs. And his father, especially, hinted at them in dozens of furtive looks and conversations that danced around the point. *Why couldn't you save Matthew? How could you have let him drown?*

That Gabe had nearly died, too, jumping in after his younger brother, was not an answer. Flint Davis was consumed by the mystery of why one son climbed out of the icy river while the other hadn't.

God knew Gabe had tried to make it up to his father. He'd turned his talent from sketching landscapes and horses to drawing precise artillery designs. He'd followed the old man into the factory out of a sense of duty and the hope that he could prove useful enough to earn his father's forgiveness, if not his love. Flint Davis never thawed, but after a time, the work became its own reward. Gabe had discovered art in three dimensions among the gleaming rows of cannon with his family name stamped on the barrels.

Until his father made him join the army and Gabriel saw with his own eyes the carnage he'd unthinkingly unleashed upon the world.

Capt. J. Cass Mason thought longingly of the well-stocked bar in the main cabin. After everything he'd done to secure this load of released prisoners, he felt uncommonly tense. But the bar would have to wait, for Capt. Frederic Speed had just asked for a private word with him inside the *Sultana*'s office.

He waved the assistant adjutant general into the small room and invited him to sit. Captain Speed, a trim, dark-haired man perhaps ten years younger than Mason's thirty-four years, glanced at the chair he'd indicated. Apparently changing his mind, he remained standing, looking ill at ease.

He'll want something for his trouble, Mason

decided. Too many of these young officers thought the steamboat lines had bottomless pockets. Never mind that the U.S. government routinely commandeered the boats and played havoc with the schedules. Never mind the fact that they'd seized the *Rowena* from Mason, all for the crime of carrying some medicine and trousers to the South. Now, two years later, every hope—and every dime—he had were riding on the success of the *Sultana*. And still, every mother's son of them came calling with his hand out.

"I'm very much concerned about the crowding," Captain Speed began. "I was just informed there are very nearly two thousand prisoners aboard."

"I thought we'd already cleared up this question in our last discussion," Mason said irritably. It wasn't his fault the military had underestimated the numbers. He'd simply reminded the officers of his line's contract and pushed for the best load possible. Now that he finally had the men on board, he'd be damned if he was going to split them. The delay would be a nightmare for both the crew of the *Sultana* and the prisoners waiting to go home.

"In some places, there's not even room enough for the men to lie down," Captain Speed added.

"The men will go through comfortably and safely," Mason assured him. "I've taken large loads for the government before."

But not this large, Mason knew. It worried him, but still, he couldn't help thinking of the number Captain Speed had mentioned. At the five dollars per enlisted man and ten per officer that the government would pay, this trip would be profitable enough to offset his earlier light loads. He was also carrying perhaps a hundred civilian passengers and a great deal of cargo.

He thought again about the loss of the *Rowena,* of how he'd been forced to sell off a large percentage of his share in the *Sultana*. He couldn't afford to allow Speed to stand in the way of a trip like this one, even if he had to pay a bribe.

But apparently Speed had only wanted reassurance, for he nodded despite his worried frown.

"Godspeed, then, Captain Mason," he said in leaving.

Speed left quickly, without pausing to shake Captain Mason's hand.

Looking after him, Mason wondered how long it would be until other impediments to either time or profit would arise.

When finally, just after nine o'clock that evening, the *Sultana* backed out into the current and began the journey north, the prisoners' rousing cheer vibrated through the decks. And J. Cass Mason felt as glad as any man among them.

Chapter Three

*If the Confederacy fails, there should be written
on its tombstone, "Died of a theory."*
—Jefferson Davis

Tuesday, April 25, 1865

My dearest Marie,
    *Perhaps it is my own guilt that makes me feel as if
God turns His back upon my prayers. So instead I beg
you to intercede on my behalf, that I might find courage
enough to expose the man who took your life.*
    *I fear he has followed me and even now lurks among
the ornate, carved decorations of the main cabin. Each
time my eyes close, I imagine I can hear him sniffing
at my scent, questing ever closer to the room where I
stay hidden, waiting.*
    *You must believe me, Marie, when I say I only meant
to warn you that he was unworthy of your affections.*

When you refused to hear my suspicions, I sought evidence that you could not refute. But only out of loyalty, my sister. Only out of love. Had I known what grief this proof would wreak, I would have gladly burnt the letter and returned to deviling the demon with my usual mischief.

Still, I often wonder how could you allow romantic sentiment to blind you to the fact that this man was an enemy? How ever did you come to love a cursed Yankee? I feel aggrieved that you pretended to disbelieve the letter, only to confront him afterward alone. Alone, where he could take your life, leaving everyone who knew you to weep such bitter tears.

Oh, Marie, how I wanted you to trust in me to see Darien Russell punished for his crimes. But since you could not accept my help and my strength before, I pray that you will now, through the power of your intercession with Him who judges all.

With eternal tenderness,
Yvette

Yvette put down her pen and blew across the drying letters. All throughout the day, as the steamboat labored upstream, she had sat inside this cramped room, thinking of Marie. She wondered idly if this was proof of the onset of madness, this short step from brooding to writing letters to a woman who could never answer. But Yvette remembered from ten years ago, when Joëlle, her toddler sister, succumbed to yellow fever, that death, though terrible, did not separate two people all at once. Rather, it descended layer after filmy layer, in curtainlike veils that gradually obscured the memory of the lost loved one.

Yvette never found it possible to think of those

she'd lost—and the climate of New Orleans ever took its toll—without feeling melancholy. Thankfully, time diminished the great tearing gouges that grief took from her heart.

Two weeks, however, had done nothing to blunt the agonizing clarity with which she recalled Marie. Perhaps, because of the part Yvette had played in Marie's death, her sister's memory would never fade, at least not until her murder was avenged.

A pang of hunger distracted her from the unsettling thoughts. Only steps away, inside the main cabin, a banquet would have been laid out, then put away by now. Earlier, Yvette had forced herself to ignore the scents that crept beneath her stateroom door and beckoned. She'd had to remain hidden, for if Captain Russell were aboard, he'd certainly watch for her at mealtimes. But now her empty stomach growled its hunger and frustration. Surely, she couldn't spend the entire journey hiding in this stateroom. Russell might not even be here.

If she were home, by now the family would have gone to table. She sighed wistfully at the thought of her favorite centerpiece, a cleverly molded nougat church, surrounded by its sumptuous congregation: steaming bowls of crab gumbo, crusty, fragrant bread, plump oysters, stuffed mirliton, suckling pig, café brûlot. Who would have imagined a week ago that today she'd be desperate to fill her stomach with coarse American fare?

Although she'd learned that even peculiar food could suffice, she still dreaded the idea of dining alone—even alone among so many strangers. How could she savor any meal without *Maman* and Papa's spirited discussions of the latest opera, her spinster

Aunt Zaza's whispered gossip, her brothers' cunningly risqué remarks?

Her stomach rumbled again, troubled by both emptiness and loss. She felt like Lucifer, cast out of paradise for all eternity, for she had to admit there was only the slimmest chance of going back. Even if Uncle André exonerated her of the criminal charges, no proper Creole family would forget the taint of scandal; her own relations would doubtless remain as aloof as strangers if they chanced to pass her on the street.

Could she ever again return to her family or New Orleans? If she proved her innocence, proved that Captain Russell had abused the family trust, surely they must accept her once more. Mustn't they? She still held proof cleverly folded and sewn into the cloth lining of her reticule. Evidence that she would use to destroy Russell in the end.

She brushed away a tear and thrust her shoulders back defiantly. Whether or not her family forgave her, she was still an Augeron, her lineage traceable to French nobility. She might be ruined, but she was not defeated—yet. Not yet and not ever, especially while Darien Russell walked this earth.

And she'd be cursed for a fool to starve just steps away from dinner. A day had passed already—broken only by reading, prayers, and her letter to Marie—since she had begged milk for Lafitte and a simple meal for herself.

As Yvette entered the main cabin, she felt as exposed as if she were completely naked. The sight of a number of crewmen dismantling the long dining tables at its center and setting up rows of double-deck cots did not disturb her. Nor did the deck passengers, who waited patiently along the edges of the

well-appointed hall. As usual, it was the Union blue,
a number of Yankee officers who were also apparently
waiting for their cots, that made her so uneasy. She
tried to maintain an air of casual indifference. She
wasn't certain if she was succeeding, especially considering that she was holding her breath. But to her
relief, Captain Russell's dapper figure was not among
the other men.

She began to think she had imagined seeing him
before. Frightened and far from home as she was,
her mistake was understandable, if vexing.

She let out a sigh to free her pent-up breath and
the rush of anxiety. Then she hurried to the rear
section of the main area, which was designated as
the ladies' cabin. She nodded a greeting to a trio
of women who sat talking together, their laughter
ringing like fork tines upon crystal. Their obvious
camaraderie and their kinship, evident in the similar
wide-set blue eyes, sent a pang of homesickness jolting
through Yvette.

After moving past them, she found the head steward, an older, surprisingly active little man, and asked
if it was too late to get a bite to eat. He interrupted
his direction of the conversion of the room from
dining hall to dormitory. Below his white mustache,
his smile looked both sincere and professional.
''There are a number of passengers anxious to bed
down in here, miss, but I'd be delighted to run to
the galley and have a plate prepared for you to enjoy
inside your stateroom.''

''That's all right,'' Yvette said. ''I'll go down there
myself.''

Cramped as she had been inside her quarters, waiting among these Union officers felt too dangerous.

She couldn't shake the idea that at any moment she might be arrested, that here, as well, no one would listen to her explanation of what had really happened.

Besides, Yankees always spoiled her appetite.

Just as she turned to leave, Yvette froze. Near the front of the main cabin, Captain Russell stood talking to some gentlemen beside the bar. He did not appear to see her, but there was nothing to prevent him from turning his head at any moment to glance in her direction.

At the sight of the man, she heard her own blood rushing in her ears, felt it pulsing hot with terror just beneath her skin. She thought she might explode if she stood here another second, simply waiting for him to look at her.

Her feet seemed so far distant from her brain, so hard for her to manage. With an effort, she subdued her quivering limbs and forced them to carry her outside onto the promenade, where Russell could not see her.

The evening air felt damp and chilly, refreshing in her lungs, and the breeze of the boat's movement quickly cooled her. The farther from the doorway— and Russell—she walked, the more she distanced herself from her anxiety.

Relieved to find that the *Sultana*'s motion didn't slow her, she hurried down the stairs leading to the galley on the deck below. After retracing her trip there yesterday, she repeated her request for a small meal to enjoy inside her stateroom. Once more, she felt a twinge of guilt for telling them she was hiding from some humiliating faux pas she'd inadvertently committed in the ladies' cabin. The cook and his assistant smiled their understanding, and within a few minutes, she emerged, carrying a covered basket.

She'd gone only a few steps when her path was blocked by a group of men who'd just come to claim the spot. Lanterns bracketed along the cabins' outside walls increased the meager starlight enough so that within the brighter circles Yvette could discern faces whittled by exhaustion and starvation. Some of the former prisoners appeared to be asleep. Or dead. *Mon Dieu.*

Show courage, she told herself. *You've already proven you know how.* She'd been brave enough to flagrantly turn her back on Marie's Yankee visitor. She'd risked arrest by painting General Butler's portrait in the bottoms of chamber pots for friends. She'd even dared to sing her insolent tunes so loudly that passing Yankees could hear each one of the rude words. If she could manage all of those feats, then she could certainly face a few sick and hungry men.

A shaft of lantern light fell across what looked to be a pair of sticks jutting from the hems of trousers. It took Yvette several moments to understand they were not sticks at all, just a man's legs, so impossibly thin that they appeared inhuman. Above the legs, the man's face stared at her, so gaunt and vacant-looking, she wasn't sure he really saw her.

The basket of food weighed heavily on both her arm and her conscience. Reaching beneath the cloth, she took out one warm roll and tucked it into the pocket of her skirt for later.

She bent so that her voice would not have far to travel. "Excuse me. Are you hungry?"

His head tipped back, and she could tell he saw her, but he simply stared. Probably because her question had been so ludicrous, she realized. She doubted he remembered a time when he had not been hungry.

In the face of such suffering, the color of his ill-fitting uniform lost all meaning to her. As she passed him the basket, the long twigs of his fingers closed around its sides.

"This is for you, my friend," she whispered. And why not? Seeing Darien Russell had completely killed her appetite.

The soldier stripped away the cloth and stared down at the food heaped on the plate. The warm scents of roast chicken and potatoes and some cheese-covered vegetable made Yvette feel nauseated, but she saw comprehension, then slow hope, dawning on the prisoner's thin face.

Another man, his face nearly obscured by a tangled thicket of a beard, sat up. "He can't say it, so I will. God bless you, miss. God bless you."

She certainly hoped so. She needed all the blessings she could get if she were to somehow avoid Russell aboard this crowded boat. She nodded and edged past the group, intent on quickly reaching her stateroom's outside door.

Gabe peered along the cabin deck and hoped like hell the dim light would obscure his features. He tried to picture his former comrades from Ohio, one level below, settling in, their backs turned toward the outer railing as they curled in slumber. He wouldn't have risked venturing this close except that the hurricane deck had grown so crowded that Zeke could not stretch out his swollen leg. Stiff in his own joints,

Gabe had volunteered to see if the steamboat's second level offered any better spots.

For a moment, he wondered if that had been only an excuse. Or did some part of him still hope he'd meet someone he'd once known willing to listen to what had really happened on that day in Tennessee? He pushed aside the question, unwilling to examine such a childish notion. He was through hoping his reputation could be salvaged. He now existed only to put the past behind him.

The steamer's whistle cut through the darkness. For a moment Gabe stood still, hearing as well as feeling the *Sultana's* wheels churning, propelling them along the main channel of the Mississippi River. As they glided northward, relief flowed through his veins, relief that they were leaving the damned South, which had cost so many lives with its futile rebellion. Away from the prison camps, empty of everything except the rows of shallow graves and the old stench that hovered thickly. Away from the burned-out shells of houses and a thousand blood-soaked fields.

And headed into what? he wondered. Though he felt certain his mother and sisters would be glad to see him after so many months of silence, would his father allow him to embrace them even once? Would he let Gabe hear their voices, so long dreamed he'd recognize them at the world's end?

But no matter how they reacted to his unannounced arrival, his family deserved to see him whole, to hear why he had run that time in Tennessee. They might even understand. He couldn't imagine their condoning what he'd done, but at least they'd comprehend his reasons. Afterward, he could disappear, start over somewhere in the West. Plenty of folks were

relocating to the rich farmland of Oregon. He'd bet
a man who could work metal into plows and other
implements would be welcome despite a checkered
past.

If the South didn't somehow swallow him, he could
move past heartache to start his life anew.

A soldier swore as Gabe tripped over his leg. He
apologized the first few times it happened, but he
couldn't help bumping and jostling prisoners every
few steps. His spirits sank. This level appeared at least
as crowded as the one above. And the only other
place to check was the main deck, where the Ohio
troops had settled.

By the time he was halfway through his circuit of
the second level, he thought of asking Seth to go
below. But the captain and Jacob had both been
asleep when he'd come downstairs. Was he such a
coward that he would wake them rather than take
this chance?

"There's a thin line between good sense and cowardice."
Captain Seth had told him that once, when Gabe
had felt the need to challenge those prisoners who
preyed upon the weak in Andersonville. Those first
few weeks, he'd had so much to prove, he'd nearly
gotten himself killed. He'd had to relearn that a man
wouldn't stay alive if he didn't look out for himself.

Was now one of those times?

Everything inside him rebelled at the idea. Damn
it, he would not continue skulking around like a
whipped pup, hoping against hope no one he knew
would see him. He was a full-grown man of twenty-
four. Old enough to have some pride left, though
the Rebels had done everything they could to strip
it all away.

He would go to the main deck then, even if that meant facing the demons that he'd hoped to leave behind. He met no one on the stairs as he descended, but below he found men huddled, mostly sleeping, in every available space as well.

As he passed the boilers, he glanced toward them, remembering Jacob's earlier misgivings. But this evening, all was quiet, empty, save for one man intently monitoring the gauges. The man, who wore the steamboat line's uniform, stood from his stool and shook his head as if to ward off sleep.

Jacob would rest easier, Gabe thought, if he saw how safe and quiet everything appeared now.

A few steps beyond the boiler area, someone he hadn't heard approach grasped Gabe from behind.

"Figured you'd be dead by now, Davis."

The man's fingers squeezed his neck painfully, but the voice dug even deeper. Before Gabe turned around, he knew the face he'd see—the wild, wavy black hair and the almost lipless mouth that slashed above a long chin like an ugly scar. He remembered eyes so black that they looked like a pair of holes drilled into meanness. Bulging and set too close together, their fathomless stare always made Gabe want to look away.

He didn't, though. Instead, he jerked free from Deming's grip and swung around to face him, struggling to keep his own gaze cool and level. He owed this bastard nothing but a mouthful of shattered teeth. He'd be damned if he'd explain or apologize to this prison bait hiding in a Union uniform.

Like the other human cargo from the Southern prison camps, Silas Deming looked worse for his incarceration. Cahaba Prison, where Gabe had found out that members of his former unit had been kept, had been a hellhole, but its captives were in far better condition than most of the men held in Andersonville. Still, the angles of Deming's face looked sharper, the black and bulging eyes more prominent. He yet towered over Gabe's six feet, but hunger or disease made him stoop forward, as if the upper portion of his spine had been bent by his confinement.

"I figured he'd be home shivering in his bed now, being as how our Gabe's so quick on his feet. Leastways when the shootin' gets too close."

At first, Gabe didn't recognize Reuben Mueller. As boys, the two had sneaked away to a nearby swimming hole when they should have been in school. When their parents put a stop to their truancy, they'd created enough mischief in the classroom to bend many a hickory stick. But they'd never been mean-spirited in their antics. Most had been directed at the bullies who gave the younger boys such hell.

But like all of the prisoners, Reuben had changed. Though he'd once been renowned for an ability to thrive on camp cooking and even nearly inedible army rations, his persistent fleshiness had been whittled away by the hardships of Cahaba. So, apparently, had the last traces of his long friendship with Gabe. Seeing Reuben allied with a petty criminal like Deming was far more painful than the fingerprints that still throbbed at Gabe's neck.

"You're lookin' mighty scrawny. Figured you bein' a namesake of ol' Jeff Davis and all, he mighta fed you better while you was his guest." Deming moved in on him again, so close that their noses were just inches apart.

Gabe withstood the impulse to strike out. Silas

Deming knew damned well he was no kin to the
Confederate president. There was no need to rise to
that bait or any other.

"Yeah, you're lookin' awful thin. But maybe those
Rebels don't give feasts for Yankee runners like we
imagine." Though the light was dim, Gabe saw his
old friend's sneer move closer. "Maybe they hate
cowards and deserters every bit as much as we do."

The bitterness in Reuben's words finally unlocked
Gabe's jaw.

"I did not desert." He straightened his back and
stared into Reuben's face. "I came back to camp and
turned myself in for discipline. But I never deserted."

"Even worse," Reuben insisted. "You were drummed
out."

Gabe shook his head. "Maybe I should have been,
but I wasn't drummed out, either. I was *sacrificed*, and
you were a party to it, Reuben. I always thought that
you, at least, might have wondered why I ran off the
field of battle. Weren't you my friend long enough
to at least wait for an explanation?"

"That day, I forgot I was your friend, Gabe. That
day, I was ashamed I ever had been."

When Reuben looked him in the eye, his gaze was
both sad and hostile. Gabe thought he spotted
remorse in the set of Reuben's square jaw. He thought
he saw the potential to mend fences. But he might
have imagined the moment out of hopefulness or
even desperation. And even if he hadn't, Silas Deming's next act destroyed the opportunity to resolve
their differences.

Deming spat in Gabe's face. Deming, a bastard so
low he stole from his own messmates and cheated
anyone green enough to try his luck at a game of

chance. Deming, who thought the war a license to loot every farmhouse their unit marched past, to rip the stuffing from tots' rag dolls just to make the frightened children cry.

Deming's spittle sliding down his cheek was more than Gabe could bear. With a howl of fury, he brought his fists up and jammed them toward the bastard's belly.

But no man spat in another man's face without foreseeing an attack. Deming stepped sideways and grabbed Gabe's wrist, then slung him forward, headfirst into a cabin wall.

The impact sent showers of light sparking across Gabe's vision and waves of pain cascading through his skull. In addition to the sharp crack of his head against wood—a sound very much like a bat striking a baseball—Gabe heard an even more unlikely sound. The scream of a woman on this steamboat packed with men.

He had no time to wonder at the source, however, for as he struggled to rise with the intent of pounding Deming, the brilliant light inside his head exploded into blackness. His knees buckled, and awareness slid away.

Chapter Four

Away down South in the land of traitors,
Rattlesnakes and alligators,
Right away, come away, right away, come away.
Where cotton's king and men are chattels,
Union boys will win the battles,
Right away, come away, right away, come away.
                                        —anonymous,
                              from "Union Dixie"

The last thing Yvette meant to do was speak up for some Yankee. She was heading toward the safety of her stateroom when she heard loud voices. She barely recognized the young man who had earlier introduced himself as Gabriel Davis when a wild-eyed scalawag spat into his face. Yvette hadn't heard their confrontation, but she saw in a trice that her Mr. Davis was both outnumbered and a far better sort than this ruffian. When Gabriel understandably swung at the man, his attacker grabbed his wrist and slung him headlong into a cabin wall.

As Mr. Davis's skull struck wood with a sickeningly solid bang, Yvette shrieked angrily, "You leave that man alone!"

No one paid her any heed. Gabriel struggled to rise before collapsing, but two men quickly hauled him to his feet. In the warm light of the lantern, she saw dark rivulets of blood dripping through his blond hair.

Just when she thought the two men had decided to redeem themselves by helping their unconscious victim, the one who'd started the incident hauled Gabriel closer to the rail. Her stomach clenched in horror as she realized the man meant to throw him overboard.

An image flashed through Yvette's mind: Marie, black hair waving in the water, where she'd been discarded as if her life meant nothing. She couldn't let this happen to this man, wouldn't let this happen to another family.

The other fellow, a bit shorter and fuller in the face, grasped Gabriel by the shoulder and hesitated.

"Much as he deserves it, you can't just pitch him over. A man can't swim in his condition—"

"You think I give a damn?" The man's dark gaze slid to lock with Yvette's and then back, as if she weren't worthy of consideration.

"It's murder, and I won't be a party to it. I-I know his people. They've already lost one son."

The black-haired devil shoved his friend aside. "He shoulda died already. God knows he's got it comin'. And there ain't a fellow here who'll say a damn thing if our runner-friend happens to slip off the side, all accidental-like.''

Yvette scanned the men crowded around and realized with horrifying certainty that the man was right. None would meet her eye. Several turned their backs, perhaps pretending that if they didn't see this abomination, it would not exist. Did this bully so frighten them that they meant to allow him to commit murder?

Outrage forced her to step forward. They might all be Yankees, the same that she had wished dead, but she refused to stand by idly and witness the death of a young man who'd treated her kindly.

''I told you once, unhand him.'' She said the words loudly, hoping that a guard would hear and come to investigate. She might be a Southerner, but she was also both a lady and a paying passenger. Those two distinctions earned her the right to expect protection.

She could hear her blood rush in her ears, and though she had to struggle to control her shaking, she did not turn away. Wisely or not, she was involved now, and she could not force herself to run.

''Only the basest of cowards would kill a helpless man. If you try to do him further harm, I shall scream. I shall scream, and then I'll tell everyone who'll listen just what mischief you intend.''

Several faces stared at her with expressions colored by a mixture of wariness and disbelief.

The black-haired ruffian pinned her with a fierce glare, apparently expecting her to burst into hysterical tears or, better yet, collapse into a swoon. Yvette rolled her eyes and sighed in feigned impatience, praying all the while that he could not hear her pounding heart.

She held her ground, her stubbornness honed by

years spent battling older brothers. Several men shifted uncomfortably, and the fellow who'd been holding Mr. Davis's shoulder spoke up once again.

"You heard the lady, Deming. Let him go—at least for now."

By supplying her with the name, the shorter man ended the standoff. She could now use it to report this incident, and she could tell that Deming knew it, too. So instead of tossing Gabriel's limp form overboard, Deming dumped him at her feet and spat on him again.

"You want the runner so bad, you can have him," he told her as he turned on his heel. Trailing a stream of curses against both Gabriel's cowardice and her lack of womanly virtues, he shoved and swore his way through the crowd.

Yvette gazed down at the heap of bleeding Yankee lying at her feet. She had him now, all right.

But what in heaven's name was she going to do with him?

"Major Fidler, might I have a word with you about the conduct of your men?" Captain Mason asked.

Fidler, the officer in charge of the prisoners, looked distinctly annoyed. A paroled prisoner himself, the major had been one of several men who'd complained about the overcrowding before the *Sultana* left Vicksburg. The hollow-cheeked man had proclaimed himself "quite unimpressed" with Mason's reassurances. This evening, his uniform hung wrinkled on his gaunt frame, and exhausted shadows formed dark smudges beneath his eyes.

Nevertheless, Fidler followed Mason into the pilot-house.

"I'm very concerned about the way the men are moving from one side to the other every time another steamboat passes or we near a town," Captain Mason began. "With this sort of weight on top, sudden shifting could capsize us or cause a boiler failure. This behavior must be stopped immediately."

Major Fidler pursed his lips, and his eyes grew as cold as chips of flint. To his credit, however, he did not remind Mason of his earlier objections. Nor did he mention the conditions, which Mason understood were less than desirable.

"I'll speak to them," Fidler agreed, his voice sounding as tired as he appeared. "All we want is to get home safely. God knows, we deserve it after what we've suffered."

Fidler left the pilothouse, and Captain Mason gazed out over the dark mass of prisoners blanketing the hurricane deck. Prisoners who, with their sheer weight, could destroy the steamboat and everyone inside it.

"All we want is to get home safely," Fidler had said.

"Amen to that, Major," whispered Mason. But his true desire was more modest still. Not home, but the prisoners' river destination, Cairo, Illinois, beckoned like a lodestone pulling at a compass needle. It was that town and not his home or his wife, Mary, that J. Cass Mason thought of when he finally whispered, "It's all that I want, too."

Gabe felt as if someone had dropped a cannonball onto his head. Experimentally, he moved it, only to find that his neck, too, throbbed ferociously from the jarring impact. He tried to force his eyes to focus, his mind to put together the jumbled images that skipped along its surface like an artfully tossed stone. One after another, he saw Matthew's face, the mangled bodies of dead soldiers, the rows of shallow graves he'd helped to dig, and then a steamboat, the *Sultana,* almost as radiant a vision as the dark-haired beauty he'd met while waiting to come aboard.

In stark contrast, the ugly memory of Silas Deming rushed at him, followed by the recollection of the man's harsh words and the solid impact that had quickly followed. Shortest fight he'd ever been in, Gabe thought, somewhat abashed.

He was fortunate he hadn't been killed, he realized, before deciding that the same fickle luck had caused him to encounter one man among hundreds who'd be hell-bent on hurting him. But where was Deming now? For that matter, where was he?

As his vision cleared, a solid shelf of wood appeared about two and a half feet above him. Gingerly, he turned his head until he could take in the narrow confines of the small room he found himself in— the two doors of the stateroom, the lamp above the table. Apparently, he was lying in a lower berth. Across from him, a young woman sat in the room's lone chair, her fingers absently fluffing the fur near a tiny kitten's ear.

A woman? He groaned, frustrated in his attempts to comprehend all that had happened. Only then did he realize she was the same woman he'd seen on the wharf boat earlier.

"What ...?" he began, scarcely guessing which

question was attempting to emerge from his confusion. "How . . . ? How did I get here?"

She frowned, as if his appearance were an unpleasant surprise to her. "My own foolishness, I'm afraid. Do you remember what that horrible, wild man did?"

"Something to my head, if I'm thinking straight."

She nodded, and the lamplight gleamed off her black hair, now uncovered. A few wavy strands had escaped a bun to frame her face. "You're lucky that you *can* think after that crack on the skull. Good thing you Yankees are so intractably hardheaded."

"That explains the way I feel, but it still doesn't tell me why I'm here." He attempted a smile despite a swirl of nausea. "I'm not complaining, mind you. I figured I'd end up in a box instead."

"Or as bait for catfish. That man meant to throw you overboard!" Her voice rose on a tide of indignation. "And if I hadn't come along, those others would have let him. I'd thought you Yankees always stuck together."

"I hear a Michigan judge gave him two choices: join the army or serve time. You Rebels saved us housing on that Deming fellow, throwing him in prison."

"But surely someone should have stood up for you against that criminal, someone besides me."

Of course, no one else had helped him. Gabriel closed his eyes tightly and wondered if he'd ever live down a simple act of—what? Kindness? Cowardice? Even after six months, he still felt uncertain of the answer.

When he looked at her again, her name rippled across his mind. *Eve Alexander,* she had said in that Southern accent he'd come to hate so much. Her words sounded silken, the same way those dark tendrils that framed her face looked.

"So why did you, Miss Alexander? What was one less Yankee to you?"

"It seemed a shame to drop the only half-decent Northerner I've met headfirst into the Mississippi."

"How'd I get in here, alone with you?"

The black-and-white kitten curled into a fluffy ball on Eve's lap.

She lifted her chin defiantly, as if she'd detected censure in his words. "I was not about to waste my grand gesture by letting those ruffians toss you in the river the moment my back was turned, so I shamed two of them into bringing you in here. However, if you're concerned about the propriety of such an action, I'm certain we can call Mr. Deming back."

He laughed, though his throbbing skull made him instantly regret it. "You misunderstand me. I'm very grateful, but I'm also confused. I've never had a lady save my life before, especially not a Southern one. I'm not too clear on the etiquette."

She tried to pinion him with an indignant glare, but the amusement in her hazel eyes dashed it all to pieces. "I believe I read an essay on the very subject in Miss Edith Willington's new book, *The Right Way to Live.*"

"Was it tucked between the chapters on 'Maintaining One's Complexion' and 'Evil Thoughts Toward Others,' chapter twenty-seven, 'Awkward and Unseemly Rescues?' " Gabe asked.

The bow of her mouth trembled until finally she gave way to laughter.

"I have two sisters who live by Miss Willington's edicts," Gabe confessed. "I'm afraid I spent a lot of happy moments mocking them for what they called 'developing their standards.' "

"I must confess, I've never put a great store by what the lady had to say," Eve told him, "much to my sister and mother's chagrin. I brought you here because . . . it seemed best at the time."

"Did you send for an officer or guard?"

"I-I didn't feel that, ah, under the circumstances, that action would be safe for you, either."

Something in the way her gaze slid away from his convinced Gabe she'd heard at least some of the conversation on the cabin deck. With the realization, he felt a rush of shame so painful that he almost wished Deming had tossed him overboard. Surely, drowning couldn't be worse than bearing this Southern woman's pity.

"I was no deserter," he insisted.

She said nothing in response, but her eyes looked expectant, as if she guessed there must be more. And in that expectation, Gabe dared to hope for something. Atonement? No, she could not offer such a thing. But perhaps the throbbing pressure in his skull was his long-silent explanation seeking its release.

Why not tell her? To her, he was just another Yankee, one she imagined a great coward, from what he guessed she'd heard. What could possibly make her think worse of him now?

"I did run once, in a battle," he began, seeking only to ease the pain by giving the true tale a voice. He searched her face, looking for some sign that she would stop him. But she leaned forward ever so slightly, as children do when an old uncle tells a frightening story by the hearth.

At least she had not recoiled. For that he felt more gratitude than for what she'd done to save his life. Before she could change her mind and leave or cry for help, he continued. "It happened in Tennessee, about six months ago. By then, the Confederates must have known the end was coming. But I'll give them this. They kept on fighting, fielding every soldier they could find. They must have been running low on fit men, though. After a while, we were fighting gray-beards. We were fighting boys as well. Kids young enough to cry when they felt homesick for their mamas."

A dim shade rose before his eyes, his brother, Matthew. Matthew laughing, the sounds of it mingling with the thin splintering of the ice beneath his feet. Unconsciously, Gabe reached out as if this time he could grab him. As if he hadn't been too far away.

"We gave the war our all, Mr. Davis," Eve told him, her voice colored by a pride undiminished by defeat. "We'll always have the knowledge that our beliefs, however wrong you people think them, have been paid for with our blood."

"Even in the blood of children," Gabe said. "It's a damned steep price for pride."

"There *is* no price too high for self-respect, sir, and I will thank you to watch your language in my presence."

He focused on her haughtiness, the contempt he imagined building in her. Only by doing so could he force himself to spill the entire story, especially the parts he'd been unable to tell Seth.

"There *is,*" he told her, "or I should say there *was* for me. Before I became an infantry soldier, I spent several years designing and testing different cannon.

I was so proud of those gleaming bronze Napoleons with my family name stamped on their barrels. Proud of their beauty and efficiency until I saw the mangled corpses on both sides.''

He could still see them when he closed his eyes, bodies pulverized by grapeshot, pulped by exploding shells. So stubbornly, he kept both eyes open to try to keep the disquieting past at bay, at least for now. Later, when the only sounds around him were the snores of sleeping men and the splashing of the paddle wheels, he knew that he would see it all once more. Once more and forever, every time he tried to sleep.

"The bodies looked the same. Didn't matter if they hailed from Massachusetts or Kentucky, from Florida or Texas. Didn't matter what color their skin or whether they ate Boston beans or black-eyed peas before the war. They all bled the same.''

He could see the disdain fading in her eyes, followed quickly by the dawning of comprehension about what this war had really been. Not some grand adventure made more noble through its inconveniences and sacrifice, but all the carnage, all the waste.

"Thank God I never had to fire any heavy weapons,'' Gabe continued. "Pulling the trigger of my Henry rifle was more than enough. Sixteen shots, that Henry had. Sixteen chances to crack open another man's chest or spew his brains all over his comrades or tear off one of his legs. But when I was called upon to fire, I still did it. To the very best of my ability. I killed my share of Rebels. Sometimes I wanted to just kill them all so I could hurry up and be quit of this place. That's all most of us wanted, to get finished and go home.''

Eve refused to meet his gaze now. Her mouth had flattened to a taut, grim line. But she did not get up and run shrieking from the room, as so many women would have. Even if she had, though, he might have gone on talking just to free the words that had lingered so long near the graveyard of his soul.

"I might have finished up a hero, the way I shot those Rebs. Might have." Gabe shook his head. "If we hadn't gotten backed into a tight spot. We were close enough to bayonet each other instead of shooting. I was fighting hard, too, because I knew the minute that I stopped, some Johnny would run me through. I didn't want to end up all in tatters like those corpses, didn't want my family to have to bury its last son. I think I was wrong, though, not to realize there *are* worse things than dying. Maybe you were right about the price of self-respect."

The kitten hopped off her lap and trotted toward him, its neck craning with cautious curiosity. Keeping its back paws on the floor, it lifted the front ones to the bunk's edge near his shoulder and stared at him, its green eyes blazing.

Gabe barely saw the kitten but wouldn't have touched it, anyway. Tiny and appealing as it might be, it remained a cat.

"You said you didn't want your family to bury its last son. Did your brother, or perhaps I should say brothers, die in the war?" Eve asked.

Her voice surprised him, she'd been quiet for so long. He shook his head in answer.

"Matthew drowned two years before the first shots. I was there. I saw him break through the river ice. I went in, too, thinking I could find him. But it was as if he'd fallen into a hole leading to the center of the earth. I never saw his face again, except . . ."

"Except?"

"Except after it became so pale and bloated I didn't even know for sure it was my brother. And then again, that last time, my last battle." He looked up at her, trying to mask his desperation for acceptance with a challenge. "I came eye to eye with a Rebel boy with Matthew's face."

Tears welled in her eyes. Dared he hope they were born of understanding? Or did she still pity him, or worse yet, fear he was insane?

He couldn't care about that. He had to get this all out, for he sensed he'd never summon the courage to tell his tale again.

"Of course, it couldn't have been Matthew. He'd been dead for years. But at that moment, I-I saw my brother. It was an awful shock." He paused and asked himself again whether his mind manufactured that vision later to excuse what happened next. No, it could not be. He remembered it too clearly. Matthew's pale blond hair, his eyes flashing with what looked for all the world like recognition.

He shuddered with the memory of it, still absolutely vivid despite the months that had passed since then. A perfectly clear moment that would last him all his life.

"I almost shot him, anyway. Just a reflex to keep myself alive, like vomiting a bellyful of poison. But my finger froze on that trigger, and then my mind—I'm not sure what went through it. I've tried to remember, but—" He shook his head, despairing of the task. "All I know is what the others told me. I threw down my rifle, and I ran like hell.

"By the time I realized what I'd done, I was wandering among a lot of pine trees. I could hear the echoes of a few last shots far in the distance. But by the time I found my unit, the Rebels had retreated. When I reported to camp, my mates had all heard how I'd run. They turned their backs to me."

He remembered the stark desolation of that moment, the realization that he'd betrayed his fellow soldiers and not just himself. "I went to the captain and reported in for discipline."

"No coward would have done that," Eve told him. Her voice was adamant, leaving no room for polite half-truths. Though he'd thought her strident earlier, he found he liked the fact that she said what she felt.

As if it agreed with its mistress, the kitten hopped onto the berth beside him. Gabe summoned the strength to sit and scooped the ball of fluff into his hands.

"This coward *did,*" Gabe said as he set the kitten on the floor. "That was the problem. I expected to be drummed out, sent home in disgrace. It was a fitting punishment. My father . . ."

Shaking his head, he closed his mouth against what his father would have done, *would* do, when he returned to Ohio.

"No one wanted to hear why I left the battle. Every friend I had turned on me. Enough to listen when Silas Deming came up with an idea. Instead of waiting for the captain to properly disgrace me, the men could drum me out themselves, run me through the Southern line. The Rebels would take care of me, he reckoned."

"Is that how you were captured?"

He nodded. "I tried my best to make them kill me,

but it didn't happen that way. Without a weapon, I wasn't even threat enough to shoot.''

"Did you . . . did you ever see the boy again? The one who so reminded you of your brother?''

Slowly, he shook his head. "I didn't, but I swear he was real. I know it. I can still see every feature, every freckle on that young man's face. And I still . . . I still wonder if somehow it could be . . .''

She leaned forward just an inch more, and the room seemed to close in around him. He'd only have to shift a bit and his knee would graze hers. He looked into her face as if to memorize it. She'd saved his life today—perhaps in more respects than one. Already he felt the pain bleeding out from the empty socket the truth had left. But the pain and blood felt cleansing somehow, as if they were preparing him for the chance to heal.

He might never repay her for what she'd done today, but he would carry her beautiful face with him, cast it into crystal as he had his brother's. As his mind took in Eve's delicate features, he grew increasingly conscious of the astonishing fact that he was alone inside this room with a very desirable woman. Awareness stole over him, and he felt his heartbeat race.

His gaze lingered for a long moment on her hazel eyes. Long enough to see them darken, just as summer clouds will to presage a violent storm.

As Gabriel sat across from her in the cramped state-room, Yvette reminded herself he was just another Yankee. Even so, she dug her nails into her palms to divert her rising tide of sympathy.

Sympathy for what? For a young man who'd admitted killing Rebel boys? She thought of the day she and Marie had been enjoying coffee in Madame Bouchard's parlor. How proudly Honorée had shown them the photograph of her husband, Emile, who had gone to war before the cursed Union took New Orleans. Then, as if her pride had drawn disaster, Yvette remembered the solemn knock at the front door, the shriek of Simone, the Bouchards' mulatto maid. Honorée's insistence, *"C'est de la foutaise!* This is nonsense—just a disgraceful Yankee trick!"

As far as Yvette knew, her friend had not yet admitted that her husband was truly dead. She could well imagine Honorée turning away all visitors who might insist she face the truth and not run to the window to peek out through the curtains every time a rider or carriage approached. She was too young to be a widow, she'd told Yvette and Marie. As if that fact could undo his death. As if the typhoid that killed him could be cured by the empty arms of his desperate twenty-year-old bride.

If that memory wasn't enough, Yvette could call forth so many others. The day their flag had been torn down, her city captured. Pierre's shame at returning home minus his right arm. Sweet François, the youngest of her three brothers, who'd been fighting in Tennessee when she'd last heard from him, about five months before. And Jules's bitterness at being the brother left behind, his heart too weakened by rheumatic fever to survive the hardships of campaigning.

Juste ciel, but she could cry a bucket for each of them, her city and her brothers and her friends. And a river for Marie, perfect, prim Marie, who'd been

misled by a Northerner with manners of silk and
morals of coarse ash.

"What's wrong?" the Yankee asked her, concern
furrowing his forehead.

She *must* think of him as a Yankee, she admonished
herself. Not as Gabriel Davis or as another young man
wounded by this war. As damaged and as haunted as
the men who'd fought on the right side.

"I am counting up the thousand reasons I should
hate you," Yvette admitted.

"It must be working. You look mad as h— You
look very angry."

She suppressed a smile at the way he'd corrected
his language to appease her. Then she shrugged.
"Mostly, I am angry with myself. A thousand reasons
should be enough for anyone. I could recite them
endlessly, but still I listen to your words and wonder.
Could it be the Yankees suffered, too?"

"War causes pain enough to go around, Miss Alexander."

"This I will concede. Now tell me how it is that you
are feeling? I have washed away the blood, but you
have quite a bump there. Shall I try to find a doctor?"

"No doctors, please. I'm feeling better now." Something in his tone suggested he was lying. He didn't
want to draw any more attention to himself. This she
understood, and it brought her to the last, best reason
she must steel herself against his story. She could not
afford the chance he might grow too curious about
her.

Still, she hesitated, though she knew she ought
to hurry him away. The hour had grown late, and
propriety bespoke one danger if he lingered, her
situation quite another.

She was a fool, she thought, even as she clutched at this opportunity to talk with someone. She'd been on the run for days, lonely among strangers, she who had never spent so much as one day totally on her own. How she missed her family, her friends! Lafitte was some comfort, for he reminded her of home, but Lafitte could never answer, and she was deathly tired of their one-sided conversations.

That was why she put aside the thousand reasons she should hate the Yankee long enough to say to him, "Tell me, Mr. Davis, what happened next to you. I've seen stories in the newspapers about Andersonville. Tell me about that place."

His polite expression melted into something darker, graver, until he looked far older than she'd guessed he could be. "I can't tell you what that place was. Not without saying things about your fellow Rebels and using language that you would certainly object to. But you don't need the words to understand. You looked around as you boarded today, didn't you, Miss Alexander? You must have seen the men with open sores, the ones without enough meat on them to make a decent soup bone. Some of them don't even speak. They gape and drool, and they make noises, but hunger and sickness have broken their minds."

"I understand there are places just as evil in the North, but I must say I don't condone it," she told him honestly. When she'd first read about the prison, she'd supposed the reports mere Yankee propagandizing, gross exaggeration. But even the tamest version was a shame unto the South. And Gabriel was right. The withered bodies of so many men could not be faked.

"But you aren't like those poor men," she told him, her gaze sweeping over him. He was quite thin, yes, but not emaciated.

"I wasn't there as long as most," he told her, "and then there were my friends."

Something changed in his expression at the mention of his friends. A warmth stole over the cool blue of his eyes, which reminded her all the more painfully of those she had been forced to leave behind. So much so that she was grateful when he continued.

"They kept me alive in every sense of the word. I remember the day I first came into camp. The smells, the sights—" He shook his head as if to dispel the images. "But I've told you, I won't describe it. At least the other captives were too miserable on their own accounts to care about the circumstances of my capture."

His gaze, which had drifted off as he spoke, rose to meet hers, then he glanced down in wonder at her hand, which she had placed atop his.

"I've known cowards, Mr. Davis," she said softly. "And I'd never number you among them."

She leaned forward, only half-realizing what she offered, only half-guessing that this blond Northerner would lean forward as well. Would raise his hands to grasp her arms gently. Would touch his lips so warmly against hers.

She felt as if a candle flame had kissed her. Its heat seared her without burning, singed her without pain. Instead, the warmth of it coursed through her, pooling in her breasts, her belly, that tiny, secret place that melted like wax heated by fire.

She moaned with the intensity of it. Never had she imagined that any kiss could feel like this.

His hand rose to stroke her hair, to cup her cheek as though she were something precious, and all the while, their kiss went on and on, opening an aching need inside her, an unguessed, ancient want. She felt the tip of his tongue taste her lips, felt them part, felt her whole mouth opening to him. Felt how easily, how eagerly, the rest of her would follow. And for the first time she understood how it was so many women allowed men to compromise them, how even her proper sister had opened herself up to this exquisite ruin.

She wondered, in her saner moments, how she would feel about it. Surely there would be shame then, even if she felt nothing but bliss now. Shame she had allowed this near-stranger, this ragged-looking Yankee to—

He moved to pull her closer, and she regained her sanity. The passion she had felt iced over, and her body splintered just a moment later, jerking her back, away from him.

"Thank you." He stood, and a wistful smile warmed the cool blue of his eyes.

She jumped to her feet and felt a fierce blush rise to heat her cheeks. Thank you? Was that how he saw her kiss—the first real kiss she'd ever given—as no more than a favor?

"You're very kind . . . and very lovely," Gabriel said, his gaze so intense she had to drop her own. "I'm much obliged to you for helping me tonight. Too obliged to try to take advantage, tempting as you are."

Her efforts at thought felt like wading upstream against floodwaters. Impossible as it seemed, she felt flattered and insulted all at once. She needed time to sort out exactly how it was she felt about their kiss, how she felt about this man, this enemy.

"I-I think you should leave now," she stammered. "I will remember you in my prayers. I-I'm not sorry that I helped you with those men."

Before she could react, he leaned to kiss her. But, to her relief, it was a chaste kiss on the top of her head, more like one of those her brothers might bestow than the cataclysm that passed before. "I don't want you to be sorry later, either; I want you to be safe. Please, stay away from them the rest of the trip. How far are you going?"

The words "St. Louis" stuck in her throat. She couldn't tell him, couldn't tell anyone, just in case someone followed her. "I'll be on board another day or two," she said instead.

His index finger brushed her cheek. Though the gesture seemed innocent enough, the pleasure that rippled through her body felt white hot. For a moment, she feared he saw the blaze the touch engendered, that he would insist on staying here to ruin her for any decent man.

The idea that he might *be* a decent man skimmed across her surface, as graceful as an egret. But what sort of decent man told his secrets to a stranger, an enemy, no less? Still, the impression stayed with her, a ghostly image of a stark white bird in flight.

He reached for her but at the last moment stayed his hand. The longing in his eyes made her heart race with a mixture of apprehension and desire.

A smile faltered, and he dropped his hand to the doorknob. "Good-bye, Miss Alexander, and once again I thank you."

He stepped out into the darkened main cabin. She

stared at the door as it clicked softly shut. She really
should have felt immense relief. Yankees were so
often vilified for their lewdness that no true lady of
New Orleans would willingly spend time alone with
one.

So why had she? And worse yet, why did she feel
so disappointed that he'd been such a gentleman and
left?

Her mind turned back to the letter she had written
to Marie, the question she had asked her: *How could
you allow romantic sentiment to blind you to the fact that
this man was an enemy? How ever did you come to love a
cursed Yankee?*

Her own words shamed her, for at last she understood how much more a man was than his uniform.
Yes, her sister had been wrong, but not for seeing
past the Union blue. Her failure had been one of
naïveté and not disloyalty.

She'd take that letter from her reticule, Yvette
decided, and she'd tear it into bits. She did not delude
herself that such an action would truly benefit Marie,
but it was the only way she could imagine of taking
back her angry words. And letters to the dead had
their own strange brand of logic.

Panic jolted through her at the realization that her
reticule was missing from the room. It contained her
letters to Marie, her small supply of money, and most
importantly, the document she'd sewn into the lining,
the letter, written in Darien Russell's hand, that she
hoped would save her life—and destroy his.

Suspicion blazed into anger as she thought of
Gabriel. Had he taken it with him? Had he played
her for a fool the same way Russell played Marie?

Her heart thundered its denial. Gabriel Davis might

be a damned Yankee, but he would not steal from her. He could not have said the things he had, kissed her the way he had, and stolen . . .

Darien Russell had kissed her sister, and much more. She wanted to grasp her chamber pot and vomit, but instead she forced herself to think.

Where had she last seen the cloth bag? When had she last held it?

Then she knew. She'd taken it with her to the galley, and she had not brought it back. She swayed with the realization that she must have somehow lost it. With her whole life riding on that reticule, she had dropped it somewhere, perhaps when she had given that poor, starving man her food.

As terrible, as frightened, as she felt, relief came, too. That she had not been so wrong about Gabriel, that he had not repaid her trust with treachery.

The thought gave her strength, which she needed desperately, for she had no other choice but to try to retrieve her reticule from the wretched prisoners, who had undoubtedly discovered it by now.

For without it, she knew she had no chance at all.

Chapter Five

*The North is determined to preserve the Union.
They are not a fiery, impulsive people as you are,
for they live in colder climates. But when they
begin to move in a given direction, they move
with the steady momentum and perseverance of
a mighty avalanche.*
—Texas Governor Sam Houston, 1859

Darien Russell had spent most of the evening nursing a drink at the bar in the main cabin. From that vantage, he could talk with a few of the cabin passengers and watch for any sign of his quarry. But as men began to claim both cots and spaces on the carpet, the smooth Tennessee whiskey lost its power to ease his troubled mind. The idea of Yvette somewhere aboard this boat, laughing at his fruitless efforts, cast his thoughts into an uproar.

It could be even worse, he realized. She could be

talking to someone instead, perhaps even a Union officer. Though it seemed unlikely she would risk such a conversation, she was both charming and articulate enough to convince a reasonable man of his guilt.

Perspiration erupted across Darien's face like a liquid pox. This same fear had prompted him to allow her the opportunity to escape in New Orleans, to put distance between her and his chief detractor, Colonel Jeffers.

At the thought of that insufferable Kentucky ruffian, Darien nearly swore aloud. The judgmental, sanctimonious yokel had despised him from the outset simply because he'd worked for the unpopular General Butler. Darien had never been implicated in any of the scandals that had led to Butler's recall from New Orleans, but the stench clung to him as if he'd been consorting with a skunk.

When General Banks, the new general in charge of the New Orleans occupation, had decided to place Darien on his own staff, Colonel Jeffers voiced his suspicions. Darien Russell, he claimed, had been fleecing wealthy Creole families. If only he could convince one of the victims to come forward.

But General Banks had not been interested in rumors, just in Darien's knowledge of the workings of New Orleans. Colonel Jeffers should have let the matter drop, but the rude Kentucky native would not let the matter rest.

Jeffers's investigation had already cost another of Butler's former aides a death sentence. Remembering Major Stolz's hanging, Darien wished to God he'd had the chance to kill Jeffers instead of the colonel's lackey, Lieutenant Simonton. But in doing Jeffers's bidding, Simonton had gotten too close to evidence that would incriminate Russell. Far too close, Darien remembered, until he'd had no choice but to mix a poison into Simonton's drink to escape the gallows.

Disagreeable as it had proved, Lieutenant Simonton's murder turned out to be a happy accident, since Yvette had been the handy scapegoat. If only she hadn't shared her suspicions with Marie as well instead of just Lieutenant Simonton, as Russell had first thought. If only he could have avoided killing his beloved Marie, too.

Her white throat, mottled with dark bruises, flashed before his eyes. He thought of how he'd kissed it, so many times before, when her family believed she was visiting her insane friend Madame Bouchard. How he'd kissed and touched her, how he'd charmed her out of her long-guarded virginity. Before he'd had to kill her.

His fingers curled and clenched, as if they could not forget the sin they had committed. Or been forced to commit by that damnable little spy Yvette. He closed his eyes for a brief moment, his mind transposing the dark splotches that ringed Marie's pale throat onto her sister, his plans drawing the noose around her neck to spare his own.

He smiled, envisioning Yvette's swift fall through the gallows, the sharp jerk as the rope stopped her, and the hideous death dance of her limbs. Just as poor Marie convulsed as he'd squeezed tight—all because of what Yvette had done.

What he intended would be in truth no murder; he merely acted as the tool of justice, as blameless as the executioner. Yvette deserved to die far more than Simonton or Marie. After all, she was the one most guilty of their deaths. If she hadn't been so damned suspicious, if she hadn't dug after his secrets so tenaciously, both of them would be alive. Their blood was on her hands.

Or more accurately, her mouth. He'd close it now, forever. Close it so she'd never sing one of her damned mocking songs again.

And then he would resign from the army so he could go home to his wife. Only this time when he saw Constance, she'd realize that he now had his own fortune. She'd be forced to admit that at long last he'd made good his predictions of success.

Finally, Darien's worries prompted him to abandon his comfortable seat. After straightening his frock coat and sleeking back his hair, he left the main cabin and ventured out onto the deck. It took him only a few minutes to find a group of men talking quietly, apparently as restless as he felt. One recalled a woman he'd seen on the wharf boat earlier.

"Pretty little thing, dark hair and a pert figure. I knowed a girl like that once back in—"

"I'm not interested in hearing how attractive she is," Darien interrupted. "The woman is wanted for questioning for serious offenses. I only need to know where she is now."

"Hell's bells, Cap'n," the short, slight young soldier answered. One shoulder was several inches higher than the other, giving him a distinctly lopsided appearance. "What kind of 'serious offenses' could a gal like that get into?"

The fool didn't think any straighter than he stood. Damned imbecile.

"Is murder serious enough for you?" Darien growled. "Murder of a Union officer?"

He could all too well imagine Yvette laughing at his frustration, immortalizing it into more verses for her song. Back in New Orleans they were still laughing at him. All except Colonel Jeffers, who was too busy investigating. Darien had to find the girl before she managed to contact that pious bastard and ruin everything for him.

The soldier's expression sobered. "I hear tell them New Orleans ladies did every goldarned thing they could think of to let our boys know how they wasn't welcome. But I never guessed they gone and killed folks, too."

If Darien were still headmaster at his own school, he'd box this laggard's ears for his atrocious grammar. But of course that was ridiculous. No young man so obviously ill bred would ever meet the standards of his august academy. Besides, the school had long since closed its doors.

How could he forget how Constance had laughed at that failure? His rage sparked hot against the memory. She'd never understood that he was destined for great things. Oh, she'd claimed to believe it when they were courting and he'd still had a healthy portion of Grandfather's money. But she'd never really shared his faith in his potential.

Darien returned his attention to the dolt before him. He had to be certain the soldier would come running if he chanced to see Yvette. "Miss Augeron is a danger to every man aboard."

"A little thing like her?" His laughter died a quick death as he noted Darien's expression. "Sorry, Cap'n. Just hard to imagine, that's all. We'll keep a lookout for her."

"See that you do, man. See that you do," Russell

responded. "I'm eager to take her back to New Orleans to face justice."

Actually, he wanted nothing of the sort. If he had, he would not have orchestrated her escape or chased after her so far. Though she'd evaded him longer than he had expected, he had her cornered now—and just the way he wished.

All alone. And as far from New Orleans—and justice—as she'd ever been in all her life.

Gabe made his way toward the bow, keeping the starlit river to his left. Each blade of the paddle wheel slapped its wet rhythm against the dark waters, carrying him that much closer to his home.

The thought of home struck him like dissonant notes on a piano, a chord that ought to resonate with sweetness but disappointingly rang sour. For more than two years his every breath had been directed toward returning there, to prove to his mother and his sisters he'd survived. To face his father if only to show him he was man enough to own up to what he'd done in his last battle.

But he knew now he'd been lying to himself. If he were really man enough, the dark splashing of the steamer wouldn't drench his soul in dread and his conversation with Eve Alexander wouldn't have churned up so much guilt and fear—and want.

As he painstakingly picked his path among the men who crowded nearly every open space, his mind navigated the varied feelings she'd stirred up. First of all, gratitude. Almost certainly, Eve had saved his life this evening not only by standing up to Silas Deming but by listening to the story that had burned inside him, as hot and lethal as a fire in a coal mine. He felt an undeniable attraction, too, a desire to explore the surge of sweetness he'd tasted with her kiss.

He smiled, remembering the way she'd felt, the softness of her lips and the warmth of her small hand as it held his. His steps faltered as his mind replayed the little sound she'd made deep in her throat. Had it been, as he hoped, a fierce hunger awakening, or was it instead the voice a woman gave to regret, a desperate desire to take back what had been too hastily offered? He sucked cool night air between clenched jaws, sure that he'd been right the first time.

She'd felt the same strong current of attraction despite the fact that she clearly saw him as an enemy. She certainly hadn't been shy about expressing her contempt for those soldiers who'd worn the Union blue. He wondered if that beautiful mouth of hers had ever offered comfort to a Rebel soldier, like the ones who had systematically starved so many men in Andersonville.

Had she been going tonight to meet some secessionist among the deck passengers? Why else had she been down below close to the boilers?

As a wave of nausea rolled over him, he wondered why it mattered. Why should he care who she was, where she was going, whom she loved? Certainly he owed her his thanks for being such a Good Samaritan, but the last thing that he needed was an entanglement with any woman, much less some damned Southerner.

His thoughts turned bitter as they circled back to Georgia, to the things he'd had to do to survive the camp. He thought of the times he and Jacob had worked their hands bloody using a knife and a railroad spike to fashion buckets out of canteens, oyster cans, or whatever else was handy. They'd sold these to other prisoners and then used some of the proceeds to buy their way onto the never-ending burial details so they could leave the camp and gain the chance to trade.

Gabe remembered digging those graves outside of camp, though at times he felt so weak, he feared he might collapse inside one and then be covered by another exhausted prisoner. The holes they dug were never deep enough, for always, always, more corpses awaited the thin comfort of their earthen shrouds and the prisoners hurried toward their stolen moments with the local farmers. For a price, guards turned their backs as food and money changed hands over corpses, even those of men the prisoners had known. But never any of the four friends. All of them shared whatever they could manage, their loyalty surviving earth that oozed with maggots and air fouled by an unspeakable stench.

And they'd all survived despite the damned Confederate guards, and especially their superiors, the men who'd decided to withhold the most basic elements of life: food, clean water, shelter. Gabe hoped to God there was a hell so that Capt. Henry Wirz, the bastard in charge of the prison, would burn there forever.

But even as the devil's flames licked Wirz's boots in his imagination, Gabe knew that a young woman as kind as Eve knew nothing of the real horrors of the war. Yes, she read the papers, according to what she'd told him, but he'd learned the hard way that the stirring accounts in the press bore little resemblance to the mud and blood and mayhem that existed in the field. Hating Eve for Camp Sumter, the Andersonville prison, made about as much sense as some Southerner cursing Gabe's mother for the Union soldiers who'd looted their way across the South.

Still, if he had good sense, he'd stay away from her. He already had trouble looking to throw him off this steamer and waiting for him at home in Ohio. He could ill afford the complication of a tart-mouthed Southerner.

". . . pretty, dark-haired girl on board, with hazel eyes. About twenty years old and stands about five feet one."

The voice wrenched Gabe's attention from what he was doing, and he tripped over a sleeping prisoner's outstretched arm. As soon as he apologized, he moved where he could hear the man's words clearly.

"Her name is Yvette Augeron, although she's likely to be using an alias. She's wanted for serious crimes against the Union."

He peered around a corner, toward the bow. Even in the dim lamplight, Gabe noted the officer's crisp blue uniform. A tall, elegant-looking figure, he held himself as straight as the creases on his trousers, as if he meant to demonstrate refined posture to his inferiors. As with his stance, his light brown hair and slightly darker beard were so perfectly well ordered, they looked like something from an illustration, not real life. The jackass looked as if his grooming hadn't suffered one whit from the war.

Or, Gabe wondered, did his instantaneous dislike of the man stem from his realization that it was Eve he was describing? Eve, or Yvette Augeron, who was wanted for crimes against the Union. Serious crimes, the man was saying. That must mean that he planned to arrest her.

The image of Eve as a criminal didn't sit right with him. She'd helped him, hadn't she? Even though he'd been a Union soldier, someone she'd barely met, she'd stepped in at her own risk to save his life. Gabe didn't know what sort of charges this dark-haired officer might have against her, but he did know he couldn't let the fellow catch her unaware.

He wished he could hear the other soldiers' responses, but all Gabe could make out was the soft rumble of their words. The next clear voice was the officer's.

"Capt. Darien Russell. If you hear anything, I expect a full report."

With that, the captain suddenly strode around the bow's curve and rammed into Gabe.

"Watch where you're standing, Private!" he snapped.

As if there were any other place where Gabe might step.

"Excuse me"—Gabe let the pause stretch out longer than he should have, until the fellow's face screwed up with indignation—"sir."

"*Salute,* you insolent laggard. You prisoners have forgotten everything that was ever drummed into your thick skulls. With men like you, it's a wonder our side won."

"I'm not sure we have yet, *sir.* I heard the guards say they'd seen muzzle flashes on the shore tonight," Gabe lied to vex him.

Captain Russell glanced quickly over his shoulder toward the east.

"Better watch yourself," Gabe said. "I hear they

fancy wider targets than us prisoners. And those pretty gold bars give them something good to aim at."

"At which to aim," Russell corrected primly. "Now stand aside. I have government business to attend."

He shoved Gabe into another sleeping soldier as he passed.

"Damn it! What the hell—!" the startled man yelped.

Apparently, Russell was in too much of a hurry to lecture the prisoner about his failure to salute, for he rushed away. Gabe trailed in his wake, leaving the soldier to continue cursing his rude awakening.

As Russell strode toward the main cabin, Gabe wondered how he could conceivably prevent a captain from detaining a woman passenger. He tried once more to reconcile what little he knew of Eve with the notion that she might be some kind of criminal. His gut feeling told him she was far less capable of wrongdoing than this pretentious fool who meant to detain her.

His mind struggled desperately to form a plan to stop this captain without getting himself in any deeper trouble than he was already in.

With a trembling hand, Yvette swiped away the tears of gratitude that blurred her vision. She had never felt such relief in all her life as when the soldier with the tangled beard handed back her reticule.

"Got me this keepin' it away from some of 'em." He gestured proudly toward a swelling eye. "But I didn't forget how you gave my friend here your dinner. What kind of men are we if we'd steal from an angel?"

The man's friend slept nearby, his emaciated body partially wrapped around the empty basket Yvette had left.

Even now, as she neared her stateroom, she could barely believe that a man—a Yankee—who had almost nothing would fight to protect her reticule. Before leaving, she'd brushed her lips across his rough cheek. In her gratitude, she forgot to worry about whatever vermin his thicket of a beard might harbor.

First Gabriel and now this ragged stranger. Perhaps Yankees varied in their natures just as much as Southern men. Or perhaps war brought out the worst in all men, she thought, too conscious of the fact that her own people had clearly starved these soldiers.

Was it possible, now that this war was ending, that reason would return and battered hearts could heal?

Perhaps hope blinded her to danger, or perhaps it was only some combination of the late hour, the dim light, and the attention required to pick a pathway through the midst of so many sleeping soldiers. Whatever the cause, as Yvette moved toward the entrance to the main cabin, she nearly ran headlong into the one Yankee that no truce would ever compel her to forgive.

Her fingers clutched spasmodically at the black reticule, which she held tight against her waist. Yvette felt her limbs begin to tremble, but she could not make them run. Her jaw dropped, but neither word nor scream would come. She was too aware of the Union officers inside the main cabin only steps away, officers who would be quickly drawn by any outburst, who would surely take this murderer's side against her.

His hand clamped firmly on her upper arm, yet Yvette barely felt the throbbing pressure points of thumb and fingers. All she could think of was the reticule that she was clutching and the folded letter sewn into its lining. Whatever happened, she must not let Darien Russell find it there.

"Strange that I don't hear you laughing now. But perhaps this time you're the object of amusement. You've led me quite a merry chase, Yvette." His voice ran dark and low, as if he, too, had no wish to draw attention to their conversation.

She jerked her arm free, breaking his grip through sheer determination. "Take your filthy hand off me, murderer!" she hissed.

"If I'm not very much mistaken, you're the one who's charged with murder, Miss Augeron."

Frustrated by an urge to slap the smugness off his face, she gripped the handle of her reticule even harder.

"Killing *you* would have been worth whatever punishment they gave me, but I have no intention of hanging for your crimes, *Captain.*" She infused the last word with all the contempt she felt, all the wounded pride that had prompted her to invent insulting songs and paint General Butler's face in several dozen chamber pots.

He flinched, and she could swear she felt how much he ached to throttle her, the same way he had choked her pliant sister. Instead, he moved forward, backing her closer to the door.

"Just remember you *did* kill them," he said. "You killed both of them!"

"Can't a fella get a drink here? You're blockin'

th'way, Cap." A soldier slurred the words behind Russell.

Yvette's gaze rode over the sharp angle of the captain's shoulder. Drunk or not, the voice sounded familiar. Hope unfurled inside her when she recognized Gabe's face. No alcohol dulled his expression. Instead, he looked grimly expectant. Did he mean to provoke Russell?

Darien glanced over his shoulder. *"You* again!" He spat the words, as derisive as Yvette had sounded. "What must I do to teach you some respect?"

"Dunno, how 'bout . . . *this!*" Gabe dropped his shoulder, then launched himself into Russell's side.

Caught off balance, the captain went down heavily.

Yvette took the opportunity to run, thanking God for Gabe's distraction. She picked her way rapidly among soldiers lounging on the deck. A few shouted rude questions or comments at her haste, but no one tried to stop her. With her heart thundering her panic, she pounded toward her stateroom's outer door. Shaking as she was, she could barely fit the key inside the lock. She expected at any moment strong arms to grab her from behind. But none did, and somehow, on the third try, she opened the door and rushed inside, then closed and quickly locked it.

"Mew?" Lafitte's cry sounded as confused as she felt.

Yvette put her back to the door, then slid down it till she sat. As if her presence could prevent a man of Russell's size from entering.

As she waited, trembling, she tried to imagine how Gabe had divined her need, her terror. How much had he overheard?

But with a beast like Russell on her trail, it was

impossible to worry about what Gabe knew or thought. Guiltily, she thought of what he'd risked by striking an officer. She might be safe now, but what of him?

If he were arrested, how could she dare help him? And if she did nothing, could she live with that guilt, too?

"Where did she go?" Russell demanded. His hands grasped the insolent private's shoulders, and he tried to shake him as a terrier might a rat.

Gabe, however, stood his ground and watched surprise steal across Russell's features. Gabe's strength was quite a change for someone who only moments ago had given the impression he was drunk.

"Didn't see her, Captain," Gabe answered clearly. "I was too busy helping you up from the floor. Sorry about knocking you off your feet like that. I got a little dizzy there for a moment. Didn't mean to stumble into you."

"You want this man placed under guard?" a voice came from his left, and Gabe looked up—and into Seth Harris's gray eyes. Apparently, his friend had come looking when he hadn't returned to the hurricane deck.

Captain Russell glanced at Seth and nodded stiffly. "Is he your responsibility?"

"Unfortunately," Seth answered. "I don't know how he does it, but he always finds himself a bottle. Maybe someday he'll get the knack of drinking without acting the part of a damned fool."

Gabe lowered his gaze in an attempt to look contrite. Really, he was suppressing a smile of gratitude at Seth's lie. He'd certainly have some explaining to do, but he felt confident his friend wouldn't arrest him.

"You better keep him out of my way," Russell ordered, glaring at Seth. "Otherwise, I'll have the both of you brought up on charges. Is that understood?"

Gabe's glance jerked upward. If there was one thing Seth Harris hated, it was high-handedness from other officers. As he expected, Seth adjusted his cracked spectacles. His spine, too, straightened, emphasizing every inch of his six feet two inches. At the moment, he didn't much look the part of the logical professor.

"They didn't strip me of my rank when I was captured, Captain." The harshness in Seth's voice iced the evening air. "I'll thank you to remember that when you're addressing me."

Russell said nothing for several moments. Instead, he glared steadily at both Seth and Gabe, as if he were committing both of them to memory.

Finally, after far too long a pause, he said, "Just keep this soldier quiet—and well away from me—and we'll have no cause for unpleasantness . . . *Captain.*"

With that, he spun crisply on his heel and strode off—thankfully, in the opposite direction of the one that Eve had taken.

Not Eve, Gabe corrected himself. Yvette. He'd have to keep that in mind.

Seth looked at him curiously. "What the hell was that about?"

Gabe nodded. "I sort of hit him, sir."

Seth shook his head disapprovingly. "Don't give me that 'sir' routine. We're way past that, Gabe. So, did you hit the pretentious bastard on purpose?"

"I did."

Seth stared at him, considering. "I thought you'd given up trying to prove yourself against every jackass that has it coming."

"It was more than that, Seth. He was troubling a lady passenger who'd just done me a good turn."

Seth's eyebrows rose. "Not that little beauty you were admiring earlier? That Rebel gal?"

Gabe shrugged the answer, ignoring the objection in his friend's tone.

"I'm not happy with it, Gabe, but I suppose that's better than what I'd imagined," the captain said. "I figured you'd maybe run into those Ohio boys."

"I did. And I'm likely to again if I don't get back upstairs."

"Then by all means let's go. You can tell me about it up there."

"I want to check on her first. I think he may have hurt her," Gabe said. "I'll explain what happened later."

"Stay out of this, Gabe. You need to concentrate on keeping out of trouble, getting home. Think logically. Or if you can't do that, think about that beefsteak you keep dreaming on and not some girl with every reason in the world to hate you. Let's go back upstairs."

"Is that an order?"

Irritation flashed across Seth's features. He shook his head. "Just good advice. Why don't you take it?"

"You've got this wrong. I'm not looking for trouble. I just need to see her for a moment. I have to." He wanted to explain what she'd done tonight to prevent him from being pitched overboard unconscious, but he had to keep it to himself. Otherwise, Seth's "good advice" would definitely become an order.

"You want me to go with you?" the captain finally offered.

"Three's a crowd," Gabe said.

Seth frowned. "Sometimes I think you're hell-bent on getting yourself killed. I don't want to hear that you've been in another fight, especially not over her. Use your head. Remember this girl's a Southerner. Expect little; trust less."

As Seth headed for the boat's stern and, presumably, the stairway, Gabriel thought on his last statement: *"Expect little; trust less."* Seth had told him those same words after he'd arrived at Andersonville. As long as Gabe had remained there, that advice made sense, maybe even helped keep him alive. But now he deliberately cast aside the notion, the same way he'd discarded the vermin-infested rags of his imprisonment.

He was a free man now, and the hellish war was over. Despite what he had done before, what he had suffered, Gabe intended to start expecting more. Maybe he could even risk a little trust.

But not on this Yvette. In the wake of everything that had happened, he didn't have trust enough to squander on a woman who had lied about her name.

Yvette sat quivering against the outer door. Before her, Lafitte tumbled and leapt, as if trying to distract her from her frantic breathing and her pulsebeats, which hammered like woodpeckers at both temples. Instead of succeeding, the kitten's antics annoyed her. Couldn't the rascal settle down and let her think of what to do?

It was no use, anyway, she realized. She rubbed at her arms, where Russell had exerted bruising pressure. How could she concentrate when his furious face kept flashing in her vision? How could she plan what to do while she worried that at any moment he might find her?

Still, snatches of ideas raced around her mind, most too swift to capture and examine. She might abandon her room and hide somewhere, perhaps among the cargo she'd seen loaded in New Orleans and Vicksburg. Or she could jump overboard with some piece of wood to float her out of danger. Perhaps, instead, she ought to find another Union officer and tell what she knew about Darien Russell and his ring of Yankee thieves. But each idea seemed more hopeless than the last until her vision blurred with welling tears.

A faint knock sent her hand flying to cover her own mouth lest she scream and give herself away. If she could only remain quiet, perhaps he wouldn't be certain she was in here. Maybe he wasn't even sure this was her room.

Hope faded as she realized that certain or not, Darien Russell wouldn't rest until he had the chance to look inside. She wondered how long it would take him to find a crewman with a key to let him in and how in God's name she could hope to escape him if that happened.

Had she fled already? And if so, to where?

Gabe tapped once more, slightly louder. His voice

rose just above a whisper. "It's Gabe Davis. Let me in."

A moment passed and then another. Though he thought he might hear some movement in the stateroom, he could not be sure. *Go away,* the voice of caution whispered. The longer he dallied, the greater his chances of running into either Captain Russell or Silas Deming and his friends.

He'd return to his spot on the crowded upper deck and stay there for the duration of the journey. He ought to feel relieved that he wouldn't have to worry about this Yvette's problems. But instead, disappointment washed over him. As foolish as it was, he'd wanted to see her again, to hear her softly accented voice, intelligence sparkling behind each word, to feel her gentle touch once more upon his hand. Longing overwhelmed him as he remembered how she'd felt when he had kissed her, and hunger rose, unstoppable as the river flooding past its banks.

And so he knocked one final time, and at last the door cracked open.

"Get away from here!" Her voice hissed through the narrow gap.

"Did he hurt you?" Gabe whispered.

Her breath puffed out, loud with her exasperation. The gap widened, and she pulled him inside. As soon as he had cleared the opening, she closed and locked the door.

"No, but he most certainly will if you stand out there pounding on my door." Anger punctuated her words, but still, she kept her voice low, as if she feared someone would hear. "Why didn't you just leave?"

Her eyes belied the abruptness of the question. In them, Gabe glimpsed something like relief. Whatever her trouble, she wasn't all that eager to face it on her own.

"I couldn't," he said, though the words did not explain his action, even to himself.

She seemed to accept them nonetheless. The anger in her voice faded to concern. "Did he hurt you?"

"He didn't, though I expect that he would like to," Gabe told her. "I overheard him near the bow. He was asking about a girl with your description . . . Yvette."

She tilted back her head, her chin jutting forward, as if she could master her emotions with a show of pride. "I had no choice except to give a false name. I am Yvette Augeron. My family always called me Yvie. 'Eve' is not so very different."

"Why? The captain said you were wanted for some crime. Something serious. But I couldn't imagine you—" He shook his head, wondering if he'd been wrong. When he'd kissed her, she'd felt so delicate, so fragile. But now, as before, he saw every indication that she had a spine of steel.

Even so, he remembered her compassion. Clearly, Yvette was a jewel with many facets. "You helped me earlier," he explained. "I figured I owed you at least the warning. But when I saw the way he grabbed you . . ."

"Now you have repaid the favor, Gabriel. You helped me out of a difficult situation, just as I helped you." She looked away from him, but not before he saw moisture gleaming in the corners of her eyes. "You owe me nothing more."

Ignoring the dismissal in her words, Gabe said, "Yes, I do. You listened to my story. It helped so much to share it. Tell me, Yvette, what's happening to you?"

She glared at him for just a moment, then dropped

into the room's sole chair. The kitten pounced onto her lap and curled into a ball. Gabe could hear his purring as she stroked him gently. Like Lafitte, Yvette seemed to have drawn into herself, for she neither looked at him nor said a word in answer.

Gabe sat on the berth's edge, as he had before. Remembering their kiss, he felt a strong ripple of desire, but once again he reminded himself that Seth was right. Nothing good could come of a relationship with a Southern woman.

If he had any sense, he'd leave now. He'd done the gentlemanly thing by offering to listen. That freed him of his obligation, didn't it?

Just as he'd decided to get up, Yvette took a deep breath. "All right, Monsieur Davis. I accept the offer of your ears."

Without further prelude, she began. "Captain Russell is an evil man."

He stared at her, studying the way her gaze kept flicking from one door to the other, as if her words might conjure up the appearance of her enemy. Though she had paused, he said nothing, sensing that if he, too, quickly filled the silence, she would not continue.

Yvette's gaze lost its wariness, and her brows beetled with anger. "He has used this war for his own profit—and, worse yet, we let him."

"Who do you mean, *we?*" Gabe ventured.

"The Creole families of New Orleans, at least the ones who took the oath. You may not know this, but when the Yankees captured our city, men like my father were given a choice: swear loyalty to the Union or lose their businesses, their homes . . . everything."

He tried to imagine his own father faced with such

a difficult decision. With his wife and daughters to support, even Flint Maxwell Davis might be forced to swallow back his pride.

Yvette continued. "My father was one who chose the oath, but it made him unpopular, even in our home, I'm afraid. So when Captain Russell came along, casting himself as a better sort than the other Union officers, Papa took him up on his offer of friendship. Russell beguiled Papa with his talk of operas and French literature. And I believe, after a time, that he began offering my father advice of a financial sort."

She shook her head, and her hazel eyes flashed anger. "Papa barely seemed to notice how one Creole family after another was falling into ruin—every one of whom had some association with this man or his friend Major Stolz."

"Sometimes we see only what we wish to," Gabe offered, but he was wondering how many on both sides had used this war to steal.

"Captain Russell even convinced Papa he had honorable intentions toward my sister, Marie," Yvette continued. "And Papa encouraged the relationship, though he well knew no decent Creole man would ever offer for Marie if it was learned she'd entertained a Yankee caller."

Bitterness edged Yvette's words. Perhaps it made her head ache, too, for she raised her hand from Lafitte to press her thumb and forefinger just above each eyebrow. The kitten rose, arched his back, and yawned, his pink mouth contrasting with his tiny ivory fangs. Gabe looked away in hopes the kitten would keep to its own place.

"We have a saying in the Quarter," Yvette continued. *"Chacun sait ce qui bout dans son chaudron.* 'Every-one knows what boils in his own pot' is the translation, but we use it to mean there are no secrets within society. Marie's secret didn't last long, so of course the only proper thing to do was see the couple wed. Even *Maman,* who hates Yankees more than a dog hates fleas, could see the necessity of that. Everyone could . . . except for me."

Gabe almost felt sorry for the captain. Little as he knew of Yvette, he suspected she could be a formida-ble adversary. The kitten leapt from her lap and rubbed across Gabe's lower legs.

"I mentioned how many families Captain Russell had befriended who had so suddenly fallen on hard times, but Papa was quite taken with him all the same. Still, I wondered more and more about the man. I suspected he was meeting Marie in secret, spending time alone with her, yet he did not offer for her hand. I . . . I began asking among the servants."

A brief smile lifted the corners of her mouth and touched her eyes with genuine affection. "But if it is true there are few secrets in society, there are fewer still among the quadroon nurses, the old house slaves, and cooks. Before very long, a letter came into my hands. A letter from this Captain Russell . . . to his wife."

Gabriel felt outrage as he imagined an older, mar-ried man trifling with one of his two sisters. He would pound the fellow into paste. Lacking the brute strength to do that, he wondered what Yvette had done and how it could have led to a criminal charge and a northward flight.

"As bad a shock as that was," Yvette continued, "the letter also confirmed my true suspicions. Captain

Russell gave instructions to his wife on how to access the accounts of the Gayarrée family's recent New York investments. I know little of such things, but even I could guess this letter would cause the captain a great deal of trouble."

"What happened?"

She poured each of them a glass of water from the pitcher. After sipping at hers, she continued. "My first thoughts were for Marie, of course. Before I showed anyone, even Papa, this terrible letter, I had to speak to her. It was very difficult. Marie imagined I had written it myself and forged Captain Russell's name. She accused me of being jealous that she would wed while I would never—"

"How could she say that?" Gabe asked. "You're so beautiful, and you're her sister, after all."

Yvette lifted a hand to stop him. "You are very kind to protest, but perhaps you have guessed already the cost of one mistake. For a young man such as yourself, there may be a second chance, but for a proper young lady—"

"What'd you do? Use the wrong fork at some fancy dinner party?" He offered her a smile, eager to lift her sadness.

She shrugged to indicate indifference, then raised an eyebrow, as if in amusement. "Perhaps I understated the number of mistakes I have made. And certainly Marie overestimated their importance. But now, *mon Dieu*, now there is no hope at all for a good marriage. Not after that monster's accusations."

Lafitte rubbed against Gabe's lower legs and mewed. He rubbed its ears. To quiet it, he told himself. He didn't want its noise to drown out Yvette's soft voice or perhaps draw the attention of a passerby outside the door.

"Did you ever convince your sister to believe you?" he asked.

"I did not think so at the time. She begged me to let her speak to this man she claimed she loved, to give him a chance to tell her this was all some terrible mistake, I suppose. I told her I would go to the Union lieutenant I had learned was investigating Russell." She shook her head. "If only I had done just that . . . But Marie began to cry then, and she begged me."

Yvette pressed her fingertips above her eyes once more, as if the memory pained her. Her jaw quivered, and Gabe heard her teeth chatter. Just as his had when he'd leapt into the frigid river after Matthew and when he'd seen his brother's face above a stranger's Rebel uniform. Mute tears slid down her cheeks, and at their appearance, Gabe rose and went to her.

She glanced up at him, her eyes full of such fear and desperation that he didn't hesitate a moment. Instead, he took her hand and drew her toward him, let her sob while encircled by his arms.

"I would have done it, anyway, but Marie—she said she was with child. She was hysterical, screaming that she would rather take her life than face such a scandal. She wanted desperately to believe the letter was some sort of fabrication, that he would marry her once he knew of her condition."

"So you didn't go to the lieutenant?" Gabe asked. He felt her head shake against his chest.

"God forgive me, I did not. I had to give Marie her chance. And then she disappeared . . . within the day. Two days later, she was pulled out of the

Mississippi River. But two days wasn't long enough to obliterate the bruises on her throat."

"He killed her," Gabe said flatly. The scheming bastard had murdered a naive young woman—and the mother of his child.

Yvette nodded. "Killed her—and the lieutenant, too. When I tried to see him, I found his body lying on the carpet of his office. And I know that Captain Russell plans to kill me also to keep his secret safe."

Dear Lord, how she had suffered, how she was suffering right now. He wanted so badly to fix it for her, to keep her safe and see her sister and the other man avenged. But neither was in his power, so instead he let her lean into his strength and weep.

How right it felt to hold her, and how natural, though he couldn't recall the last occasion he'd held a woman so very close. He bowed his head and brushed her jet-black crown with his lips, but gently, very gently, so that she would not pull away. Comforting this woman, who had eased his pain such a short time before, felt like a balm for all that ailed him, a salve upon his soul.

To his utter amazement, she lifted her face toward his, as if her lips felt drawn by the same force that seemed to pull his own. He kissed her, once again feeling some soul-deep connection, feeling her woman's curves against him, imagining her opening like pale magnolia petals.

His body responded to her need with want, to her softness with almost painful hardness. His mind reacted, too, part of it appalled by the recklessness of this attraction, part of it realizing that for all their differences, their losses had a striking similarity. Her sister, his brother. Her Louisiana, his Ohio home. As long as the kiss lasted, he felt convinced that both were dim reflections of something stronger that had been touched off by their connection. When she broke the kiss, he felt diminished, a fragment of that newfound, greater self.

"That was very foolish," Yvette said, though she seemed to be admonishing herself, not him. Despite her words, she did not step out of his embrace. "I thought that perhaps I'd grown beyond such rashness."

He touched her cheek and gently kissed her temple, then smiled as he felt a shudder ripple through her. "It didn't feel at all foolish," he whispered in her ear. But he knew exactly what she meant.

"Each of us has trouble enough alone," Yvette declared. This time, she turned away.

Gabe felt her absence, as sharp as pain. Lust, he told himself. No more than physical lust. A stallion felt it for every mare it scented. What he felt could mean nothing more.

Yet he could not still his reckless tongue. "Each of us needs a friend now."

She risked a cautious smile, though it vanished quickly. "I have had many friends, Monsieur, family friends and young ladies from the convent school. *That* did not feel like friendship. It felt like something other, something we must not allow."

He returned her smile. "I'll admit, it felt like something other to me, too. Something very . . . pleasant."

She shook her head emphatically. "I watched another Yankee ruin poor Marie. I'll be cursed if I learned nothing from her error."

Offense wiped the smile from his face. "You take me for a Captain Russell?"

She did not immediately answer. Instead, she studied him keenly. His anger and disappointment steeped a bitter brew. How could he have imagined she'd see past this uniform, that the kisses she'd bestowed meant more than either impulsiveness or pity?

He turned for the door and unlocked it. Her silence gave him all the answer that he needed.

The door was halfway open before she caught him by the elbow. "You have to understand how hard this is for me. I have never kissed a man before today." Color rose into her face with the admission. "I scarcely know how I feel about it. Except that . . ."

She turned him toward her, then leaned against the door until it once again clicked shut, isolating both of them amid a crowd of thousands.

"Except that what?" he prompted.

She glanced up at him through her long lashes. "Except that I am frightened and alone for the first time in my life, and I can't imagine I am thinking very clearly."

"Must be brain fever," Gabe told her, despising the irritation in his voice, hating the fact that her admission so disturbed him. "Only a damned fool would want anything to do with a man like me. I hope you get your troubles ironed out, Yvette. I hope you get to go back home again. But until you manage that, I hope our kiss will give you something to remember. Something to make you wish for more than lonely nights."

Without waiting for her reply, he strode out of the room, pausing only long enough to hear the door lock in his wake.

* * *

After Gabe sent for the head steward, he wondered if Seth had been right. Maybe he was only tempting trouble. As if he found it preferable to returning home. He held on to the thought, picked it up, and turned it, examining the possibility from every angle.

Despite the unpleasantness he knew he'd face from his father, he didn't want to die. The dream of Oregon glittered brightly as a star on his horizon. His inheritance from his grandmother's estate, though modest, would be enough to get him there, half a world away from Father's ever-present, unasked question: *Why in God's name did you live instead of Matthew?*

With that thought came relief that no one in Oregon would know he'd had a younger brother. No one there would wonder why he hadn't gotten to Matthew in time, dragged him out from that hole in the ice, and brought him home. No one would ever ask why, unable to be the hero, he had instead run like a coward in the war.

Gabe swallowed past the painful lump of his delusions. At the edge of the Pacific, no one would know what happened. No one except him. The harsh truths of his life would shadow his journey across the continent like a pack of hungry wolves, always waiting for him to stumble so they could pounce and savage him.

The thought angered Gabe. He'd had a bellyful of running. Whatever slunk up behind him, he'd rather turn around and fight. Why else would he have left a safe deck to scout another place to sit? Why else did he feel the need to help Yvette with her problems?

Gabe glanced around uneasily. If either Capt. Darien Russell or Silas Deming caught him before he made it back upstairs, he'd have the opportunity to see how much he really wanted trouble.

After about fifteen minutes, the head steward finally met him outside the main cabin. A slight man with a thick, white mustache, he looked distinctly annoyed.

"We're very busy settling in deck passengers and the officers. Before you ask, I cannot do a thing about the overcrowding or the distribution of your rations. Those are military matters. My concern lies mainly with our civilian passengers. So tell me quickly, what is this important matter you must discuss?"

"One of the lady passengers, a civilian," Gabe emphasized, "confided in me that she is experiencing a, ah—delicate problem with one of the high-ranking officers aboard, a Captain Russell. Apparently, she—ah, discouraged his attentions some months ago, and ever since he has been sending her alarming notes, troubling her on the streets, and so forth. Finally, she decided to flee north to stay with family for some time. Unfortunately, he followed her on board the *Sultana*."

"Have there been problems here?" the steward asked, his irritated expression dissolving into interest.

"I saw him grab the girl myself. I think he might have harmed her if I hadn't been able to distract him. Of course, since he's a captain, this is an awkward problem. I'm afraid he may invent some wild story and convince crew members to help him search the staterooms."

"He most certainly will not!" The steward's voice bristled with indignation, and he straightened his spine, adding half an inch to his modest height. "I will alert the cabin crew immediately that no information may be shared and no civilian passengers disturbed."

"The young lady will be very grateful."

The steward peered up at Gabe, his sharp-eyed gaze appraising. "You're a fine young man to stick your neck out for a stranger. Wait here. I'll bring you something for your trouble."

"That's all right, I—" Gabe began, but the older man whisked away.

Once again, Gabe peered nervously up and down the deck and hoped to heaven that none of the men crowded nearby had overheard his story. If any of them related it, he could add military prison to his list of worries. He realized now that Yvette had never said what crime she'd been accused of committing. If he were abetting someone charged with something serious in nature, he might even be risking a hanging.

And for what? For those brief moments that their kisses felt like something real? Those moments before she'd wondered aloud how she could allow herself to feel attraction to a Yankee?

He shook his head, disgusted with his own foolishness. Not wanting to risk staying here another moment, he started toward the stairway.

"Wait!" someone called from behind him.

Gabe's pulse roared in his ears until he realized it was only the old steward with the flowing white mustache. Noticing the covered basket the man carried and the delicious scents that rose from it, Gabe could not suppress a grateful grin.

Food. He'd never tire of eating, but this meal would be shared with his friends.

If he could make it back up to the hurricane deck without being hurled overboard or arrested.

Chapter Six

*On the Avenue in front of the White House were
several hundred colored people, mostly women
and children, weeping and wailing their loss.
This crowd did not diminish through the whole
of that cold, wet day; they seemed not to know
what was to be their fate since their great benefac-
tor was dead. . . .*

—Gideon Wells,
after the death of Abraham Lincoln

Wednesday, April 26, 1865
On the Mississippi River, north of Helena, Arkansas

The *Sultana* had to fight the river's current to carry
them northward, just the way Gabe fought his misgivings every mile of the trip. Everything about the journey felt precarious, from the possibility of Rebel
snipers to the enemies aboard the steamer and his
ill-advised attraction to a Southern woman.

He'd tried so hard to put Yvette out of his mind, to focus on the problems at hand instead of those his attraction to her represented. This morning, he'd succeeded, at least for a while, when they'd had that scare back near Helena. Someone had shouted out that a photographer was taking their picture from the shore, and every fool aboard had crowded to the port side, trying to get his face into the photograph. Top-heavy with prisoners, the steamer had listed over so far that it nearly capsized. The officers quickly shouted orders for the men to keep their places for the duration of the journey. But sticking to one spot was difficult, especially with the lack of the barest requirements for human comfort.

In spite of both the scare and the conditions, it was hard not to take cheer from the way the morning sun slanted through the trees to their east and the sky shone sapphire-bright with promise. If he had a thimbleful of sense, he'd cast last night's temptation to the river and leave it safely behind him in the South. He needed to fix his thoughts instead on his new beginning.

With that admonition firmly in mind, he tied a long rope to the handle of a borrowed bucket, then cast it far over the boat's side. Within moments, the bucket splashed into the Mississippi, and Gabe almost wished that he could follow. It might be a bit nippy yet, but a swim would feel like heaven after all the time he'd spent cramped on the upper deck. Opting for sanity instead, he settled for the exercise of hauling the full container back up, pulling the rope hand over hand.

Jacob joined him.

"Zeke's not doing so well this morning." Jacob leaned over to pull the bucket over the railing. Half the water had sloshed out the sides during its journey past the lower two decks. "He feels hot as hell."

"Fever? Damn. Is it the leg?"

Jacob ran strong fingers through his dark brown curls. Frustration was evident in the set of his square jaw. "Yeah. I think so. It doesn't look good, Gabe."

"It's infected, isn't it?"

His brown eyes filmed with emotion, Jacob looked away. "I have to get him home, Gabe."

Gabe put a hand on his forearm. "We'll help you do it, both Seth and me. You know that. We're going to get Zeke back to Indiana. He'll be all right then."

"It's a damned disgrace," Jacob growled, his impatience bubbling through the worry. "Packing us on board this boat without water or decent food or even a damned privy we can get to. Then telling us, 'Be still. You'll roll the steamer.' You notice most of the ones saying that are sleeping in their fancy staterooms or on cots in the main cabin. They aren't jammed on top a bare deck with their legs rotting off."

"Is that what you're worried about? That Zeke will lose the leg?"

Jacob shook his head, his features taut with tension. "No, not now. Now I'm worried he won't let them take the leg if they have to. He swears he won't do it. . . . I'd make him, anyway, but there's something you don't know. Something in our sister's letter, the one that caught up to us in Vicksburg."

"What? What is it?"

"Our pa's real sick. It's his breathing. He's always had his troubles with the dust from the grain, but not like this. It's bad enough so Eliza was worried we won't make it home in time."

"I'm-I'm sorry, Jacob. Why didn't you say something before?"

Jacob shrugged and stared at the swirls and eddies of the river. At length, he spoke again. "Zeke and I both think the world of our pa. We didn't want to imagine what might have happened in the month since that letter was posted, much less talk about it."

Gabe nodded. Jacob, especially, valued his control. Discussing the possibility of his father's death might put that at great risk. Respecting his friend's feelings, Gabe changed the subject.

"Seth said he asked around about a doctor last night. No luck, though."

"Damned army. All the half-starved, sick fellows on board and they can't even spare a doctor."

"The military's been one treat after another," Gabe allowed, "but at least we're heading north."

"Yeah. Still hardly seems real sometimes. We're finally going home."

Gabe grasped the bucket's handle. But before he started back toward the place where Zeke was slumped beside Seth, he made a promise, one that he meant with all his heart. "All four of us, Jacob. Every single one."

Capt. Darien Russell could not resist a smile of satisfaction at the chief mate's frown. Especially since that expression was directed at the supercilious little steward who'd been obstructing his efforts. Russell couldn't help appreciating the nervous twitch of the steward's white mustache.

"I don't like to be bothered about these matters." The chief mate paced the section of deck cleared for this discussion, his hands clasped behind him as he walked. "Captain Mason wants a good time and a safe journey, Mr. Beecham. With a record load like this one, those—and only those—are my concerns this morning. As far as I know, the country's still under martial law. If Captain Russell wants to search the staterooms, let him do it. He shouldn't have to come ask me."

Beecham straightened, as if that might fool anybody into thinking he was more than five feet two. When he glanced toward Russell, his dark blue eyes glittered with disdain. "I have reason to believe the captain's motives may be less than honorable."

Fear jolted through Darien's system. What could this man possibly know about his motives? He glared at the steward, and he determined to grind this professional lickspittle under heel.

"As I've told you before, this woman is a criminal against the Union!" Russell shouted. "Are you in league with the Confederate traitors, man? It's well within my power to detain you, too."

Behind the snowy mustache, Beecham colored instantly. "I was born in Illinois, sir. I once shook Mr. Lincoln's hand. I tell you, I'm loyal through and through. But I also have a duty to my passengers. And I was ... given to understand that this young lady is no criminal, just the unwilling object of your affections."

"What?" Not far away, heads turned toward Darien's exclamation. It took every bit of control he could muster not to swear at the outrageous lie. "This— this woman is a murderess, I tell you! I have written orders to arrest her, signed by the general in command of New Orleans!"

Withdrawing a folded piece of paper from his frock-coat pocket, he thrust it toward the chief mate. There was no chance at all either of these civilians would recognize the signature for the forgery it was.

The chief mate, who looked distinctly as if he'd rather be attending other duties, made a show of examining the paper. "This appears to be in order, Mr. Beecham. I want you to cooperate. The captain will be most unhappy if he is disturbed with this matter."

He passed the so-called orders to the steward, but the man refused to take the paper. "I don't need to look at it. I'll do what I can to assist you, Captain Russell. If you have intelligence about this woman's hiding place, I'll gladly let you search any stateroom. I hope you'll understand that I was only trying to act in the best interest of a lady. I had no desire to appear disloyal. I did check the passenger list after you spoke to me before, and I answered truthfully. There is no person registered by the name of Augeron on board."

"Oh, Miss Augeron is far too clever to register under her real name," Darien explained. But he smiled as he said it, thinking how Yvette would soon find that even cleverness had its limits against a superior foe.

My darling sister,

Some might accuse me of using these letters as a way to pretend that you yet live. But I assure you most emphatically that I never for a moment forget the grating of your coffin sliding into our family tomb. Never for a moment do I forget our maman's cry of pain or our grandmére's stern face wet with tears.

Today I imagine you in heaven; I see you laughing

*at the way temptation has been thrown into my path.
"How could you love a cursed Yankee?" Like a fool,
I asked you that, never guessing that a man cannot
be defined by his birthplace. Never guessing till today.*

*Our family would disapprove of the young man I
have met, much as all but Papa disapproved of Captain Russell. Society would raise its lofty eyebrows that
I would even speak to such a personage and turn its
back upon me for allowing him a kiss.*

*And such a kiss it was! Every little hair upon my
nape and arms rose as lips touched mine. Every ounce
of my resolve melted like a candle left too close to the
hearth. Did it feel like that for you, too? Did it ignite
your very being?*

*Only by remembering your errors did I manage to
break away from the enchantment, to pull myself out
of the flame. And only by imagining your laughter at
the sanctimony of my earlier letter, the smugness of my
naïveté.*

*I swear to you, Marie, I will no longer judge your
actions, will no longer demean those things you did
under the intoxicating spell. I promise you instead that
I will be strong for both of us, strong enough to put
aside the pleasures of the flesh. I will not allow this
Yankee to distract me from my path.*

Your somewhat wiser sister,
Yvette

Though the new day was already hurrying toward
noon, Gabriel's last words hung over Yvette's mood
like a pall: *"I hope our kiss will give you something to
remember. Something to make you wish for more than lonely
nights."*

She could scarcely imagine why she would find such

a prediction troubling. Unless she somehow managed to avoid Captain Russell until she reached Uncle André, she would die soon. Too soon to worry about whether she had hurt a Yankee soldier. Too soon to regret a life of loneliness.

Yet, as she teased the kitten with a loose scrap of lace or tried in vain to concentrate on the French novel she was reading, she realized she was lying to herself. Whether she lived another hour or many decades, she would worry over what had happened on this boat. And what had almost happened with a Yankee prisoner, a young man of unknown background whom her family must despise.

But did they not despise her, too, now? She winced as she remembered *Grandmère*'s words:

"The best thing you can do is leave and forget you ever were an Augeron. God knows we will spend our whole lives living down the scandal you have brought upon our name."

Always the scandal. If Papa had taken Russell's investment advice and lost every last picayune he'd ever made, if Marie had been ruined by a married Yankee, no one in the family would have ever spoken of it, as if disgrace kept from the papers were no disgrace at all. But now, with Marie's death in the news and, even more shockingly, Yvette's public murder accusation, there was nowhere in New Orleans to hide from gossip.

Even Papa had withdrawn his support. His reputation ruined, he would sell the coffee brokerage, he explained, and buy a plantation in the country. There the Augerons could live in tarnished splendor, a fine society unto themselves. He offered his youngest daughter, a girl he had cherished and spoiled all her life, not a word of invitation, not even one last crumb of love. She'd been cut off from her family as completely as if she were already dead.

Except for the possibility of Uncle André. Long removed from Creole society, he had embraced American culture as completely as if he'd been born to it—and in doing so, had prospered. At least that was what her father always claimed. Yvette wondered if her uncle yet remembered any French or the Gumbo Creole he had learned from his Negro nurse.

But perhaps Uncle André remembered enough to realize what grief Yvette had caused the *famille*. Perhaps enough to banish her as well.

A pang of terror made her drop her book. Without any family, then what would she do? How could she hope to make Captain Russell pay for what he'd done when she was all alone? And even if by some miracle she succeeded, how would she survive?

Heart pounding, she went to her bag and once more counted her money, but she had no more than she'd had yesterday, after Gabriel had left her.

Once more, her thoughts circled back toward him, settled on his handsome features, allowed the caress of his lips. She had to admit that she'd thought herself too fine to be a poor soldier's diversion. Despite his obvious intelligence and consideration, she never would have dreamed of entertaining such a fellow in New Orleans.

But now, stripped of her family and her fortune, she wondered on what grounds she based such pride. The amazing thought slashed through her consciousness that a penniless fugitive such as herself might not be good enough for him.

A tap came at her door.

Against all reason, she thought, *Please let it be Gabriel.*

But fear that Captain Russell was the more likely visitor followed on the heels of that impulsive thought.

"Anyone inside?" The voice, though muffled, was distinctly female.

Yvette decided to risk a peek.

A woman of about her own age carried a folded stack of towels and a water pitcher. The crimson birthmark covering her left cheek reminded Yvette of a hand slap, but the blonde's smile belied the impression of fresh violence.

"Good morning," she said brightly. "I've come to freshen up the stateroom for you."

Yvette detected a faint Irish lilt to the woman's voice. Her father ignored the sentiment that Irishmen were drunken laggards. Sometimes he hired them as teamsters to deliver sacks of coffee. Yvette was more used to Negro slaves and servants, yet she stepped aside to allow the chambermaid inside. The door swung closed behind her.

"I'm Kathleen Rowe," the young woman said with more familiarity than Yvette thought proper. Yet her blue-green eyes sparkled with both warmth and good sense.

Although Yvette didn't answer, she continued. "My husband's one of the crewmen. It's so crowded I was asked t'help out with the staterooms. Have ya been to the cabin yet, now? The cook's serving a glorious breakfast, and the day's a bonny one."

Ah, so this woman wasn't properly a servant. Perhaps that explained her unusual demeanor.

"I'm afraid I'm a bit seasick. Or maybe river sick's the right term." Yvette hated being forced to lie once more, but entering the main cabin would be far too dangerous.

Kathleen nodded emphatically as she refilled the stateroom's water pitcher. "I've just the thing for it. Let me drop these fresh towels, and then I'll bring some toast and tea."

The Irishwoman smiled at Lafitte, who batted playfully at the hem of her black skirt. "And perhaps I can find a wee bit of a treat for him as well."

Yvette found herself liking this amiable young woman and wondered for a moment if class had too long blinded her to a diverse host of good people.

Gabriel dreamed of her hazel eyes again and the smooth dark brows that arched above them. His palms slid along Yvette's raven hair as his lips tasted the warmth of her fair skin, the desire of her pink, kiss-swollen mouth.

He awoke with a groan and blinked in the bright sunlight. Bored with sitting still, he must have dozed awhile.

Eagerly, he gazed toward the trees and noticed how many of their bases were blanketed by brown floodwaters. Yet the shoreline seemed unchanged, unmoving. Only the endless splashing of the paddle-wheel blades and the smudged gray trail behind the smokestacks assured him they were truly moving north.

"Hey, Gabe, how 'bout some water?" Zeke's voice surprised him. He'd been asleep all morning.

Gabe pushed himself up on his elbows and yawned until his ears popped. "Sure. Let me find the bucket. Those Tennessee boys borrowed it."

"I'll get it," Jacob offered. "If I sit here one more minute, my knees are gonna rust."

Despite the clear attempt to hide his concern, worry for his younger brother strained Jacob's voice. When Gabe looked at Zeke, he understood. Zeke's straight brown hair hung in damp strings, and perspiration sheened his pallid face. His green eyes still looked sharp, though, as if he were plotting some sort of diversion, the way he had in prison.

"You've got that look again, Zeke. Planning another championship season of louse racing?"

"Naw. Those Sisters of Charity picked off my best vermin. Besides, I don't think it would be so popular outside of Andersonville." His humor sounded forced, his voice exhausted.

"How's the leg?"

"Just fine." Zeke's words had an exasperated edge to them, as if he'd been asked the question once too often.

Gabe shook his head. "Maybe we should get off in Memphis. They'll have some good food at the Soldiers' Home there. Doctors, too."

"God damn it, you sound just like my brother— and Seth, too. He went to see if he could find some fresh bandages. I'll tell you what I told him. I'm *better.* Anyway, I heard you groaning in your sleep. You see the damned doctor."

"Sawbones can't fix what ails me," he admitted. Zeke managed a laugh. "I hear you're courtin' trouble."

Gabe smiled, for Zeke's sake, then shrugged. "I can't get her off my mind."

"You don't want any Southern woman. You come on home with us. Jake and I'll introduce you to our sister. You're already just about a brother. You could be our brother-in-law for real."

Jacob laughed and knelt beside him with the water. "You must be delirious for sure. There's not a man alive could pry Eliza off that farm. Not with a pitchfork. And you'd best keep her name out of the conversation when Captain Seth gets back."

Seth had grown up near the farm where Jacob and Zeke lived. He'd been friends with Jacob for years before he'd gone off to teach mathematics, and he had some sort of history with Eliza, too. Gabe had never gotten the whole story, though. Apparently, the subject was still a sore one as far as the captain was concerned.

Zeke nodded to his brother, his green eyes closing as he drank from a dented tin cup. The same one he'd had in prison, Gabe recalled. Like the rest of them, he'd resisted giving up the implements of his survival. Just as well. Hell could freeze over before any of the paroled prisoners aboard could get a cup.

Water began to drip out of Zeke's slack lips. That quickly, he'd fallen back to sleep.

Jacob Fuller lowered his brother until he lay half-curled on the deck. Jacob's long sigh shuddered, as if he were fighting his own exhaustion—or an urge to weep.

Gingerly, he shifted and then began to unwrap the cloth around Zeke's foot and ankle. The wound looked red and angry, and moisture oozed along its edges. Gabe couldn't smell it—yet, but he'd seen enough at Andersonville to dread the coming stench.

"Maybe they can save the leg in Memphis," Gabe suggested. "I'll bet they have good hospitals there."

Jacob's brown eyes were dark with pain and pent-up anger. "I promised him I'd get him home, but this . . ."

Gabe helped him bathe the wound. "You look like you could use a walk."

"You heard what the captain said. They need us to keep still. And Zeke—"

"You know we'll take good care of him. Besides, I have a thing for you to do. You remember what I told you about that Captain Russell, who's looking for the Southern girl?"

"What's the matter? It's not enough you've gotten yourself into trouble? Now you're working on me, too?"

"If half of what Yvette told me was true, *he's* the criminal."

"Do you realize you're taking this Southern girl's word against a Union officer's? She's a goddamned Rebel, Gabe. The whole idea stinks of treason. How can you be sure of anything she said?"

"She's not some Confederate operative, Jacob. She's just a very young woman, and she's scared as hell. Look, I'm not asking you to spit on Lincoln's casket. All I want you to do is find this Russell and tell him you saw her hiding down below, among the cargo."

Jacob shook his head. "*You* do it if you're so damned certain of this girl's word. You're the one always spoiling for a fight."

"I'll get more than that if I interfere with him again. Maybe prison time. I'll tell you what. You've always been the best judge of character of the four of us. Go meet Captain Russell. I've heard he's in the main cabin trying to buy some information. You can act like you know something, and maybe he'll buy you a drink. Then, if he doesn't strike you as an arrogant son of a bitch, make up some excuse and come right back. But if he does, if he seems to have something to hide, tell him what I said about the girl."

Seth returned with a sheet he'd commandeered. He sat down beside them and began to tear it into bandages.

"I'll wrap this time," Gabe volunteered, peering furtively at Jacob Fuller. Seth would give him hell if he knew what Gabe had suggested.

Jacob rose. "I'm doing this for my stiff knees, Gabe, not because I think it's smart."

Without another word, he began making his way toward the bow—and the main stairwell.

"What was that about?" Seth asked. "You aren't stirring up more trouble, are you?"

"Not me. I just told him about the rumor they had some extra rations in the main cabin."

"Hell, we don't have any way to cook those cheap hog jowls they gave us. More of the same won't do us any good. Now if he could get more food like you brought last night . . ."

Gabe grimaced, his stomach growling at the thought. "Not much chance of that."

"You never told me how you came by that meal."

Gabe busied himself wrapping Zeke's ankle. "You're better off not knowing, Captain."

Seth smiled. "I'm not one to look a gift horse in the mouth, especially one that comes bearing real food. But since you were involved, you're right. I don't think I want to know."

Gabe finished his task and used an extra length of cloth, dipped in the bucket, to wash Zeke's face. All the while, he was thinking that Seth would probably tie him to the deck rail if he guessed what Gabe meant to do tonight.

Chapter Seven

Were these things real? Did I see those brave and noble countrymen of mine laid low in death and weltering in their blood? Did I see our country laid waste and in ruins? . . . Did I see the flag of my country, that I had followed so long, furled to be never unfurled again?

—Sam Watkins
First Tennessee Infantry, CSA

"Keep to your place," a guard warned Jacob as he neared the stairway. "Cap'n's orders."

Jacob's gaze swung toward the brusque voice. Damned if it wasn't that overbearing sergeant who'd herded them through Vicksburg.

"I've been asked to report to Captain Russell in the main cabin," Jacob told him, not bothering to explain it had been Pvt. Gabriel Davis—and not the officer—who had done the asking.

The broad-shouldered young sergeant stepped forward and warned with a pointed finger. "I find out you're lying, I'll have you shackled to your place."

Jacob felt his temper rising. After putting up with the poor conditions for the past two days, he hadn't a lick of patience to spare this blustering fool.

"You'd best take that finger out of my face before you lose it."

The sergeant stepped out of his way, which didn't surprise Jacob in the least. He'd never been certain what it was about him that prompted men to back down, but in his whole life, he'd rarely had to fight to make his point. Perhaps it was the darkness of his stare or maybe the matter-of-factness with which he spoke. Once he'd thought it was his muscular blacksmith's build, but he realized now that wasn't it at all. Despite his current gauntness, men still acquiesced to his rare demands.

Another guard stopped Jacob as he tried to enter the main cabin. The short redhead's gaze swept disdainfully over Jacob's rumpled, ill-fitting uniform.

"Where do you think *you're* going?" the guard asked, showing a set of teeth so chipped, it looked as if he'd spent the whole war champing hardtack without bothering to soak it first.

"Got some important information for Captain Russell," Jacob told him. This mission of Gabe's was something he'd enjoy.

The red-haired fellow looked skeptical, but he told Jacob to wait while he checked with the captain at the bar.

A few minutes later, the guard reluctantly showed him into the main cabin. After two years in the army and seven months in Andersonville prison, the room's opulence nearly overwhelmed Jacob. He set his mind to ignoring the fancy gingerbread woodwork, the chandeliers, the plush carpet, and fine bar, but they made him want to shout: *There's starving men on every deck, men who've lost their limbs or eyes or best friends. What are you people doing bothering about all this?*

Russell turned his head as Jacob approached. Jacob managed a halfhearted salute. Just as Gabriel had suggested, he meant to make up his own mind about this man, so he could at least begin by showing what the military deemed respect.

The captain flicked a glance in his direction, but he neither stood nor stopped fidgeting with the length of string he held. "Don't waste my time with idle chatter. If you've seen the girl, say so right now."

Jacob's anger surprised him, as did his immediate dislike for Captain Russell. The man stank of high-dollar whiskey, along with a two-bit case of contempt for common soldiers.

Jacob made up his mind immediately. Gabe didn't have to drag him into sending this arrogant ass on a wild-goose chase. "She's down below, on the main deck. Saw her heading into the stern cargo room."

The captain turned and focused on Jacob, his gaze hawklike, measuring. Jacob held that gaze, and Russell fidgeted, straightening his spotless frock coat and smoothing his perfectly trimmed beard.

"You're certain?"

Jacob nodded. "Just like the one you've been telling us to look out for. Small woman, only about twenty. Black hair, pretty face, fine figure. Shame to think that she'd do wrong."

A smile lifted the corners of the captain's mouth without touching his eyes. He gathered his string—

now tied into a slipknot, like a snare for rabbits—
and shoved it deep into his pocket. His hand extracted
in its place a silver coin, which he flipped toward
Jacob.

Jacob watched it flash by, but he did not follow its
arc onto the carpet. Nor did he bend to pick it up.

"I'm not saying I couldn't use that," he told Russell.
"But I only told you because I thought it was my
duty."

"Surely you don't think it's wrong to profit from
doing the right thing?" the captain asked, his brows
lifted in an expression of incredulity.

Jacob shrugged, then turned his back to Russell.
As he began to walk away, he said, "I reckon that's
why Mama named me Jacob and not Judas."

As he exited the main cabin, his final sideways
glimpse caught Russell stooping to retrieve the money
from the carpet.

Darien Russell strode downstairs to the main deck,
eager to investigate the curly-haired Indiana soldier's
report that Yvette Augeron was hiding among the
cargo. Damnable girl was causing him an ungodly
amount of trouble.

In spite of his irritation at the delay, he had to
admire the story she'd concocted for the steward earlier. It demonstrated the kind of shrewdness he'd
only seen in one woman before.

Constance, his wife, the very woman who had gotten
him into this situation in the first place. She had
forced him into all of it. Her appetites and expectations had nipped at his heels until he moved forward.
Not willingly but as if to escape a jabbing prod.

The investment scheme might have been Darien's idea, but now that it had gone so sour, he hated Constance for it. Not for those he ruined, for like her, they'd all been born to wealth, to believe the fine things their due for merely breathing. He hated her because she'd infected him with her tastes and battered him with disappointment at his defeats.

Most especially, she scoffed at his *failed* academy. That was how she put it. Time and time again.

As much as he resented his wife, with her red hair and her blue blood, he still derived enjoyment from the skill he'd used to carry out his plan. She might enjoy the money, but he'd been the one to take it. And he didn't take it in the manner he'd described to Constance.

For all his frustrations of the past few days, he smoothed his light brown beard and felt a smile tugging at it. What *would* Constance say about his methods, about the delectable little virgin he'd seduced in his quest to claim her father's wealth? He wondered how his perfect wife would like that or if she'd only laugh before going back to her plans to host the club's next foxhunt or renovate the house on the New Jersey estate.

Her estate. How often she'd reminded him of it, of how successful her father had been in the import business, of how he'd hired caretakers to maintain his family's grand tradition of horse breeding. The businessman, gentleman farmer, and later politician, Frederick Worthington had been all a man should be. Not a failure like her husband, a man who'd squandered his inheritance by opening an academy he was ill suited to manage.

It was no wonder that when he'd choked Marie,

he'd found himself imposing his wife's features on her dying face.

But right now Yvette was the problem at hand. He still recalled the stinging words he'd overheard her singing in the parlor when he'd come to visit Marie.

> Yankee Doodle came to town,
> Just to loot the treasure,
> But when he saw New Orleans' girls
> His fancy turned to pleasure.
>
> Yankee Doodle, keep it up,
> Yankee Doodle Dandy!
> Butler's come back in disguise
> To pinch whatever's handy!

There were other verses, those he'd tried so hard to forget, but soon they were on the lips of every child in town. He heard servants—Negroes—singing them in the streets! All of them laughing at him, many of them guessing at the hints Yvette had woven through the lyrics.

Colonel Jeffers guessing, too, and sending Lieutenant Simonton to ferret out the truth. Until he'd been forced to murder Simonton and sweet Marie as well. But Darien finally realized it was not those killings he wanted to avenge. It was that detestable, crude song and all its mocking accusations.

He would damned well kill Yvette for that song.

"Captain Russell."

He recognized the voice at once and turned toward the diminutive figure of the head steward. The man's expression was sour, as if he found this conversation a distasteful task.

"What is it, Mr. Beecham? I have a report to investigate."

"Let me add another. The wife of one of the crewmen saw the girl. She's in a stateroom on the cabin deck."

"The cabin deck," Russell repeated as he fingered the bit of string inside his pocket. "Can you show me where?"

Beecham hesitated, as if he still harbored distrust. But at length he nodded. "Those are my orders, sir."

By early evening, Yvette had finally managed to slip into the gentle stream of the French novel she was reading. A knock at her door disrupted the illusion of safety. Instantly, she jumped up, irrationally certain that at last, Darien Russell had come for her. Lafitte, who had been sleeping on her lap, barely managed to twist around in time to land on his feet. He hissed at the rude awakening and darted beneath the lower berth.

A familiar voice identified the crewmen's wife, Kathleen Rowe. Yvette breathed a quick sigh of relief, for the woman's amiable chatter had broken up long hours of isolation.

"Feeling better, miss?" Mrs. Rowe asked, but her words sounded more guarded than curious. The hand-slap birthmark stood out sharply against her noticeably pale face.

Something had changed, Yvette sensed. Someone must have filled Kathleen's head with lies—and a description.

"Yes, I do," Yvette told her, trying to keep her voice as natural as she could. "Thank you for bringing me the tea and toast this morning. It was very kind of you."

Not to mention it was the only meal she'd had today, since she'd been too afraid to leave her stateroom.

"I've brought you some clean towels and fresh water." Her blue-green eyes, so merry earlier, flicked toward Yvette anxiously.

"But you already came this morning," Yvette told her. There appeared to be something else tucked between the white squares, perhaps a wooden box.

Kathleen went about her business, saying nothing. Before, she'd been so friendly. They'd chatted about the war's end, and Kathleen told several amusing stories about growing up sandwiched among eight brothers in Ireland. Were circumstances different, Yvette thought they might have become close friends. Away from New Orleans's French Quarter, Yvette began to realize America was a different world in which one might choose to step outside social boundaries.

Once she'd finished her chores, Kathleen straightened her spine and looked Yvette directly in the eye. Nervously, she tucked a loose strand of fine, red-blond hair into her bun. "Is there—is there anything else you might need . . . *ma'am?*"

Something about that last word, after their earlier informality, struck Yvette as a warning. Did Kathleen mean to tell Russell where she was? Or had she already done so? Yvette didn't dare ask, but Kathleen's tone all but screamed she must get out of this stateroom right away.

"Sometimes," Kathleen continued, her voice little more than a whisper, "sometimes I've no choice but to look out for my husband's career, particularly when I'm asked a direct question.''

''I-I believe I'll step out for a walk,'' Yvette said, though her mouth had grown almost too dry for speech. She bent to capture Lafitte, intent on placing him inside the handbasket. Perhaps the kitten recalled his earlier incarceration, for he scooted away from her whenever she moved close.

''Leave him. I'll see to him, don't you fret.'' Kathleen's words were soft, imploring, and this time there was no mistaking the admonition in her voice. ''Oh, and I nearly forgot.'' She pulled a box out from between two towels. ''I packed you some food. I thought you might want to take it with you . . . for later.''

Kathleen passed it to her. Yvette nodded gratefully, unable to speak past the knot of terror in her throat. Snatching up her reticule, she hurried out the door.

A slow grin spread across Darien Russell's features as he caught sight of Yvette's retreating form. Though the steward had been called away to attend to some other matter, the captain was pleased that he had found her on his own.

Darien followed the young woman onto a relatively clear section of deck reserved for paying passengers. Noting the rank apparent from his uniform, a guard saluted him and stepped aside so he could pass.

Unconsciously, he paused to smooth his beard lest the uncharacteristically wide smile had left it in disorder.

Yvette's presence on this deck confirmed his suspicion that the steward had been lying. If Darien could prove it, he ought to have the stubborn little man arrested. Unfortunately, that would be not only difficult but unwise, for it would bring too many others into this affair. And too many questions, which he could ill afford right now.

He quickened his pace, both eager and relieved to end the game he had begun when he'd allowed her to escape. A game he meant to end now with a decisive victory.

Despite his elation, Yvette's carelessness surprised him. After their last encounter, he'd expected her to be wary. Yet she hadn't even looked around to see if anyone was following.

He set aside the thought, instead planning how he'd deal with this woman who had caused him so much grief. He could lay not only Colonel Jeffers's suspicions and two deaths at Yvette's feet but his mangled pride as well. He intended to restore it by shredding hers to ribbons as she died.

Though his school's failure had drained him of his family money, Darien considered himself a man rich in refinement. He had not particularly enjoyed the murder of Lieutenant Simonton, and he still regretted the way Marie had died. He took a certain pride, however, that both deaths had been bloodless, neat, precise. He'd left not a single clue to connect himself to either. If one meant to do murder, one must plan it carefully.

He must plan Yvette's as well. But this time felt so different. In her case, the killing went so far beyond the required punishment, it qualified as sport. His heartbeat accelerated, and he began perspiring as he drew closer to the woman. He lengthened his strides, thinking how she had scored the first point in this

deadly contest, had drawn blood with her witty little
song. But as Darien drew nearer, he vowed that she
was finished. From now on, the only points scored
would be his.

He had finally beaten the haughty little Creole.
And if he could prevail against this woman, he could
ultimately prevail against his Constance, too. He knew
instinctively that just as when he'd killed Marie, while
Yvette fought through death spasms, his mind's eye
would rearrange her features into his wife's face.

Excitement thrummed in his veins as he drew close
enough to touch her. His skin felt flushed with heat,
and impending triumph aroused him. He'd question
her inside her stateroom, and who knew what might
happen next? The thought occurred to him that he
could take her if he wanted and she couldn't do a
thing about it.

Let her sing her goddamn ditty as he defiled her.
Let her hum a few bars as her eyes bulged and her
face transformed in a gruesome parody of twilight—
scarlet to indigo, then black.

He sucked in a breath of cool air to dispel the
memories of Marie's nearly endless death. Yvette had
killed her, he remembered, Yvette's interference, not
his hands. And it was time now that she paid in full
for all she'd wrought.

Unable to wait a moment longer, Darien rushed
toward her. His right hand shot forward and firmly
grasped her elbow. "You belong to me now," he
hissed as she tried to jerk away.

The woman spun toward him, her blue eyes round
with terror, a scream already cutting through the
deep murmur of men talking a short distance away.

Darien's left hand was halfway to clapping over her

mouth to silence her when he realized he hadn't caught Yvette. Instead, he'd grabbed a woman perhaps ten years older. Though she was petite and had dark hair like Yvette, she was also obviously with child. Frantically, she tried to jerk loose from his grip.

Instead, his fingers tightened on her arm. She must let him explain!

"I-I'm terribly sorry! I thought you were—" he stammered uselessly. The woman's screams drowned out his attempted explanation.

As the guard approached, Darien released the woman and tried to calm her.

"Please, madam, I apologize profusely. I mistook you for another woman."

But she was sobbing now, her palm pressed to her heart. Her whole body trembled, and she collapsed against the guard.

Just what he needed, a hysterical ninny and one more humiliation. Damn Yvette for putting him through this!

Farther down the deck, a giant of a bald man pushed his way through the crowd and shouted, "What in God's name are you doing to my wife?"

Before Darien could offer a word of explanation, the huge man swung at him. Darien ducked the massive arm and stepped back. In one swift motion, he withdrew his Navy Colt and leveled it at the man's chest.

"Now, perhaps, you'll feel more inclined to listen."

The woman quieted abruptly, and the bald man might have turned to stone, he stood so still. Darien Russell felt power coursing through his veins. He was in control here; they'd have to listen now.

His calm restored, he offered a cold apology for the

inconvenience. The matter settled, he spun crisply on his heel and strode away. As he did so, he swore to himself that no matter what obstacles rose up in his path, he would have Yvette Augeron.

He would have her before the night was out.

Like most of the other men around him, Gabe stood as the *Sultana* glided into Memphis at seven in the evening. As they drew nearer to the wharf, he looked down at Zeke.

"You sure you're doing all right?" Gabe asked. "It's safe enough here. Union soldiers, Union doctors even."

"I've told all of you, I'm going home . . . as fast as I can get there," Zeke snapped. His color rose—a good sign after this morning's pallor. "And for the last damned time, I'm feeling fine—fine enough to belt the next one of you who asks me how I'm doing."

If Gabe didn't think Zeke would try to make good on his threat, he'd lean over and touch his friend's forehead again just to reassure himself that the fever was gone for good. If they didn't get Zeke off the boat now, he'd have to wait for Indiana to get decent medical attention.

"What I could do with is some food," Zeke complained. "I'm so hungry, I'd settle for hardtack."

Jacob smiled. "Maybe I can do better than that. How about if I slip off the boat and get us something decent? We still have some money left from what Eliza sent us."

Seth and Gabriel each dug into their pockets and offered Jacob more money and advice on where he might go to avoid the crowds of other hungry soldiers.

"Just don't eat my portion on your way back to the boat." Though Zeke's voice sounded irritable, he was grinning at the thought of a real meal.

As the steamboat was made fast, officers shouted orders for the men to remain aboard while the cargo was unloaded. They might as well have been commanding a cloud of locusts to ignore a fresh green cornfield. Hundreds of soldiers swarmed to escape the overcrowded vessel. Many of them spoke excitedly about the prospect of obtaining hot food at the Union-controlled Soldiers' Home. Others made no secret of their desire for a stiff drink and the chance to break up the monotony of their long trip.

Gabe could hardly blame them. He'd do the same if he weren't so damned worried he would miss the chance to see Yvette once more. Try as he might, he couldn't escape the fact of his attraction. Attraction, hell. She'd grown to an obsession in his mind.

There was probably nothing to it. But he had to see her one more time, before the chance was lost forever. Before Yvette faded into his past, one more regret that he was powerless to change.

Yvette's spirits sank at the thought of all the things she'd left behind in the stateroom. In her haste, she'd abandoned her jade-and-ivory rosary beads, a gift from Papa after her confirmation, along with all the clothing she'd brought with her when she'd fled New Orleans. There were other personal items as well, all the little things she needed to maintain some modicum of hygiene and beauty. All of them could be replaced if she had money, but her last few dollars wouldn't even serve to take her to St. Louis if she left the boat. And then there was the matter of Lafitte.

Her brother, Jules, had brought the kitten to her after finding him abandoned in their garden. He was a pitiful bit of fluff, Jules told her, probably not worth her effort. She'd accepted the challenge of saving him as if her brother had thrown down a gauntlet. The tiny kitten had been so thin and listless that for days she'd risen several times a night to warm milk to feed him. Alone in the kitchen, she kept careful watch, for *Maman* would have been incensed to find an animal inside the town house.

Within two weeks, the kitten's strength returned, and he turned into a rambunctious terror. By that time, she'd grown too attached to the black-and-white bundle of energy to give him up, to leave him behind when she'd left home.

But now she didn't seem to have a choice. If she understood Kathleen Rowe's cryptic comments, Darien Russell would find her if she went back to her stateroom. Her best chance of escaping was to leave this vessel now.

Yvette felt bad for the animal, which would be abandoned for a second time in his short life. She tried to reassure herself with the thought of Kathleen's promise to look after him. But the thought was cheerless, and she felt bereft, surrendering the last vestiges of her former life.

The sun had set only minutes before the *Sultana* came into Memphis. Twilight was fading rapidly as the crewmen and a few of the stronger prisoners began unloading hogsheads of sugar from the cargo. Small groups of soldiers bolted down the gangplank onto the wharf boat and the cobblestones beyond.

Watching them, Yvette wished uselessly that she were a man so she could blend in. Even so, the confusion offered her the best chance to escape.

Or so she thought until she spotted Captain Russell. He was keeping to the shadows, watching everyone who left the *Sultana*. A couple of soldiers appeared to be talking to him, but his hawk's gaze never lessened in intensity. Yvette knew beyond a doubt that if she stepped into sight, he'd swoop down on her in a moment and haul her off the boat, where he could see to her in private.

She harbored no illusions that he really meant to take her back to New Orleans. The journey and a trial would offer too great a chance for her to speak, to show someone the letter she kept hidden in her reticule, carefully folded and sewn into the lining. The damning letter Darien had written to his wife.

If he ever found that letter, he'd destroy it, and she'd hang. No Yankee would believe her story without written proof. She became more and more convinced he couldn't take the chance that anyone might listen. If he got his hands on her, she would not live long enough to hang.

She thought once more of her stateroom and realized that if Russell were here, he could not be there. Her belongings beckoned her, especially Lafitte. Now was her best chance to retrieve them, and perhaps when she had finished, Captain Russell would have given up watching the gangplank. The plan seemed worth a try.

Quickly, she hurried upstairs to the cabin deck. Her knees were shaking by the time she reached her stateroom door. What if Russell had left someone inside to guard it, someone who would arrest her the moment that she stepped inside? For a long moment, Yvette hesitated, feeling vulnerable, almost naked standing out here on the deck, yet reluctant to risk walking into what would be a perfect trap.

"Miss Au— Miss Alexander?"

Quiet as it was, the voice still made her jump. By the time she turned to face it, the speaker was almost close enough to touch her. Certainly too close to flee with any real hope of success.

Her pent-up breath gusted out through painfully clenched teeth. *Gabriel Davis.* She ought to feel upset at his appearance, for the last thing she needed was another complication now. Instead, she felt relief at seeing him, someone she could trust with all her burdens.

Ridiculous to feel such absolute faith in a Yankee soldier she had met just days before. Yet she did, and for some unfathomable reason, she felt certain that her surety had nothing to do with desperation and everything to do with the warmth she saw in his blue eyes.

"Please," she breathed, "would you step inside ahead of me? I'm afraid—afraid that someone unpleasant might be waiting."

He nodded his assent, and she slipped past him to wait. Her every muscle tensed, prepared for flight, as he pushed open the stateroom door and peered inside.

The kitten tried to dart between his legs, but Gabriel scooped him up and grinned at him.

"Here's something unpleasant for you," he told her, passing her the squirming creature.

"Oh, Lafitte," she crooned. She carried him inside

and felt a renewed surge of relief when Gabriel followed.

Yvette placed the kitten into her handbasket and latched it. Then she began gathering necessities as quickly as she could.

"Are you getting off in Memphis?" Gabe sounded disappointed.

She paused to stare at him. "I'm in a great deal of trouble, Gabriel."

"Russell?" he guessed.

She nodded. "I believe someone has told him which stateroom I'm using. I hid on the main deck for a while, and I'd decided that I'd have to leave the *Sultana*, though I really need to travel farther north. But when I approached the gangplank, I saw him waiting—watching for me to disembark."

"Then you'll have to stay on board."

"But how? He'll find me if I stay here."

Gabe looked at her strangely, then placed his hands on her shoulders.

"Please . . . we have no time to waste on kisses."

"I don't consider kissing you a waste, Yvette." But he did not lean toward her. Instead, he slowly spun her all the way around so that when he'd finished, she was facing him once more.

"Laissez-moi tranquille!" she said, her anger for the moment pushing past her English. She took a deep breath and shook off his grasp. "Let go! I'm trying to collect my things!"

"And I'm trying to help you. You're going to need to take those clothes off."

Her French came in an angry torrent, words that would have turned her mother crimson. Even her brothers would have been shocked at the way she handled expressions she'd only overheard them saying among themselves. Unfortunately, their meaning was quite lost on the insolent Yankee. Even worse, she'd never learned to swear properly in English.

To her surprise, Gabe laughed and held up his palms, as if in surrender. Shaking his head, he told her, "I'm sorry. I'm sorry. Th-that's not what I meant."

The *imbécile* was laughing so hard that he could barely speak. Yvette felt a flush of rage and shame heating her face.

Gabe regained control. "I'm not sure how I'll do it, but I'm going to see if I can find you something else to wear. Men's clothes—maybe we can dress you like a roustabout. I don't know much French, but from your tone, I'd guess you have the right vocabulary."

"Mon Dieu! You mean to disguise me as a man?" The idea was so absurd, so shocking, it nearly took her breath away.

"Well . . ." he began, his gaze appraising her once more. "As little as you are, maybe a boy. Let me go quickly and see what I can round up. I'll need to commandeer a cap, too, since we don't have any way to cut your hair so quickly."

Yvette blinked, wondering who would ever believe the fiction that she was male. But even a ridiculous idea was better than nothing, so she nodded mutely. At least then he'd leave her alone to finish packing the remainder of her things.

"Do you have money or anything to trade?" Gabe asked her. "Some pretty trinket? Something a soldier or a crewman might want for his sweetheart? I'd play the gentleman about this, but I just gave most of my money for the promise of real food.''

''Real food,'' Yvette repeated, thinking for the first time of the box Kathleen had given her. She went to the table where she'd left it and opened the top. Apparently, Kathleen had been afraid that she'd go hungry. Inside she found wrapped meats and cheeses, several oranges, half a cake, and a loaf of bread, still faintly warm. ''Do you think this might do?''

Gabe stared at it with poorly disguised longing. ''Good Lord! There are men out there who'd strip naked for a share of that.''

She couldn't help smiling at his expression. ''Careful, Mr. Davis. Salivating in the box might lower its trade value.''

''What?'' At last his gaze shifted from the feast to her. ''Oh, sorry. I'd better go now.''

''Please hurry,'' she told him as he moved to leave. ''I don't know how long I have before he returns.''

Gabe hesitated, then abruptly took her into his arms. How wonderful it felt to have him squeeze her, how safe and comforting! She was glad when he followed with a kiss, one so full of promise that she began immediately to melt, to wish that he would stay with her despite the danger.

Too soon, he pulled away. ''Do you still think it's a waste of time?''

She shook her head, too overwrought to deny the power drawing them together. He grinned at her and left. She blinked at the closed door for a long moment before returning to her packing.

And all the while, she prayed Gabe's help would come in time.

* * *

Gabe hurried toward the stateroom, a rumpled wad of clothing tucked beneath his arm. Hurried not only because Yvette needed him but because he wanted her.

Every time Gabe saw her, his hunger grew to see her one more time. But that craving was as nothing compared to the clear conviction that coursed through him when he held her in his arms. Implausible as it seemed, he knew that she was meant for him. The reality of it went soul-deep, unchangeable, as if it formed the kernel of his beating heart.

A jolt of fear that the one woman who moved him was too far beyond his reach rode hard on the thought. A French-speaking Southern woman and a Catholic, too, if the rosary she'd stuffed into her reticule was any indication. A fugitive from Union justice. He imagined his father's reaction if he dared bring her home; the thunder of artillery would pale in comparison to the old man's disapproval. The rest of his family would react with utter disbelief, and he knew beyond a doubt they would abandon Yvette to chilly isolation, excluding her from the warm circle of their favor.

He nearly laughed aloud at the idea. Bringing home a woman—any woman—wouldn't change their welcome one iota. He'd be disgraced with her or without. With her, however, he could feel hope flutter into wakefulness inside him. They could both make a fresh start.

In Oregon, together. With Yvette beside him, he

could survive his exile. Together they would both have love, and in time they could begin their own new family.

Excitement coursed through him as he thought of their future. The first real excitement he had felt in such a long, long time. Now all he had to do was convince Yvette that he was not insane.

At his knock and soft words, she let him back into the stateroom. She wrinkled her nose at the bundle in his arms.

"Those Illinois boys might have sold their souls for all that food," he told her as he spread out the clothing on the chair. "But I settled for a jacket from one fellow, a pair of britches from another, and this cap. All too big, I know, but we'll do what we can. There are plenty about dressed worse."

Yvette picked up the jacket's empty sleeve. She used only her nails, as if she loathed touching it. "This doesn't smell too clean."

"Don't worry. These clothes came from Vicksburg. Vermin-free, you have my word." He hoped it was true. He winced at the image of her on deck, trying to hide among the men, then erupting into shrieks at the sight of a flea or louse.

She looked dubious. "What about my feet? Surely, I can't go barefoot."

"You won't be the only one." He felt exasperation growing at her stalling.

She folded her arms across the swell of her bosom. With a shake of her head, she told him, "Thank you for your efforts, but I simply cannot put these on."

"Why not?"

"I will not wear the Union blue. You told me you'd find some roustabout to trade with."

"Nobody's hungrier than the soldiers. Yvette, you have to do this. Unless you don't mind Russell catching you."

"I'll hang before I dress as a Yankee."

Gabe's dream of a future with her withered. What in God's name could he want with such a damned fool, stubborn woman?

"You'd hang?" he asked. She'd said that Russell meant to kill her, but hanging sounded more like execution.

She nodded. "He's had me charged with murder. The murder of the lieutenant looking into his affairs."

"So you're going to let him win?" Gabe argued. "You're going to let this Yankee, this man who you say killed your sister, take you?"

He shook his head, disgusted, before muttering. "And I thought you had spirit. I thought you had sense. Turns out you're not a damned bit different from all those other Rebels, ready to die over your puffed-up pride. More concerned with appearances than winning. No wonder your side lost. No wonder—"

She slapped him, and he felt the sting of it along his cheek, heard the sharp crack of her palm against his flesh. Her hand shook, and she stared at it as if she were surprised at what she'd done.

He grinned and resisted the impulse to rub the burning flesh on his face. *"That's* what a fighter does. And you're a fighter now. Not some little girl just playing at it. I don't care about the war, Yvette. I only care about you winning this one. I . . . I care about you. Now put on the damned uniform or I'll strip those clothes off you and dress you myself."

Her face flushed crimson, and her eyes blazed hazel fury, but she didn't back away.

"You wouldn't dare," she told him.

But she wasn't certain. He heard it in her voice. Good, then. That made two of them. He called her bluff, stepping forward until he was so close, her folded arms were touching him.

It took every bit of self-control that he could muster not to reach out and grab her then, not to rip her dress off. He'd be doing it to save her, he swore to himself, but he remembered the desire between them, and he wasn't certain that his motives were completely pure.

Before he had the chance to find out, she relented.

"All right," she spat the words and turned from him. "But step outside. I certainly won't have you watching."

"What in God's name makes you think I'd want to?" he asked her, hoping that lightning wouldn't strike him, for he'd never uttered such a lie since he'd been born.

She stared at him and held his gaze, and he could tell she knew. Knew how he wanted her not only now but for his whole life.

Tears welled up to soften the fierceness in her eyes.

"Thank you. Thank you for helping me," she said, though her voice faltered beneath the weight of her emotions.

He had to force himself to turn away from her, had to remind himself that Russell could come here at any moment. Only that kept him from kissing her again, from caressing her, not stopping until both of them had had their fill.

Instead, he waited outside while Yvette Augeron, proud daughter of the Confederacy, transformed herself into a Union soldier.

Chapter Eight

They are everywhere, these Yankees, like red ants,
like the locusts and frogs which were the plagues
of Egypt.

—Mary Chesnut,
A Diary from Dixie

As Capt. Darien Russell stood near the steamboat's
gangway, he made no attempt to halt the exodus
of former prisoners from the *Sultana*. Instead, he
watched with a mixture of fascination and disgust
as the dregs of the Union army loped or limped,
depending on their condition, onto the wharf boat
and then the cobblestones beyond it. No order at all
to them, he noted, except to disobey.

He was glad he had decided to do nothing to stop
the departing men. In their minds, they were no
longer military, as if in the wake of Lee's surrender all
obligations had dissolved. They would have certainly

ignored his orders, just as they had ignored the orders of more familiar leaders. Some might have mocked him, and at his current level of frustration, he scarcely trusted himself to keep his temper reined.

His temper. It had always been his loaded gun and mockery its surest trigger. As the hours crept by, he thought of how it had caused his academy to fail. Although he'd loved to lecture, he could never handle boys. Remembering their sniggers still made his hands fist into hammers, his hands, which had not learned from the fateful blow they dealt to William Charles.

Certainly, he'd boxed boys' ears before—and often. But when he'd caught Will mimicking his lecture in the corridor in tones so pompous and speech so flowery, when he'd heard the others howl with mirth, Darien—quite literally—saw red. A bloody veil of rage obscured both his vision and his reason, and before he could regain control, his fists pummeled the boy, again and again.

That time there had been no neat precision; there had been blood. Blood streaming from the boy's ears as William lay unconscious on his classroom floor. The other boys stood motionless, mute with disbelief and horror. It was only by the grace of God the child didn't die. But he would never hear again from his left ear, the one that Darien's right fist had struck.

Darien's temper had cost him his school in the end, along with every penny he'd ever sunk into it. Every last cent of his inheritance. William's parents had accepted an apology and a modest settlement in lieu of filing any criminal or civil charges. But when they withdrew their son, others followed, many others, until Darien had no choice but to close his academy. Close it and forever afterward listen to his wife harangue him for his failure.

Even in the military his temper hobbled him. He could no more abide the laughter of men than boys, and his harsh brand of discipline inspired muttering far more often than heroics. His superiors explained he had no gift for leadership. A man of his intelligence and background might well be a colonel by this time, or even a general. But Darien instead was a captain serving generals, seeing that their food was hot, even on the battlefield, and that their orders were delivered. In other words, despite his rank and education, despite the grandness of his ideas, he functioned as a lackey.

Until New Orleans taught him to use the role to his advantage. Until he saw how others prospered and decided to drink from the same well. He felt a surge of pride at the thought of how he had manipulated wealthy men so deftly. So deftly that the last one handed him his lovely daughter as if she were a bright bow atop the gift of the man's fortune. And if, at the end, he hadn't quite succeeded in separating old Augeron from his wealth, he had at least enjoyed despoiling Marie and the heady feelings of deception and revenge upon his harpy of a wife.

Darien smiled, thinking of his brilliance. It helped to pass the time far more agreeably than dwelling on his failures. He'd leave this war a very rich man, never again to fear his Constance—or the noose. All he had to do was silence Yvette Augeron, to make certain she never left this steamboat.

At least not without him.

* * *

Jacob decided to avoid the long line at the Soldiers'
Home in favor of trying to buy food elsewhere. He
wandered down a seedy-looking side street near the
riverfront. He'd heard someone say there was a riv-
ermen's saloon there, but nothing about the dilapi-
dated wooden structures looked inviting. Jacob had
just about decided to turn back when he spotted a
sign hanging above the doorway of a severely leaning
structure. Ma Abbot's had been painted in crude,
uneven letters, as if a child or a drunk had done the
job.

Jacob had misgivings about entering the place.
Someone had used wooden props to keep the saloon
from keeling over. Strips of paint peeled from weath-
ered outer walls so full of knotholes that anyone who
took the notion could easily peer inside. Neither the
rectangle of dingy yellow light nor the out-of-tune
piano music coming through the open door seemed
inviting in the least, but Jacob Fuller was not a man
to turn away from anything over a few hairs rising
along the back of his neck.

Instead, he raked his fingers through his thick curls,
as if to straighten them, before striding into the
saloon. The moment that he did, the odors struck
him. Smoke and liquor combined with stale sweat
and old grease. But something more enticing over-
powered those unpleasant scents, something that
smelled of baking bread and maybe onions. His stomach rumbled, oblivious to the suspicious, dark-eyed
gazes of the trio of rough-looking men standing by
the bar. In a corner, another pair stopped laughing
at his entrance. Only the piano player, who had his

back turned to the door, continued as he had been, plinking out a badly played rendition of "When Johnny Comes Marching Home."

Jacob approached the bar. A hooknosed man stood behind it, gazing at him over the paunch of an enormous belly. Unlike the patrons, his smile offered welcome.

"Whatcha have to drink, soldier?"

"I'm more interested in food right now. What's that I smell cooking?"

The smile stretched into a grin. "My wife—Ma's—cookin' meat pies. I swear she keeps the place in business. Can I sell you one?"

Instead, the bartender sold him a sack of meat pies and a half-full jar of pickled eggs. But when Jacob dug into his small cache of coins, he sensed eyes devouring his every movement, eyes that hungered for money more than food.

Four soldiers from the *Sultana* burst in noisily, all shouting orders for whiskey. One was an enormously tall fellow that Jacob had seen aboard the steamer. This close, he reckoned the fellow might be seven feet tall.

Happy for the distraction, Jacob took his leave. But as he did so, out of the corner of his eye he saw the three men who'd been standing at the bar walk out behind him. The same three men who'd been watching him so carefully when he'd paid for the food.

It would be a long walk back to the *Sultana*, Jacob realized. A long, dark walk alone.

Gabriel and Yvette stood in shadow in a spot on the main deck that had been vacated by a group of men who'd gone into Memphis. Yvette took Gabe's hand and squeezed it, sending a brief but powerful current of desire through his entire body. A current he could no longer ignore. She meant to leave him now, forever. He did not delude himself into thinking that, once parted, he'd ever again find her.

Apparently, she was thinking along different lines, for she released his hand to point out Captain Russell ahead of them. He stood watching the gangway, his back to them, his posture rigidly alert.

"Maybe he'll give up soon," Yvette wished aloud. In her borrowed outfit, she looked like a drummer boy. But only if she stayed out of the light, where her delicate features and the sweet curves of her body would not give her away.

"I hope . . ." Gabe began, not knowing how to voice his thoughts without angering her. But the passing moments beat away at him like eagles' wings. There was no time to woo her gently, to gradually chip away at her resistance. No time to waste on doubts. If he wanted her, he'd have to say so now, while there was still some fragment of a chance.

"Got no use for a goddamn coward," Silas Deming's voice reminded him. Deming had been wrong when he'd said it, but now the statement urged Gabe into action. His heart told him that if he listened to the voice of fear instead, or even to Seth Harris's voice of reason, he would regret it to the end of his days. That his body might yet inhabit the earth, but the last vestige of his wounded soul would die a slow death of self-loathing.

So he risked putting into words what he'd been thinking. "I hope he *doesn't* leave."

Yvette glared at him. "Do you *want* me to get caught? After all you've done to help me?"

He shook his head. "It's not that. It's, well . . . I want *you*, Yvette. If I had time, I'd do this right. I'd court you slow and proper, like the lady that you are. But you're about to leave now, leave for somewhere I can't help you. About to go where I can't ever hope to hold you in my arms again."

Her eyes rounded, and she blinked rapidly. Perhaps she blinked back tears, but in the poor light, he could not be certain.

"You feel it, too, don't you?" he asked her. "There's something strong between us, something we might never feel again. I could love you, Yvette. No, I may as well risk everything and tell you, I *do* love you—now. I love the way you fit against my body. I love the way you listen and you talk. I love the way you take a stand, whether it's against a thieving officer or against a bunch of soldiers about to kill an unconscious enemy. You put what you believe on the line, the same way the best soldiers have, on both sides of this war. I don't only love you, I *respect* you for it, and that's a combination you don't come by every day."

He paused and took a breath. God, how he wished she'd say something in response that would stop him from making a damned fool of himself. But as the seconds stretched into a brittle silence, he decided that having gone so far, he had little else to lose.

"Don't go, Yvette. Come with me, to Ohio. I don't intend to stay there. I mean to start a new life afterwards, in Oregon, where Union and Confederacy are just words from the papers, where a man's skill is as good as money in the bank. It'll be rough going for a while, but I mean to make a living forging metal,

anything but cannon. I won't take a damned dime
on tools made to kill men."

"Gabe," she breathed, "what are you saying?"

"I'm asking you to make a new start, as my wife."

"Your wife . . . ?" The words were choked, the voice
tight. "No one has ever . . . ever made me feel so . . ."

When words failed her, she put down the basket
that contained Lafitte. Rising, she then draped her
arms around his neck and leaned into his embrace.
Gabe felt such joy, such expanding relief, that he did
not hesitate to enfold her in a kiss so genuine, so
generous, that it made his body ache with need.

Yvette's cap slid off, and her dark waves cascaded
nearly to her waist. Coming to his senses, Gabe broke
away to retrieve the kepi and hand it back to her.

"We can't do that again," he warned as she tucked
her hair back into hiding. He grimaced at the thought
of what might happen if he were seen kissing what
appeared to be a drummer boy. They'd both be catfish bait for certain.

"No . . . we can't," Yvette said, and from the sadness
in her voice, he knew she meant forever, not just
now.

He had opened up his heart to her for nothing.
He had played his finest hand—and lost.

As men unloaded a hogshead of sugar, Darien Russell heard a crewman's voice.

"That's near the last of it. Blow the whistle now
and give them boys a chance to get back on board
afore we shove off. They'll be wantin' to get home,
and no mistake."

A warning jolted him back to full awareness, an

instinct that Yvette was somewhere close by, waiting for the passing hours to lull him into inattention. Waiting, perhaps, for him to give up and return to the main cabin to bed down for the night.

He could almost hear her thinking that now would be her best chance to flee the steamer. The day had long since faded into moonless darkness, broken only by lit torches. Faces would be hard to distinguish by the dim, flickering light, although with so few women about, he didn't think he'd have much trouble discerning her.

Darien smoothed his hair and beard to hide his anticipation. From the looks of Yvette's stateroom, which he'd checked before they'd tied up, she'd fled in a hurry, leaving nearly everything behind. Everything except the damning letter he suspected she still had. Surely she would try to leave before the *Sultana* resumed its northward journey.

Perhaps she'd spotted him. He'd thought he was well hidden, here in the shadow of the cabin deck, but maybe she had seen him and been frightened away. He moved to the opposite side of the gangway, into another dim spot. Hopefully, she'd see only the place he had vacated and think he'd given up.

The steamboat's whistle cut through the sounds of conversation, of singing from somewhere on the decks above. This was her last chance then—and his last chance to catch her this evening, as he'd sworn.

Despite Jacob's sense that he was being followed, their attack had still surprised him. Maybe it was only the way he had been raised, but he always felt a cold ripple of shock when someone meant—on pur-

pose—to do him bodily harm. Someone that he
didn't even know, that he'd given no excuse whatsoever for the action. Maybe that was why the whole
idea of this war had made so little sense to him. Jacob
could never see the reason why so many folks would
want to venture so far from their homes to hurt and
kill each other.

These thoughts spun through his head as he was
coming to. Or what was left of his head, anyway.
Gingerly, he touched a throbbing spot. His fingers
came away coated with warm, sticky blood.

Damn. He felt in his pockets and found the remaining coins missing. Not that there'd been many
in the first place. Surely not enough to jump a man
and pound him till he lost consciousness. But there
you had it. What foolishness was not provoked by war
was begotten out of greed, he figured.

Cautiously, he tried to stand. His world careened
crazily, tilting farther over than Ma Abbott's saloon.
He sank down on his haunches so he wouldn't flop
face first into the trash-strewn alley. That was when
he noticed they'd left the sack with the meat pies.
The jar of pickled eggs had rolled out of the bag and
broken. Fearful of glass shards, he reluctantly decided
he would have to leave the eggs behind.

Picking up the sack with the pies, Jacob made a
second attempt to regain his feet. Though his head
pounded and he still felt dizzy, this time he managed
to remain upright.

He heard a blast from a steamboat's whistle. The
Sultana! Was it leaving him in Memphis? He hoped
like hell that he was wrong.

As quickly as possible, Jacob shambled in the direction of the river.

* * *

Beyond Gabriel's broad shoulders, stars burned themselves indelibly into Yvette's memory. Sparkling like his diamond hopes, glittering like tears.

She knew in that moment that she would never forget the words that he had told her. That forevermore, when she looked into the night sky, she would see them written in the constellations, blazing out of the cold depths of space beyond. And like those stars, the memory of his love would offer a bit of light amid the vastness of the emptiness that lay before her.

But could it possibly be true? Yvette remembered laughing with her friends at the absurdity of the stories about strangers who fell helplessly in love after a single glance. Yet here she was, drawing declarations and proposals from a young man she hadn't known three days before.

How could it be that the impossible words she was hearing and the improbable emotions she was feeling were more real to her than all the dreamlike years she'd lived in New Orleans? Had fear and loneliness made a muddle of her senses, leaving her vulnerable to this mad spell of attraction?

As she looked into Gabriel's shadowed face, she could feel his nervousness, his desperation. That much, at least, was genuine. He loved her, and she began to believe she loved him, too. But that love did nothing to diminish what she felt for her family, the equal shares of pain and affection, of loyalty and pride.

She was still an Augeron, as Marie had been. Marie, who had been killed because of the letter Yvette showed her, and by the same soulless brute that now stood watch near the gangway.

She had sworn that she would see to it that the man who killed Marie was punished. Even if, in doing so, she had to sacrifice the possibility of a future with Gabriel. Yet she would always love this young soldier for the offer, and so she tried to think of how to soften what she had to say.

"A part of me wishes that I could stay with you," she whispered. "But we both know this plan would never work. I make a poor Yankee soldier, do I not? Sooner or later, this deception must fall to pieces. And then they would arrest you, too. I cannot risk that."

"But Yvette—"

She hated the pain in those two words, so she rushed to cut him off.

"No, Gabriel. You mustn't say more. Look, the captain's left his post. He will go to check my stateroom, or he will go to bed. That means it is time now. Time for me to go."

"Then I'll come with you," he offered.

"No. I will not have it. I mean to finish this with that devil Russell. I have proof of his crimes, and I am the only one. And if I fail, I fail alone. No one else must pay this time. I have already hurt too many others that I love."

She paused to let her final words fill the space between him, to give him time to realize she'd just said she loved him, too. Loved him but would never have him, would never press her lips to his again.

Pain welled up, bled over from the wounds left by Marie's death and by the loss of both her family and her home. Pain so intense that it could only spill over in her tears.

"Yvette . . ." he told her, and her name on his lips made it seem much harder, caused her to wonder if anyone had ever said the word just so.

She said nothing more, instead choosing that moment to turn away and hurry toward the gangway. Praying he would love her too much to call out after her. Wishing at the same time that he would risk everything to try to stop her.

She never knew for certain what he would have done, never knew, for at that moment, Lafitte began to meow.

Darien would not have understood that he was looking at Yvette if not for her hesitation. While he heard the animal's muted cry, he could not be sure of the direction. He was so intent on finding the belled outline of a skirt that he would not have noticed the boy walking toward the gangway.

But when that "boy" pulled up short, looking so very ill at ease, he found himself shocked once more at Yvette Augeron's audacity. He sprang out of his place among the shadows, eager to grab her before she saw him coming.

"Run!"

A shouted warning from the opposite side of the gangway ruined Darien's plan. Yvette whirled around, saw him, and took off running. But because he was closer than she was to the gangway, she fled in the direction she'd come from.

She fled with him—that insufferable blond soldier who'd interfered before. Clearly, the two of them had formed some sort of bond. Sly little bitch was probably flipping up her skirts for his protection.

The two of them melted into the hordes perched along the deck, their dark uniforms blending into the shadows cast by the lanterns bracketed along the outer walls. He pursued, trying to keep his gaze fixed on their movement and thread his way through the men, too, but where a gap opened to Yvette and her accomplice, it as often closed for him.

"God damn it, stand aside or I'll have the lot of you arrested!" Darien ordered, hating the loss of his composure nearly as much as Yvette's escape.

"Mister, here's your mule!" called one soldier, referring to that idiotic camp song about a farmer led on a merry chase as he searched for his errant equine.

"Arrest away, Cap'n," another man called, his voice slurred by liquor. "After Georgia, any federal prison's bound to seem like paradise!"

Tin cups were raised, and the shouts of laughter that followed served only to inflame Darien's temper more. How in God's name had this rabble gotten whiskey?

From all along the deck, mischievous former prisoners took up the raucous cry.

"Mister, here's your mule!"

Every goddamned one of them seemed to think himself hilarious. Their laughter made Darien want to ship the whole worthless lot back to the Southern prison camps and let the Rebels finish what they'd started.

Ignoring them, he tripped past outstretched legs, but by the time he escaped the mob, the pair he sought had vanished like candle flames blown out by the wind.

Again he swore and returned to guard the gangway. At least he knew she was aboard, still trapped within the crowded confines of a two-hundred-sixty-foot-long boat. Once they left Memphis, she'd have no way of escaping. No way except the cold and swollen waters of the Mississippi River in spring flood.

Chapter Nine

It is well that war is so terrible, lest we grow too fond of it.

CSA general Robert E. Lee,
to Lt. Gen. James Longstreet,
Battle of Fredericksburg

April 27, 1865
Just north of Memphis, Tennessee

"Damn it!" Jacob shouted at the stern of the retreating steamboat. How was he to catch up with Zeke and his friends now?

He could feel more blood oozing through his scalp. He tried to wipe the drip tickling his forehead, but he suspected all he'd done was smear his face.

With a frustrated sigh, he turned and nearly missed another Indiana soldier who was bargaining with the owner of a skiff.

"I have to get back aboard," the soldier insisted. "I'll pay you to row me."

The skiff's owner, a man whose arms were corded with hard muscle, bargained with him until he set a price.

Jacob stepped closer. "Mind if I come, too?"

"You gotta pay," the riverman insisted.

"I was just jumped. They took my money."

"You're still bleeding," the soldier pointed out. Then, turning to the riverman, he said. "Go on and take us both, why don't you? I paid you more than fair for two."

The skiff's owner frowned, then glanced toward the receding steamboat. With a curse, he agreed, probably because he realized the longer he spent arguing, the farther he would have to row.

"Much obliged," Jacob told the other soldier. "How about a meat pie for the journey?"

The two ate in near silence, never taking their eyes off the *Sultana,* which was pulling steadily away.

Capt. J. Cass Mason tripped on his way out of the main cabin. *Pull yourself together,* he admonished himself, *or they'll imagine you are drunk.*

Though he had been drinking, Mason was a man who knew his limits—and his boat's. The thought chilled him that this crowd may have exceeded the *Sultana*'s.

A steamboat was a fragile means of transportation. Few survived as many as five years. They hit snags and sank. They caught fire and burned. They blew apart in spectacular explosions. The only strategy for a riverboat captain was quick profit. Pay for the vessel and bank every cent you could so you could build a new one when she died.

The war had interfered with that bold plan. Mason had no savings, only a meager one-sixteenth share in the *Sultana*.

As he made his way toward the stairs that would take him to his quarters, a nightmare vision rose before his eyes. Bodies floating in the river, illuminated only by the hellish flickering of a burning hulk.

His mouth went dust dry in spite of the drink he'd just imbibed.

One of the prisoners, a lieutenant, asked Mason if he knew a spot to sleep.

Ignoring the question, Mason said only, "I'd give all the interest I have in this boat if only we were safe in Cairo now."

Yvette didn't know how much time had passed before her shaking subsided enough to allow her the power of speech. It seemed an eternity, hiding in a place that felt nearly as dangerous as the gangway. She wondered, Would there ever be a time when she felt safe again?

"Can't we find somewhere else? It smells bad here." Yvette wrinkled her nose at the pungent odors of horse sweat and manure.

The culprits, tethered so close that she felt the heat radiating from their bodies, shifted on restless hooves. They loomed frighteningly in Yvette's vision, gigantic shapes carved from the darkness. As a child, her ribs had been badly bruised by a kick from Pierre's pet pony. She'd been suspicious of all equines ever since.

The nearest of the animals nickered and flung its

huge head up and down. Yvette flinched and took a step back, into the wall of Gabe's chest.

"Shh. It's all right." Despite his quick and heavy breaths tickling her ear, Gabe's voice was calm and reassuring.

Yvette wondered if he meant to soothe the horses or her. She was surprised by the way his words formed misty puffs along the outside border of her vision. After running in the woolen uniform, she felt so warm, so damp with perspiration, that she hadn't noticed that the temperature had dropped.

"We can't very well stay here all night," she told him. Following his lead, she pitched her voice lower. "I have to get off now, while there's still time."

"Look, Yvette." He reached over her shoulder to point toward the lights on shore, which were receding. "You've already missed your chance."

She forced herself to stillness, noticed for the first time the familiar churning of the paddle's blades, the deep rumble of the engines, and the steamboat's forward motion. Down here on the main deck, the sounds were louder, so much so that she could not imagine why they'd failed to register before.

The two of them had found a section of deck reserved for cargo, not all of which had been off-loaded in Memphis. They had slipped past a sleeping guard to hide among the horses and mules being transported.

"I-I don't much care for horses," she admitted. Gently, she set down the handbasket with Lafitte. Thankfully, the kitten had grown quiet.

"Could've been worse, Yvette. They drove off the pigs in Memphis."

"You don't understand," she whispered. "They're so awfully huge. I-I'm afraid of them."

His arms wound around hers to cross her body, and she felt his solidity behind her. Bolstering her strength and courage, making her own breath puff out in swifter plumes. Making her conscious of the effect their nearness was having on his body, the growing hardness that pressed against her. She felt reassured and excited all at once, and far less mindful of the horses, which had by now grown complacent in their presence.

She shifted her arm to swing around the reticule she had tied behind her back, beneath the dark blue jacket. When it no longer lay between them, she leaned toward him once more, enjoying his quiet gasp beside her ear. Enjoying the way fear melted with the tingling heat ignited by his warm breath, only to ripple through her body, everywhere.

She could not suppress a sigh, as if she'd stepped into a warm bath on a frigid day.

"Still frightened?" Gabe whispered. The words kissed at her ear, or was that the heat of his lips instead?

Some part of her looked on in disbelief. Here they stood, among a score of dozing horses, hiding from a man who meant to have her hung. Yet her body still took pleasure from this illicit contact, this man's loving touch.

He must be caught up in the spell of it as well, for his lips traveled along her neck. His hands reached up beneath the army jacket. And then he held her breasts, which no other man had ever touched. He seemed to scoop and lift them, and his fingertips played lightly at their almost painfully hard tips.

"Mon Dieu . . ." she whispered, her whole weight leaning backward, her whole being possessed with this new pleasure. And she knew in that moment there would be no pretense of denial, no abandoning whatever little miracle had taken hold aboard this boat. She would lie down if he asked her, right here among the horses' steel-shod hooves, for she would rather die of trampling than live without fully understanding what love offered.

She turned, suddenly desperate to kiss his mouth, to know how it felt to touch him, too. But in a moment, he grasped her hands to stop her, then pulled away his lips.

"Yvette, honey," he whispered. "You have to stop now. We have to stop before I can't."

"What if . . . what if I don't want to?"

"Hiding here won't do us much good if we spook the horses."

She could hear, rather than see, the smile behind his words.

He let go of her hands so he could hold her, then bent to kiss her head. "You deserve better than this—"

Tears made the receding lights of Memphis swim in Yvette's vision, and she felt the breeze of their passage chill her face. "What if we never get the chance at anything better? What if Russell captures me before I reach my uncle?"

He squeezed her tighter to him. "I won't let that happen. I swear it, Yvette."

She shook her head, suddenly feeling desolate. "Russell planted evidence. He left the poison in my room. No one in New Orleans believes I didn't kill that lieutenant. They didn't even want to see my proof. They're going to hang me, Gabriel. And I don't want to die without being with you first, without knowing—"

"You won't die," he interrupted, as if he were convinced his words could make the situation better. As if he thought his love could stop the future from opening before them, a somber banner unfurled by a baneful wind.

She laid her head against his shoulder, felt the itchy wool against her face, the way her tears dampened the fibers.

"Say you'll come with me to Oregon," Gabe told her, his every word throbbing with his need. "Say you don't care that I'm a Yankee and you don't mind that I couldn't kill that boy in Tennessee. Tell me that you'll marry me, Yvette. I don't care if you don't mean it; I want to hear it from you, anyway. Give us both a future we can look foward to tonight . . . even if it isn't real."

She pulled away from him, but her hands sought his. Her hands, which, like the rest of her, hesitated to break their connection. "I couldn't lie to you. I couldn't do that to myself. Can't you feel how much I want you? I don't care about those other things— where you're from and what you did or didn't do before we met. I think people must change into something different in war, something separate from their better nature. I know that I did, but I've only seen it in these past few days. I've only noticed it since meeting you."

He withdrew a hand to touch her cheek. "You're not like me. You're innocent."

She shook her head once more. "I didn't kill Lieutenant Simonton. But I *am* guilty. Of being jealous of my sister's love. Jealous enough to bring the whole world crashing down upon our heads."

"But you were right about Captain Russell, weren't you?"

"I was right, yes, but my reasons were all wrong. And I was wrong about a lot of other things as well. But I'm not wrong in saying this. I love you, and I'd give anything for the chance to marry you. If only I hadn't thrown away that chance before I knew you."

"You said that you had proof, Yvette. Proof that Captain Russell is not the man he claims to be."

"I do. I have it right here with me, and when— *if*—I can get it to my uncle, he might know how to make the Yankees listen."

"Will it prove your innocence as well?"

She shook her head. *"Non,* it cannot do that. It can only cast suspicion on my chief accuser."

"Then come with me. Don't risk it!"

She shook her head once more. "I must do this . . . for my sister. And I must do it for myself. I could never be happy in Oregon, even with you, if I failed to make the murderer pay."

"Then I'm going to help you," he answered. "I swear, I'll never leave your side."

She wasn't certain whether his words increased her burden or relieved it. Though she could hardly bear to think of him hurt or imprisoned on her behalf, some part of her exulted that she would not have to go through this alone. That she would not have to die alone, if that came to pass.

Selfish, that desire. To have someone who loved her in the end. Too selfish, for in the end she would be just as dead as if she were alone.

And she would destroy this kind man, too.

What sort of woman was she to even think of causing him such grief? The thought shamed her, so deeply that she knew that she must say no.

But not yet. Not now, while he was holding her so tightly. Not when this man's touch might be her last.

With the thought, waves of exhaustion nearly overwhelmed her. The hour was very late, and her day had been so troubled.

So was it too much to ask that she should rest now? Rest and let him hold her before she said good-bye.

The skiff owner grunted at Jacob's thanks. The hour was late, and the row out to the coaling barge had apparently drained him of whatever civility he might possess.

The Indiana infantryman scrambled aboard the *Sultana* but paused to offer Jacob a hand.

"I appreciate you talking him into letting me come, too," Jacob told him.

The two edged along the crowded deck. Jacob looked for an opening that would eventually lead him to his friends and hoped there would be room for him to lie down.

The infantryman turned, clearly intent on another path. "After all we've been through, seems like every mother's son of us ought to make it home."

As his hand stroked her back, Gabriel thought how Yvette's situation was yet another tragedy of war. So fine a woman, with her beautifully made dresses and her fancy stateroom, ought not to have to hide amid the livestock tethered near the stern. She ought not to have to lean against a ragged soldier, either, and a damned poor excuse for one at that.

"I love you, and I'd give anything for the chance to marry you."

Strange how little comfort her admission brought him. He felt like another Yankee looter taking advantage of her dire straits. Because that's what he had done, was doing even now. He knew damned well that even though his family had prospered during this war, he didn't have the kind of pedigree her family would demand. He knew it as soon as he had heard her speak and had noticed the expensive trim of the violet dress she had been wearing when he met her.

Certainly he loved her, but was taking advantage of her gratitude and desperation right? Or could their connection, which both had felt almost from the first, transcend their different backgrounds and the terrible things both had experienced?

He tightened his hold on her and kissed her temple. Though he'd imagined she was dozing, she answered softly, with a murmured sigh. And in that sigh he heard others in their future, ten thousand sighs of pleasure in the wake of making love.

There might be at least that many reasons why this love between them could not work, but her one sigh was enough. For on the power of its promise, he knew he would stand by her and do whatever he must to keep her safe from harm.

"You there!" Deep with authority, the voice boomed in the dark stillness.

A nearby horse tossed back its head and snorted with the suddenness of the interruption. Its warm breath formed twin plumes of steam. Another shifted restlessly, and the lantern light flickered across its rolling eyes.

He felt Yvette stiffen, more frightened than the animals around them. For an instant, he wondered if she might bolt and climb over the railing. But after her initial jolt, she stood stock-still, as if that would hide her.

"Come out of there and get back with your unit," the guard ordered.

"Just trying to keep warm near the horses," Gabe lied as he turned toward the man. He glanced behind him and saw Yvette, her head lowered as if to hide her face.

"This boy's teeth were chattering so loud I couldn't sleep," Gabe explained. "Thought this might be a good place to take him till he got to feeling better. It's almost toasty here."

The guard took a step nearer and peered over Gabe's shoulder at Yvette. The dark beard wagged as he nodded.

"Had a hard time of it, haven't you, son?" The deep baritone resonated with both sympathy and anger. "Those bastard traitors ought to be lined up and shot for what they did to all you fellows. Bet you'd pull the trigger if you could. Wouldn't you, boy?"

A pause stretched taut as he waited for an answer. Gabe prayed that Yvette wouldn't choose this moment to rail against Yankee atrocities. Finally, as Gabe prepared to spin some yarn about the "poor boy's" muteness, she murmured her agreement.

Now the guard sounded apologetic. "I got orders to keep the men away from these animals. But you might try back by the boilers. It's plenty warm there.

Some of the real sick fellas already staked out spots, but there might be room to squeeze in."

Yvette picked up Lafitte's basket as Gabe thanked the man. Then the pair left their sanctuary.

When they were out of the guard's earshot, Yvette whispered, "This crowding is terrible. Where can we go?"

He thought about two decks above, where his friends lay sleeping. He imagined explaining that he was helping her first to Jacob, who would question his loyalty, and then to Seth, who would question his sanity. Of the three of them, Zeke was the only man likely to support the idea. He'd see the notion of smuggling a Southern girl as a grand lark and nothing more.

But whether or not his friends approved, Gabe couldn't imagine any of them reporting this strange "drummer boy." Their very silence would put all of them at risk, should Yvette be discovered. Gabe shook his head at the thought. He was willing to accept the price he might pay for helping Yvette, but he would not—could not—involve his friends. Better they should wonder, even worry, about what had happened to him than become embroiled in this mess.

"Maybe we should try the cargo hold," he suggested. He thought about the darkness and the dirt. Once more the thought assailed him that Yvette deserved far better than this ratlike scrabble for survival. "I warn you, it won't be too pleasant down there."

"I don't care at all." She tried to mask her anxiety, but beneath the thin veneer of boldness, her voice quavered. "I will do what I must if at the end of it I can make Captain Russell pay for what he did."

He admired her determination. Most women would by now be in hysterics.

Or perhaps not. Perhaps women were no frailer than circumstances allowed them to be. He thought of his father's sister, Aunt Agatha, who had buried first a husband, then her three children, one after another. And survived. She had not only survived but had taken over—and expanded—the family business, a prosperous millinery. Predictably, his father bragged it was the Davis blood that made her tough, shrewd, and resilient. But Gabe suspected it had been necessity instead.

Gabe and Yvette edged along dark, blanketed humps of sleeping men. Occasionally, from somewhere along the deck, they heard the outcry of a former prisoner erupting with some nightmare. Gabe was so used to the eerie night cries that he scarcely would have noticed except that Yvette stiffened and looked around each time she heard a scream.

There were other sounds as well, snores and sometimes moans. The moans of men who suffered every ill, from the phantom pains of amputated limbs to the cramps of diarrhea. The inescapable noises of exhaustion and of suffering that Gabe had ignored for months and months.

A new sound broke the darkness. Different, unexpected, yet unmistakable. The metallic click of a revolver. He froze, listening for direction. It had sounded all too close.

A shadow separated itself from the others. Before Gabe could recognize Captain Russell, Yvette's gasp assured him that their worst fear had come to pass.

She glanced about herself, as if looking for an escape route. Her body shifted, and in an instant,

Gabe realized she would go over the rail and leap into the river.

Russell pointed his pistol at her chest. "You'll be dead before you hit the water. At this range I won't miss."

"That would save you the trouble of dumping me there yourself," Yvette told him, "as you dumped Marie."

"Come along. We'll discuss this upstairs, in your stateroom."

"Did she tell you she was carrying your child?" Yvette continued, fearless in her fury. "Or did you kill her first?"

Russell flinched visibly. "Liar!" he accused. "Come now, before I'm forced to fire."

"She's not going anywhere with you," Gabe swore.

"You won't have anything to say about it. You'll be under guard. Helping her was treason. I'll have you up on charges for aiding this murderess. Perhaps you'll hang as well . . . unless . . ."

"Unless what?" Yvette asked.

Russell was still staring at Gabe. "Unless he turns around and walks away from this right now."

Gabe didn't realize he was moving toward Russell until he felt Yvette grasping his arm, restraining him.

"No, Gabe! Don't! Just do what he says! Go . . . please go back to your friends, go home," she pleaded.

He patted her hand and loosed it from his shirt. They both were offering him freedom, the chance to tuck his tail between his legs and walk away. But neither Russell nor Yvette could hear the words that still rang in his head, *"Got no use for a goddamn coward."*

Neither one imagined what such an act would cost him.

But Gabe Davis knew, and in that instant, he realized what had happened on the battlefield had been something unexplainable, but it had not been cowardice. As it would be if he left now.

"There is no price too high for self-respect, sir."

Yvette had spoken those words to him, and he saw now that she had been right. There was no price too high, not even death.

With that thought, he launched himself at Darien Russell.

But he never reached his goal.

Chapter Ten

All was still; no one thought of danger by the resistless power of that element which has enabled men to triumph over the mighty force of wind—the steamer was on her way. . . .

— Rev. Dr. George White,
from his sermon of April 30, 1865

Clutching his stomach, Jacob staggered toward the railing. It hardly seemed fair that he was the only one who'd taken ill from the meat pies after all the trouble he'd gone through to get them. Several yards behind him, both Captain Seth and Zeke slept peacefully, clearly untroubled by the nausea that plagued him. Of course, neither one of them had been cracked on the head this evening, either.

Jacob wondered once more what had become of Gabriel. He'd bet his bottom dollar (if he had one, he thought ruefully) that it had something to do with that Southern woman. And knowing Gabe, he'd have trouble nipping at his heels. Jacob disapproved of Gabe's involvement with a Rebel, but he hoped that whatever his friend was up to, it would inconvenience the hell out of that jackass Captain Russell.

Jacob leaned against the deck rail and stared out over the dark water, illuminated only by the meager light of those few stars not hidden by the clouds. A chill night breeze stole across the hurricane deck to give his curls a playful tousle. Inhaling deeply, he smelled the damp, muddy river scent. Despite the coolness, there was a hint of spring as well, of translucent green, unfurling leaves, of blades pressing upward through the soggy soil.

The fresh air settled his stomach and made the pounding in his head more bearable. The hour was late now, so that most men slept, and the boat felt for the first time quiet, still. Jacob let the rare peace soak into him . . . one split second before it was shattered by the loudest sound he'd ever heard.

The gunshot reverberated through Gabe's body, through his brain and through his world, all-consuming and as unending as the heaviest artillery barrage. He'd expected it, of course, expected Russell would fire. Expected, probably, to die, to give Yvette the chance to get away.

But he had not anticipated the way the sound would seem to lift him, to send him spinning into darkness. He had not expected that dying would feel anything like flight.

Cold enveloped his whole body, pressing in on him. Cold liquid. The realization sank in that he had fallen into water. A dark river without landmarks, without up or down or any frame of reference whatsoever. The shot must have flung him over the steamboat's railing, down into the Mississippi, where he would bleed to death or drown.

His body provided him with a direction. Some instinct sent it struggling toward air, limbs pumping as efficiently as if there'd been no bullet. As if he were yet again a truant boy swimming in the pond near home.

He gasped and sputtered at the water's surface, his mind grappling with his surprising strength and the utter lack of pain. He remembered hearing that the soul separated from the body at the moment of death, but he still felt sensations: the chill wetness of the river, the expansion of his lungs, the disorienting dizziness of his rapid tumble through empty space, then water.

His eyes began to focus, and he saw shapes around him, floating: odd fragments of flotsam, a swimming white horse, what looked like a man's body, limp and facedown, bobbing amid wavelets. The horse neighed frantically and struggled closer to Gabe. With an effort, he made a few strokes, then grasped the animal's thick mane.

It dragged him along toward a huge hulk in the water, a black shape lit by . . . flame? And all at once, the pieces spun together in Gabe's mind. He had not been shot at all. Something must have happened to the *Sultana*. Perhaps a Rebel shell had struck it or a boiler had given out. Whatever the cause, some sort of explosion must have blown him off the deck.

And not only him. Now that his senses were returning, he could hear desperate cries all around him in the water, shouts to God for mercy or to curse his name. Other shrieks, less clear, were coming from the steamboat, and the fire silhouetted masses of humanity leaping from the stern, clutching at each other, going down beneath the flame-lit water in writhing, screaming clumps.

A shaft of fear impaled him so fiercely that he nearly lost his grip on the white horse. Yvette was in this somewhere. Had she, too, been blown off the deck, or was she part of the madness on the burning steamer?

Not ten feet from him, men fought for purchase on a floating plank, clawing as viciously as mad dogs. Yvette, who might be five feet tall and a hundred pounds at best, would never survive such savage chaos, never—unless he found and helped her. Yet how could he locate one small woman in this hellish nightmare? Was she even still alive?

He thought, too, of his friends, of Seth and Jacob and Zeke, whose infected wound had cost him so much strength. Dear God, after all that they had suffered, would any of them live?

The panicked horse, whose mane he held, was making directly for the stern, as if it thought it could climb up onto the ruin. Gabe realized that if the horse swam close enough, men would try to scramble onto it and overwhelm it. He grasped its halter with one hand and fought to pull its head to redirect it away from the *Sultana,* but the animal was oblivious to everything except the instinct to return to what it remembered as a place of safety. One thrashing hoof struck Gabe's shin painfully, and he gave up the useless struggle.

God help him, he would have to let the horse go, Gabe realized. He scanned the river's surface, but every floating object he saw was being fought over by other swimmers. Even so, he pushed away from the white beast. He had no other choice, not if he wanted to live long enough to find—and save—Yvette.

The revolver must have misfired, Darien Russell thought. The flash and sound of it reverberated in his skull, filling all the world with heat and thunder, sending him reeling toward the blackness. Tumbling, grasping, clutching. His left hand grabbed something wooden, and with a painful jerk, his body came to rest.

It took several moments for him to realize he was hanging by one arm from the railing. If he slipped, he'd be in the water—in the dark.

Shrieks of pain and terror splintered the air around him. Far too many to be explained by a misfiring revolver or the young soldier's attack against him. Smoke thickened the air, gripping his chest as painfully as talons. Coughing hurt, but the breeze shifted, and his breathing eased.

Still wondering what happened, Darien reached up to grasp the railing with his right hand. Only then did he realize he had lost his gun. Pulling himself higher, he saw ruptured interior walls and flickering blue flames. Men were leaping pell-mell off the stern, and moans and screams added to the nightmare quality of the scene.

Had a Rebel unit, one too stubborn to surrender, somehow fired upon them? Or had they struck another boat? Surely there must have been some sort of explosion. His mind worked desperately to make sense of what was happening until he realized that his questions must wait for later, till a time when he'd found safety.

He hesitated, wondering if he should drop into the water or climb back aboard the *Sultana*'s deck. He shuddered at the thought of the black and swollen Mississippi flowing beneath his feet and at the image of Marie as she had slipped beneath its surface. He didn't want to go there, not with the river sprawling cold and endless under the night sky. He'd never survive it unless he found some floating object and kept it to himself.

Darien struggled for several minutes to pull himself back over the rail. Panting with exertion, he scanned the gangway for any sign of Yvette or the private who'd befriended her. Perhaps if one or the other had been wounded, he could pitch them overboard and let nature take its course. Panicked soldiers rushed about, desperately snatching up anything that might float, and he knew no one would take any note of what he did. Certainly no one would bother to try to stop a murder.

But neither one remained anywhere in sight. It seemed likely that both Yvette and the soldier had been hurled into the water by the blast.

"Please, you have to help me! It's burning me alive!"

Russell turned his head and looked down. A pile of rubble pinned a man's midsection to a half-collapsed stretch of deck. Darien moved closer, hoping the trapped fellow would prove to be Yvette's friend. But the man reaching toward Russell was gray-haired and not blond, and Darien recognized him as one of the guards.

"Please!" the soldier repeated.

Darien hadn't meant to come near enough for the man to look him in the eye. Yet he had, and he nearly gagged on the sharp odor of scorched flesh. That was when he realized the guard's legs were covered by a red-hot sheet of twisted metal.

All around him, heaps of glowing coals gradually smoldered their way through both the deck and fragments of shattered interior wall that lay scattered like kindling. Flame licked at the debris that trapped the soldier, and his pleas abruptly changed to screams of agony.

"Dear God! Dear God! I'm dying!"

A lump formed in his throat as Darien used his shoes to try to kick some of the debris off the guard. He quickly realized that nothing in the pile was large enough to make a proper float. Even so, the man's pleas prompted Darien to kick a few more times until flame ignited the hem of his wool trousers.

After using his hands to beat out the fire, he turned away, heedless of the rising volume of the guard's agonized screams. Nothing to be done about it, Darien told himself. Not unless he wanted to die, too.

Distinctive female cries drew his attention. He spun toward the sound, hoping he would have the chance to settle accounts with Yvette. But the woman running down the gangway was clearly not her. The tall blonde's eyes were wild, and by the firelight, he saw what looked like a large red burn on her left cheek. Despite the apparent wound and the tears streaming down her face, she was moving with swift determination, clutching two boards as if for dear life.

He couldn't stay and burn to death as the guard had, and he couldn't face the river without a float. This might be his best chance. Darien grabbed the

larger board as she tried to pass him. She shrieked
and swung the other toward his shoulder. He wrested
it away from her as well, but she clawed desperately
in an attempt to regain her treasure.

With all his strength, he smashed the smaller board
into her left temple. Hard enough for the force of
the impact to send shafts of pain shooting through
his arm. Hard enough to send an arc of bloody droplets flying across the boards. Did he only imagine the
sound of the liquid sizzling against hot coals?

The woman crumpled at his feet. *His third murder.*
But unlike the others, this one had neither neatness
nor precision to take pride in. Only ugliness and the
base instinct to survive no matter who stood in his
way.

Before anyone could serve him the same, Darien
stripped off his frock coat and climbed over the railing. After pitching his boards into the water, he leapt
after them, barely noticing that the screaming of the
burning man had finally ceased.

Sharp, exquisite agony was all that kept her focused.
Without it, the shock of the concussion might have
rendered Yvette unconscious or stunned her until it
was too late to try to swim. Her left elbow, struck by
some heavy flying object, instead drew every bit of her
attention, even as she plunged beneath the water's
surface.

The wound throbbed a dark warning. The cold
Mississippi meant to swallow her, just as it had Marie.
Already its chill ebbed away her strength and pulled
her bare feet toward the bottom.

No! Yvette rose on a wave of outrage, aided by her

kicking legs and her right arm. She refused to sink,
to feed the river yet another unprotesting Augeron.
Her face broke the surface, and she took angry gulps
of air.

What in the name of heaven had thrown her off
the steamboat? What had struck her hard enough
to cause such sickening waves of pain? Putting her
questions aside for later, she tried—and failed—to
use the injured arm. The effort made her vision cloud
with blackness and her head dip once more beneath
the surface of the waves.

God, no! She sputtered to the surface once more
and knew she mustn't try again to use that arm. Surely
it was broken. Yet without it, how would she ever keep
herself afloat?

Gradually, she became aware of other swimmers in
the water, their heads lit intermittently by the flickering of flames upon the burning steamboat. Some
sort of fire or explosion, she decided. But right now
that didn't matter. All that mattered was the plank
she saw illuminated, not twenty feet away.

As she set out toward it, she prayed that she would
reach the plank before anyone else saw it. And before
her strength gave out.

In those first few instants, Capt. J. Cass Mason
thought it a nightmare, the result of too much worry,
maybe even too much drink. But the *Sultana*'s violent
shudder soon shook him awake, and he quickly realized this was something far worse than any nightmare,
far deadlier as well.

If not for the tremendous boom, he would have
thought they'd struck a bar or snag. Either would

be enough to end the *Sultana*'s life and ruin him financially. But the blast meant an explosion, unless he missed his guess. As Mason pulled on his clothes and shoes, he thought first of Confederate artillery. But he soon dismissed the idea as nonsense. When he'd gone to bed perhaps two hours before, they'd been near the river's center, too far from either shore for shells.

Too far, also, for an easy swim to land and safety. He would have to calm these people before a panic led to a mass drowning. He'd seen hysterical passengers leap to their deaths from boats that still might float for hours more.

As he hurried from his room on the hurricane deck, he saw plumes of steam rising into the night and flames already erupting like a brightly colored pox. He realized then that his earlier thoughts of grounding or artillery had been merely wishful thinking. There was only one thing this could be.

An angry face flashed across his vision, that of R. G. Taylor, the boiler mechanic who had come aboard in Vicksburg to set the boat to rights.

"Why did you not have this repaired in New Orleans?" He pointed at the leaking bulge as he spoke, his tone accusing Chief Engineer Wintringer.

Wintringer took offense, as he had drained the boilers and had them scraped and cleaned while they were in the Crescent City. Afterward, he'd nursed them all the way to Vicksburg.

"But they weren't bulging or leaking earlier," Wintringer insisted. "Can't you patch them up enough to last us to St. Louis? We've got to get on quick if we're to make our load here."

"If I do anything at all, I will make a job of it or

have nothing to do with it," said Taylor as he stalked off the boat.

Mason had ordered Wintringer to go after him, and somehow his chief engineer had changed Taylor's mind. While the men had quickly patched the bulge to stop the leak, Mason had kept busy securing every passenger he could.

Securing passengers that might die because of his decisions.

As he expected, the deck was a chaotic swirl of motion. Men leaping overboard, fighting for the largest and sturdiest-looking boards and planks. He edged past a gaping hole blown in the deck. Steam and smoke billowed out of it as though it were a shaft down into hell. Apart from his own room, much of the Texas cabin, where the boat's officers slept, had been blown to bits. He tried not to think of the men who had been sleeping there.

He had only one priority left now, the responsibility of saving as many as he could. Nothing else mattered. Especially not his life.

Absurdly, Gabe thought the small boat was coming to save him—him alone, among the hundreds now struggling, dying in the water. He would climb aboard the rescue and find Yvette in time.

The delusion exploded as he realized the men aboard—crewmen, by their uniforms—were beating with oars at other hopeful swimmers as they grasped at the boat's gunwales to pull themselves inside. One shrill voice cut through the cacophony of moans and screams and pleas.

"You can't leave me, Edmund! My God, you're my husband!"

It was only then that Gabe understood. These crewmen had taken the sounding yawl, the boat sometimes used to test the depth of channels for the steamboat. They were stealing it and abandoning everyone else. Even one man's wife.

As he clutched the empty cracker box he'd found, he thought again of Yvette, tried to imagine leaving her—or any of his friends. Impossible. If he found any of them, he would rather drown than live without them.

He heard a shrill scream, one he thought he recognized. Was that Yvette he saw in the water? He saw only a dark head, smaller than the others. He kicked frantically, trying to maneuver the crate nearer.

As he began to close the distance, he could make out the plank that she was clutching and the two men trying to wrest it away from her.

"No!" she screamed, as fierce as either of the men. But one of her arms dangled limp and useless, and it was obvious the men would overpower her.

"Yvette!" Gabe tried to shout, but instead, unexpectedly, his mouth filled up with water as arms clamped around his ankle, the arms of a drowning man, dragging him beneath the water's surface.

Yvette screamed in pain as a flailing hand struck her injured arm.

Pain turned to fury as a second man grabbed onto the plank she held, then shoved her away.

"No!" she shouted.

She tried to regain her hold, but it was useless. If

she stayed and fought here, they would drown her. She was neither big enough nor strong enough to stop them. Resentment boiled in her veins, nearly overcoming the chill water. If she'd ever had any illusion that Yankee chivalry existed, this behavior cured her of the notion!

As no Southern gentlemen were present to rescue her, she would have to use her head to save herself. Reluctantly giving up the struggle, she kicked away from the two men. She saw other floating debris nearby, each piece surrounded by groups of struggling soldiers. Every moment, dozens more splashed into the water. Some clutched each other, as if their bodies might form a raft. Instead, they writhed, then sank almost immediately beneath the river's surface. Yvette looked away, sickened by the sight.

She'd have no chance at all here. The best thing to do would be to swim into the darkness, away from the *Sultana*. She thanked God for the summers she'd spent with her family at Grand Isle and for her mother's insistence that every one of her children learn how to swim.

Since she was ten years younger, *Maman* made sixteen-year-old Pierre give her lessons. Annoyed and impatient, he had tossed his little sister into the waves beyond the third sandbar.

Frightened half out of her mind, she splashed and clawed uselessly, then sank twice beneath the warm Gulf waters.

Pierre had dragged her out. "First lesson: never panic, or you die."

A harsh lesson, but one she had never forgotten.

Grimly, she forced her mind to calm. With careful deliberateness, she put her later lessons into practice, using only legs and her uninjured arm. She began to make slow progress, trying to ignore the question that throbbed at her left elbow: *How long can I possibly go on?*

"The hull's not damaged! We'll be landing soon!" Captain Mason shouted.

But the soldiers on the hurricane deck swarmed past him, heedless of his words. He could do nothing to save them, he realized. They were an animal-like mob now, most of them too insensible with panic to harness their energies to attempt to put out the spreading fire. God help them all, he prayed as he turned away.

They might not listen to him, but the women and children on the cabin deck might still be reassured. He climbed down to the second level, where he found a group of ladies kneeling behind the main cabin. Over the screams of the trapped and drowning, he could barely hear their prayers.

"Help will be here soon," he assured them. "Please, don't give up hope."

They looked up at him as if his voice had been God's, giving them the answer that they sought.

Unable to bear their gazes, he turned and rushed inside the elegant main cabin. Steam swirled throughout the shattered deck in scalding clouds. The front of the room tilted, forming a deadly ramp into the fiery center of the deck below. Glancing down into it, he saw bodies strewn amid the flame and wreckage.

As the smoke thickened, he began to realize he'd

been wrong. The *Sultana* would never regain the shore; nor would the rescuers arrive in time. She was burning far too quickly.

Keeping toward the rear, Mason dashed about, alternately stopping to try to free those trapped amid the wreckage and to hand passengers everything that he could find that might float. A few soldiers and officers were composed enough to join him, and together they passed chairs, stateroom doors, and even sheeting from the cabin's interior walls to be thrown overboard.

On one trip to haul a door out onto the deck, a bone-thin former prisoner clutched him by the arm. As Mason turned to look, he was startled by the darkness of the man's eye sockets, the skull-like contours of his face.

"My brother's dead! He's *dead!*" Even as the prisoner sobbed the words, his pale face transformed into a mask of fury. "You bastards have gone and killed us all!"

Ripping free of the man's grip, Mason recognized the grain of truth in his ranting. But with the thought came a renewed surge of energy. He stepped into the steaming cauldron to see who might be saved.

Gabe kicked at the strong arms that held his ankle and dragged him ever deeper. He felt the man's grip slipping to his foot. With one last, powerful kick, he lost his shoe and sock to the poor fellow, then struggled toward the water's surface. His lungs burned with the terrible need to inhale, and black dots with bright outlines began to cloud his vision.

Too deep, he realized, he'd been dragged too deep to make it back without a breath. In a moment, he would pass out and take in water, anyway.

Just as Matthew had, back on that cold December day. An image flashed before him of his brother's face after he'd been pulled out of the river. So pale and swollen he couldn't recognize the features.

The memory gave him strength enough to hold back the blackness for another instant, during which he finally broke the water's surface.

Gasping and coughing, he looked about him, hoping against hope he'd find the cracker box. But it was gone now, along with any sign of Yvette; he saw only the plank she had been holding, now claimed by the two men who must have drowned her.

Grief cleaved him like an ax, sending sharp pain shooting from his chest and out his limbs. But on its heels came even more powerful denial. It could not be true. He had not seen her go under.

Perhaps she'd swum away. Or she'd found some better raft. Somewhere in the dark and moonless night she still lived. She hadn't yet slipped under; she hadn't yet drowned.

Over and over, his heart preached the message, irrational as it was. He ignored his mind's whispers that he deluded himself, that he'd held out the same insane, impossible hopes the day that Matthew disappeared beneath the ice.

Though his strength was fading, he swam away from the burning steamboat in the hope of avoiding anyone else who might clutch and drag him under. Farther away, the flickering firelight illuminated a dark mound in the water, too rounded to be a plank, too large to be a box. He prayed silently that he hadn't located the crew's pet alligator.

He did not stop swimming toward it, for his arms and legs now felt so heavy that he knew this mound to be his only hope. Instead, absurdly, he pictured himself riding the gator's back to safety. He nearly laughed aloud despite the realization that only shock and exhaustion could lead him to find any humor in his situation.

At last he reached the floating mound and threw one arm over it. It was a drowned mule, its body still warm from its futile struggle. He thought how strange it seemed that he'd traded a live mount for a dead one and how that choice might yet save him.

If it floated downstream fast enough to keep other men from latching on and swamping him.

After pulling himself against its belly, between the front and rear legs, Gabe leaned his face into the dead mule's wet hide to draw the last warmth from its cooling body. And as he did, he tried to convince himself that both Yvette and his three friends still lived.

Jacob realized he should be glad that he survived, that of all the men who'd gone over with the stage-plank, he'd been one of the few who'd bobbed back to the surface. He felt no joy in it, though, no great cheer that he'd been stronger than many of the other soldiers who'd clawed at the long wooden walkway for purchase.

He hadn't even meant to jump. He'd still been searching for his brother, Seth, and Gabe. But the flood tide of men leaping at the stageplank had swept him along, then forced him overboard before he could veer out of its path.

The current and the remaining men clinging to it conspired to take him farther from the burning steamboat. As his makeshift raft began to move away, the last clear image Jacob saw was that of Captain Seth running, then leaping from the main deck.

Jacob's brother wasn't with him.

Captain Mason coughed to clear his lungs of smoke. As the fire progressed, he'd been working like a madman to save all he could, but now his arms hung like anchors at his side. All he wanted to do was to sink down onto the deck and sleep, never again to open his eyes, never again to face the devastation he had wrought.

But still passengers struggled in the water, so he forced himself to resume the task of tossing pieces of wood into the water.

"Captain, help me!" a new voice shouted.

Panting, Mason turned toward a man he thought might be a guard.

"Please, he's still alive!" The guard beckoned him to follow.

Mason strode after him, along the outer promenade. The man led him to a spot where the hurricane deck had fallen onto this level. A pair of legs jutted from beneath the wreckage. Surely the man couldn't be alive.

But when the guard touched the outstretched legs, they kicked. Mason tried to help the man lift off the deck, but exhaustion had drained him utterly.

He shook his head. "I can't. I can't."

Then he shuffled back in the direction of the stern, hoping to throw overboard a few more pieces of debris, not caring that when the fire forced him to leave the *Sultana,* he'd held back not an ounce of strength to swim.

Chapter Eleven

Exult O shores, and ring O bells!
But I with mournful tread,
Walk the deck my Captain lies,
Fallen cold and dead.

　　　　—Walt Whitman,
　　　from "O Captain! My Captain!"

Over and over, Darien felt the awful jolt leaping from the woman's skull into his arms, conducted by the plank he'd used to strike the woman's temple. One of the same planks he now gripped to save his life. As he drifted blindly through the darkness, he saw the ebb and flow of his act: the drawing back of his arms with the stolen length, the swing and follow-through of the deathblow. The second woman he had murdered.

"Did she tell you she was carrying your child?"

Yvette had asked him that, and the possibility it

might be true rose in his thoughts like gorge. *My child.* Could Marie have given him the son or daughter that Constance never had produced? The darkness and the river resurrected Marie's face, but this time one cheek was marred by a red discoloration like a hand slap, the same mark that bloomed on the face of the blond woman he had struck.

Cold wavelets lapped against his back, but none came colder than his recollection of the crack of the wood against her temple. The sound washed over him, again . . . again . . . again . . . And then a voice rode over the memory, his grandfather's deep baritone, saying, *"This boy's going to be the finest Russell ever. I can tell he's destined for great things."*

Great things. Like murdering two women, perhaps even his own unborn child? *I might have been a father.* No, it couldn't be. Yvette had been only striking out at him with the only weapon at her disposal, a hideous, cruel lie. He had to put her words out of his mind now and instead focus on the ones Grandfather had uttered.

Darien had never questioned the old man's proclamation or paused to wonder if it had been less the result of patriarchal foresight than a consequence of shattered hopes for his only son. But now, as the current carried Darien downriver, he at last comprehended his grandfather's loss and the tremendous blow to the old banker's pride. His only son, Darien's father, had been stabbed behind a tavern in some sordid misadventure involving a loose woman. Jonathan Russell had bled to death there, leaving behind nothing except gambling debts and a pregnant wife.

Darien's thoughts turned to his mother, a hollow shell of a woman. With her own family dead, the beautiful young widow had been forced to live as a permanent guest of her husband's father.

From the time Darien had been able to speak, he'd been aware of an almost overwhelming strain between the two. He'd seen Grandfather touch her cheek once, gently. His mother had cried out and fled the room.

Grandfather, seeing the child's wide-eyed confusion, explained to him. "Sensitive woman, your mother. But she knows I mean you both the best."

Beyond that, neither ever spoke of their disagreement within his hearing, but the tension was so palpable that Darien often watched them carefully for any sign of the explosion he knew must surely come.

But it hadn't. Instead, one evening when Darien was five years old, his mother had kissed her son good night. Tears had glistened in her eyes, but his mother had often seemed so sad that he'd gone right on babbling about the pony Grandfather had promised for his birthday.

Later, Nora Russell slipped quietly into the night, taking only a small carpetbag and not her son. He had never heard from her again.

". . . *the finest Russell ever.*" Putting aside the disturbing memories of his mother, he focused on Grandfather's words instead. How many times had he spoken them in that ringing voice that sounded like the thunder of God? As a child, Grandfather *had* been God to Darien, and his prediction had become a holy prophecy, made all the more sacred by the old man's death six years ago.

For the first time ever, Darien wondered about Thomas Russell the *man*. Could his proclamation have been no more than wishful thinking? Had he

seen Darien only as a final chance to leave a better
legacy than his wastrel of a son?

That couldn't be right, could it? For if Darien
weren't really destined for great things, then that
would mean that there had been no reason to build
his fortune as he had, no excuse to take three lives.
Instead of succeeding on his dead father's behalf, it
would mean that Darien had instead far exceeded
him in villainy.

No! Why else did he yet live when so many had
burned to death or drowned? Why else had fate always
protected him from calamity, from the battlefield to
this very night?

He held on to the two planks and to all he had—
the certain knowledge that he was meant to live
beyond this. He was meant to survive and find that
grand fate in his future.

Gabe didn't know how long he had dozed, only
that his fingers ached where they'd been cramped so
long in one position, knotted in the dead mule's
mane. His legs felt numb and his brain logy with . . .
what? Exhaustion? Cold? He could barely think.

He peered around a world of velvet darkness, cold
darkness, without the flickering *Sultana* to add light.
Had the steamboat burned completely, or had he
drifted far downstream?

He lifted his head from the mule's cool belly and
noticed for the first time the way the backs of his
hands and forearms stung. Maybe he'd been burned
in the explosion, or maybe it was only the night's
breeze blowing across exposed, damp flesh.

Even more disturbing than the darkness and the

pain was the eerie quiet that had descended upon the river. He wondered if it might be possible that he alone survived, that no one else was clinging to flotsam. A more frightening idea brought him fully awake. Had he dozed through a rescue? Had the others all been picked up by passing steamboats while he'd drifted past?

The idea so unnerved him that he was glad to hear the splashing of another swimmer's approach. He felt a body thud against the mule's back, opposite him.

Recovering his senses, Gabe hoped that it would be just one. The mule could certainly float two of them to safety. How many more than that, he couldn't guess, and he lacked both the strength and will to fight off others.

The other person bumped his arm while seeking a handhold.

"Are you alive over there?" a hoarse voice asked.

Despite the hoarseness, he recognized the Southern accent. His heart gave a leap, and he instantly awakened fully.

"Yvette?" he asked.

A pause stretched on and on, so long that he was certain he'd imagined it was she.

Across the mule's ribs, a hand gripped his arm. He bit back a yelp as flesh pressed his burned flesh, but in a moment he forgot his pain completely.

"Gabriel!" she cried. *"Je ne comprends pas!* How can this be, of all these people? My float was sinking, and this was the only thing to grab, and—"

He released the mule's mane with one hand to stroke her cold fingers. "Maybe we were meant to find each other. Oh, Yvette, I thought I'd seen two men drowning you, but at that moment I was pulled under as well."

"Those ill-bred ruffians didn't drown me, but it was not from lack of effort on their part."

"After I broke the surface, I couldn't find you anywhere. I— Please, marry me, Yvette. You didn't answer me before, but do it now. Promise that you'll marry me when this is over. Promise me."

When she didn't answer, he continued, his words suddenly in flood. "I'm sorry. I know I made a mess of that, but—"

"Let me guess. You neglected to read Miss Willington's chapter on the etiquette of proposals over a dead horse floating on the Mississippi River."

Her absurd comment, in the face of all that had happened, took Gabriel aback. But the moment passed, and he found himself laughing, more from relief that they had found each other than at her statement

"I—well, I did read that one," he said after he recovered, "but this is different. It's a dead mule, actually."

"In that case, I shall forgive your ignorance," she told him, her voice now so hoarse that he could barely understand her.

"So will you? If we can get out of this?"

Another pause. As the water lapped at them, he tried to read her face by starlight, but the moonless night had shrouded her expression.

Finally, she answered. "Yes, I will, Gabriel Davis. I *will* marry you."

"I love you more than I ever believed it was possible to love anyone, Yvette." He squeezed her arm.

"You're so cold. Give me your other hand. I don't want you to slip off."

"I can't lift my left arm. I think it's broken. Something must have struck me when I fell from the boat."

"You should have told me you were hurt! Are you injured anywhere else?"

"I don't think so ... hard to tell with this chill. What about you?" she asked.

"I'm not sure, either. Maybe a few burns."

He released her fingers to unwind a length of rope he'd wrapped around his upper arm. "I'm passing you the mule's lead rope. Let's wrap this around your good arm in case you fall asleep. Don't try to tie it, though. If this animal goes under, you'll want to be able to break loose."

She murmured her thanks and accepted his help.

"Will someone come for us?" she asked.

"They probably heard that blast all the way to Memphis. Don't worry. They'll come for us. . . . I swear it." He spoke with more certainty than he felt, but the words helped reassure him, too.

"But what if they can't find us? It's so dark."

"Look that way, where the sky is getting a bit grayer. That must be the east, then. Once the sun's up, they'll find us for certain."

"It's a big, big river, Gabriel."

"You found me, didn't you?"

"I did. And I promise, *mon cher*, that I won't let you go again."

". . . he's destined for great things."

Grandfather's voice kept Darien company, but it could not keep him warm. By this time, he was shiv-

ering so violently that he could barely keep hold of
the two planks that he had killed to get.

His mind was playing tricks, too, pushing him again
and again into the past, forcing him to watch more
of the things that he'd been forced to do. Telling
the old Creole he knew a way to make profitable
investments in Union industries secretly so that his
neighbors wouldn't guess. Dropping poison into
Lieutenant Simonton's drink. Choking the life out
of Marie, the only woman who had ever really loved
him.

"This boy's going to be the finest Russell ever."

He had to hold on to those words, had to use the
power of Grandfather's voice to float him like a raft.

Out in the darkness, Darien heard a new sound, a
deep, repeated splashing, a pulling of oars through
water, a distant voice shouting, "Hallo! Call out if
you can hear me!"

He felt such shock at it that he could not respond.
Or perhaps the cold and the long swim had numbed
his mind.

The sounds drew steadily nearer. Darien was con-
tent to simply listen, without doing anything at all.

But he finally came to himself long enough to shout
out, to wave until they found him and hauled him
from the water. He had to, for it could only have
been his destiny that provided this escape.

It must have been, or all his actions had a darker
meaning than he could bear to face.

Cold. So very, very cold. If she could only get dry,
she might feel better. Must get out of these rain-
soaked petticoats. Must get out of this rain.

Yvette woke with a start, wondering where on earth she was and how she'd come to be there. One thing had certainly been right about the dream. She was soaked through, but, she realized with a jolt of horror, her condition had nothing whatsoever to do with any rainstorm.

She was floating in a broad, cold river. Her arms both ached ferociously. The right, where it was wound up tightly in some sort of rope. When she tried to move the left, pain shooting through her elbow made her cry out sharply.

Fresh agony exploded upon her senses, and she remembered that greater blast aboard the steamboat, the struggle to survive, the clumsy swim with one arm injured. Finding Gabriel out here floating, holding on to this dead beast. Promising she would become his wife.

"Gabriel," she called softly.

When he didn't answer, fear coiled in her belly. She spoke his name once more, her voice tight and anxious.

The sky had lightened somewhat, enough to turn the drowned mule an indistinct dark gray, the color of a particularly wet fog.

She used her good arm to pull herself up slightly so she could see over the hummock of the bloated equine corpse. She prayed that she would be able to reach over the beast's ribs to shake Gabriel awake.

But there was nothing save the water, which must have taken Gabriel.

Yvette screamed, a long, painful shriek that fractured into sobs. *Gabriel was missing. Gabriel was gone!*

Though her throat felt as if her grief were tearing it to pieces, she sobbed with loneliness and loss. And

all her losses crowded in upon that drifting island in
the Mississippi, an island made of misery and death.
The loss of her possessions, from all her clothing to
poor Lafitte, who surely must have died.

So many, many losses, but none worse than Gabriel.
Yvette screwed shut her eyes, now blinded by a haze
of tears. Blinded to anything except her horror. But
closing them did nothing except isolate her with her
grief and make her wonder why on earth she still
held on.

"Hello out there! You fellas holler out if you can
hear me!"

Yvette looked up, wondering if in her exhaustion
she might have imagined the man's voice.

"Hello!"

The second shout convinced her, but the voice
seemed to float above the water, coming from
nowhere and everywhere at once. She turned her
head to try to see a boat or perhaps a nearby shore.
She had grown so stiff, the action caused her upper
body to slide off the mule's back with a splash.

She tried to flail her legs, but her clumsy efforts
had little effect. Had it not been for the lead rope
wound around her forearm, she would have gone
down like a stone. But even with it, she could barely
manage to push her face above the water's surface.
Once, then twice, she fought her way to air, then
coughed and sputtered with the effort to breathe.
She couldn't think of shouting out; the struggle to
keep from sinking again consumed every ounce of
energy. She could hold nothing back.

But it wouldn't be enough. The cold hours in the
water had weakened her too much to pull her head
and shoulders up on the dead mule's back. Fight

though she would, eventually the river must win out, and someone far downstream, perhaps as far as New Orleans, would find her, dangling from the lead rope of a drowned army mule. Once more, she submerged.

Something snagged her hair, then pulled it sharply, yanking her head free of the river's grip. She could see a dark shape just above her—a little boat, a man leaning far over the side. The man still clutched her hair near the scalp.

It hurt badly, and she wanted to shout at him to stop it, to cease tormenting her while she was dying. Instead, she felt him shift his grip to her midsection. With one huge hand, the black man drew her from the water and into the bow of a small sounding yawl.

"God's sake, it's a woman. And look at this. She's got up like a soldier. What do you suppose . . . ?" A bristle-bearded white man wrapped her in a blanket as he spoke to his two mates.

Other drenched survivors were lying in the bottom of the yawl, each one wrapped in a wool blanket. Some were moaning, maybe crying. She raised herself up on her good elbow and tried to see their faces.

"Gabriel?" she called out. Then more loudly, "Gabriel?"

No one answered.

Curling her body tightly within the blanket, Yvette wept until exhaustion overtook her. Her last conscious thought was a fleeting image of Gabriel, his hair waving in the murky waters of the Mississippi, like Marie's.

Chapter Twelve

"There in the bosom of the Mississippi they found their last resting place. . . . [F]lowers are strewn over the graves in the cemeteries of our dead, but there are no flowers for the dead of the [people], who went down on the Sultana. *But let us remember them."*

—Maj. Will A. McTeer,
adjutant of the Third Tennessee
Cavalry, which lost at least
220 men aboard the *Sultana*

God forgive him, he had lost Yvette. Even now, Gabriel wasn't quite certain how it happened. Only that at some point cold and pain and shock had conspired once more to lull him to sleep. His grip on the mule's mane must have eventually relaxed, and he'd slipped easily beyond the safety of the float made by the creature's air-filled lungs.

He awoke as water closed over his head and struggled to the surface. But not before he'd taken in a lungful of the river, which caused him to choke and cough so badly that several minutes passed before he could call out.

He doubted that Yvette had heard him, that she had awakened. By this time, the mule's body had caught an eddy that spun it away from the main current, which had swept Gabriel downstream.

He tried to fight the river to reach Yvette, but his limbs felt as if they'd been cast in iron. Within moments, he realized that his mad attempt to swim upstream would mean certain death. Shouting once more to Yvette, he gave up and turned his gaze downstream to find something—anything—he might hold on to.

A keg drifted not ten yards away. Even that felt like a mile as he floundered toward it. When finally he reached it, he found it difficult to hold. No matter how he tried to grasp its rounded sides, the blasted thing rolled and spun and bobbed out of his grip.

"Over here!" a man's voice shouted. "Get over here and hold on!"

Gabriel turned his head to see a trio of soldiers around a floating bale of hay. They weren't much farther than the keg had been, but to Gabe the distance looked impossible.

"Come on, soldier! Swim for it!" another man shouted. "You'll drown for sure on that thing."

He was right, Gabe knew. He had no choice but to try. Summoning the last of his reserves of strength, he clumsily paddled toward the raft.

He'd nearly made it when his legs cramped. He fought the pain and with a flurry of his arms kept his head above the water's surface. But he could no more reach the hay bale than he could sprout wings to fly.

A hand extended outward from the hay bale. He focused his gaze—and his efforts—on those fingers.

"God damn you, grab on!" the soldier screamed at him.

He did, and the soldier dragged him closer, so close that he could grasp the twine that held the bale together. Two men, the soldier who had offered him his hand and a man with a gash extending from the corner of his mouth to his cheekbone, hauled Gabe up onto the bale.

"Rest up here a spell," the third man told him. "We been takin' turns."

"Damn awful cold up there," the man with the cut said. "Breeze cuts right through them wet clothes."

He was right, Gabe realized. Though his exertions had sent warmth flooding through him, it took only moments for him to begin shivering. His forearms and hands, exposed to air once more, began to burn intensely. He ought to crawl back in the water and just hold on to the side. But he could neither move nor speak now, so within moments he succumbed to his body's desperate need for sleep.

Yvette was barely conscious of the strong hands that passed her from the yawl to something larger. It might have been another steamboat, or it may have been a military cutter. She knew little more than the shivering that had overtaken her body, not a delicate shudder, as if she had been chilled, but a powerful, palsied quake that threatened to shake her all to pieces.

As more survivors were brought aboard the vessel, she began to take some notice of the swirl of activity around her. Her thoughts coalesced into concern, not for herself but for the one she'd lost.

She wanted to ask one of the men about Gabriel, whether they had seen him, whether they would look. But no matter how she tried, her jaws worked only at their chattering, and her voice failed her completely.

By the pearl-gray light of early morning, she saw a man kneeling beside her, his hair pale silver, his expression grim. She noticed he wore a Union uniform. "We'll have you feeling better in a trice, miss."

But his words barely registered, for her gaze fell upon the wicked-looking knife in his right hand. Though her limbs lacked coordination, she struggled as he moved the blade in her direction.

"Sorry, but it's needful," he told her. "I'm a surgeon, and I'm obliged to get you out of these wet things to warm you."

Somehow she clutched the blanket wrapped around her in the hopes he wouldn't take it off. No one—not even a medical officer—was going to strip her of her clothes! Sodden or not, Union blue or not, they now composed the sum total of her possessions.

He pulled harder, so hard that the blanket drew tight around her injured elbow. She gave a hoarse cry and let go, then wept silent tears as he carefully cut away the jacket.

"Smart of you to put on a boy's clothes before you went overboard," he commented. "Something would have likely caught your skirts and drowned you if you'd kept to female dress. You're the first live woman we've pulled out of the river."

Clumsily, she tried to cover her exposed breasts with her left arm.

"Here. Allow me, miss," the surgeon told her as he wrapped her in another, drier blanket. It effectively shielded her from view as he pulled something from the remnants of her jacket. "What's this?"

Yvette stared at the sodden black mass in surprise. Her reticule, which she'd swung behind her back beneath the jacket, remained with her. Incredibly, her reticule, with its precious secret in the lining, had survived. She loosened her grip on the blanket to clutch the ruin of her bag.

Fresh tears blurred her vision, for what good would the pulpy mass of Russell's letter do her? After hours in the water, every damning ink stroke would be river-washed, destroyed. She choked out a sob of frustration as the surgeon removed her trousers. Even the possibility of revenge had been lost now.

The silver-haired man tried to console her. "I've a daughter your own age back home in Michigan, and I promise, I'll watch after you just as I would her. My name is Henry Millard. When we get back to Memphis, I'll take you to the hospital and see to any wounds. In the meantime, you'll need to drink from this. It will warm you from the inside out."

He pressed a flask to her mouth and tipped it. Yvette swallowed reflexively and felt the whiskey burn a path from throat to stomach. She coughed and spat, trying to clear the awful taste of both the whiskey and humiliation from her mouth.

"Now, you just rest here real quiet," he admonished, and she realized that this Yankee, like her Gabe, was a kind man. "I have to see to others now."

Once more, she tightly shut her eyes against both

pain and grief. How could she rest here when her thoughts were still out *there,* focused like a ray of sunlight through a lens upon the future—and the man—the Mississippi River had snatched away from her?

Despite Yvette's pain, despite the whiskey and exhaustion that blurred the ragged edges of her consciousness, that focused beam tightened and intensified until she felt her very heart burst into flame. Instead of using tears to douse that fire, she lay very still, imagining she watched it burn away, leaving behind only a layer of fine white ash that could not conceal the glowing coal of hatred beneath it.

By daylight, the Memphis waterfront boiled with activity. Surgeons, nurses, and medical attendants of every sort had gathered, along with representatives of the U.S. Sanitary Commission. Rescue boats came in and disgorged drenched, half-frozen passengers from the *Sultana.* The survivors were covered with dry blankets and assessed for transport to several area hospitals. The dead were merely covered and left in long, grim lines.

Darien Russell, a blanket wrapped around his sodden waistcoat, strode amid the chaos, searching each knot of survivors for a familiar face. If Yvette Augeron had by some miracle survived this, he had better damned well find her before she started talking.

Darien had always deplored the aftermath of battle, with its bloody puddles and its shattered limbs, the muteness of the corpses, the wails of the survivors. The scene at the riverfront this morning was equally revolting but very different. Instead of gunshot wounds, many of these victims suffered the peeling, reddened flesh of scalds from the boiler's steam or fractures caused by the explosion. Nearly all of these men, many of whom were emaciated wrecks to start with, shuddered with the bone-deep cold of the river and the night. The keening cries of the living rose hideous around him. Only the stillness of the corpses was the same.

For all his searching, he could find no woman, only prisoner after prisoner and the occasional guard or male passenger. Had fate solved the problem of Yvette Augeron? Would her body, like her sister's, surface in the Mississippi after a few days? Or was it here already?

He decided he must check among the corpses. As he walked among the rows, lifting cloth after cloth, he felt gorge rise to his throat. It wasn't the ashen pallor of the dead that did it, nor was it their hollowed cheeks or pitiful condition. It was instead the half-lidded stares, both vacant and somehow accusing, that looked up at him as if to ask, "How is it *you* still live?"

Did they know, then? About the ugly act that he'd committed to ensure his survival? Fear conjured up the blond woman he'd struck down on the promenade.

"I've been watching you." A female voice rose just behind him, strong and flat and with the broad tones of New England.

Darien nearly jumped out of his skin. But when he turned, he had to stifle the impulse to laugh out his relief. No living soul could possibly be less a threat. Round-faced, stout, and with her brown hair streaked with gray, the woman wore the somber colors of a Sister of Charity.

He shook his head at his own foolishness. Exhaustion had him imagining every sort of fancy.

She placed a plump, stub-fingered hand upon his still-damp sleeve. "While your efforts to locate your comrades are admirable, you'll do none of them any good if you take chill and perish. Truly, you should have been stripped of those wet things when you were pulled from the river."

Strange to hear a woman of God speaking so matter-of-factly about the need to strip a grown man, but he supposed the sister had undressed her share of wounded soldiers since the war began.

Darien hesitated only a moment before deciding that, for the time being, a lie would be his best course of action.

"I must find my fiancée." He struggled to strike the right note of desperation, and he could see by the change in her expression that he'd succeeded.

Emboldened, he continued. "We were separated just before the blast. I'm afraid we had some foolish quarrel. She may not even wish to see me."

"You poor man," the woman crooned.

"I don't ask her forgiveness," Darien told the nurse. He would swear he saw tears welling in the foolish woman's eyes. "I only ask to see that she's alive."

She grasped his hands in hers. "You must have faith, sir. Would you like me to pray with you for her safety?"

Pray for Yvette's safety? His overtired mind wondered if lightning would strike for such a ruse. But in an instant he dismissed the thought. The only divinity he believed in was his grandfather's prophecy. Surely praying with an old nurse could do no harm. On the contrary, it might help bolster sympathy. Who knows to what lengths such a woman might go to help him find his lost "fiancée"?

He nodded, trying to keep the smile from his lips. He thought perhaps she might take him somewhere more secluded, but this maelstrom of activity offered its own brand of privacy. Amid so many prayers and screams, she merely took his hands and bowed her head.

Fearing he'd be observed otherwise, Darien closed his eyes. And as the old nun prayed that his fiancée would be found safely, he found himself whispering his own, slightly different version. He prayed that he would find her shrouded with the dead.

Yvette awakened to the protests of a badly scalded soldier as two deckhands carried him off the boat at the Memphis waterfront. Staring after the huge men, she felt mortified by the thought of their hauling her nude body like a burlap sack of coffee. She'd have to walk if she wanted to avoid that indignity.

Although she'd warmed considerably during the trip, her elbow throbbed so intensely that she wished for the comfort of the surgeon's flask. She sat up, arranging the blanket to cover her, and tried to imagine how she was going to manage her reticule, her arm, and her dignity at the same time.

The silver-haired surgeon returned to see to her.

"Don't try to get up," he told her. "I'll carry you myself."

Gratefully, she nodded. Although she'd prefer to

walk on her own two feet, the idea that she might drop the blanket had begun to seem an alarming probability.

"Please be careful of my left arm. It's terribly painful."

"May I have a look?"

She felt heat rise to her face. "Surely, not here."

He smiled sympathetically. "I can see you have a lady's sensibilities, but unfortunately, this disaster has left many without clothing. I assure you, no one is going to be unduly shocked by your bare arm."

Reluctantly, she rearranged the blanket to let him look at the injured limb. The inside of the elbow joint had blossomed with angry black and purple bruising. Swollen to twice its normal size, the arm looked as if it belonged to someone else.

Yvette had to look away. The sight of the damage made her head whirl and her stomach lurch.

He asked her to squeeze his hand. She managed, but when he asked if she could bend the elbow, she turned and glared at him.

"No, and if you attempt to do so, I promise I shall utter the least ladylike language ever to scorch your ears."

She could see him struggling to fight back a smile.

"Very well," he told her. "Instead, I'll see what I can find to make a quick sling so we can get you to the hospital without having you pass out."

Less than ten minutes later, Union surgeon Henry Millard carried her off the cutter and onto a crowded wharf boat. Crossing it, he hurried ashore. Instead of stopping to place her among the wounded soldiers, he carried her directly toward a hack that had been hastily converted to an ambulance.

Yvette peered over his shoulder and caught a glimpse of something that nearly tore her breath away. Darien Russell, head bowed and eyes closed, his hands clasped between those of an older woman in dark dress. An instant later, he disappeared from sight behind the backs of a group of similarly dressed women carrying blankets to the new arrivals.

Had that really been Russell, or was she hallucinating? That possibility seemed more likely than the thought of that Yankee demon in an attitude of prayer.

"I think this one's dead. Hasn't twitched a muscle since we pulled him off that bale." The speaker lifted his wrist, then dropped it.

Gabriel wanted to respond, wanted to shout that yes, he was alive, but his body refused him. He began to wonder, Was it possible he *had* died? Did his spirit merely linger, not understanding that his life had dissipated in the dark, cold water?

He felt a slight weight settle on his face. Whatever it was itched like wool. They'd pulled a wool blanket over him. His whole body twitched in repugnance.

The blanket was pulled back. "Damned if he ain't still breathin'. I didn't feel no pulse. He's mighty cold, though. Let's get him one more blanket and send him on the ambulance."

Thank God they wouldn't bury him alive. The thought should have relaxed him, but something that he must do nagged him urgently. What? What could it be?

Yvette. She was still out there, floating with the mule. How much longer could she last? He had to tell somebody! He had to send them back to find that floating mule before it was too late. Before she slipped down beneath the river's surface, just as he had. Before she was lost to him forevermore.

Shouted orders reached his ears, and all around him he saw people moving. Other survivors had been brought here, too, he realized. Could his friends be among them?

By focusing every shred of energy he possessed, Gabriel managed to croak out, "Must find them!"

But his effort went unheard amid the confusion and exhausted him so utterly that he plummeted into a deep sleep.

Darien laid his hand on one of the two attendants loading the young private into a waiting ambulance.

"Where are you taking him?" he asked.

The brawny, towheaded fellow paused.

"I'm his commanding officer," Darien lied by way of explanation. "I'll need to notify his family."

The man nodded. "They'll find him at the Soldiers' Home, providing that he lives."

"He doesn't look too badly burned."

"Hard to tell. Cold water'll kill plenty. Excuse me, but we need to move along."

Darien nodded and watched the two men load the modified buckboard wagon with several injured men. He didn't even know the name of the unconscious private. All he knew was that the man had twice helped Yvette escape him. If she were still alive, she would likely check on him. Yvette's flaws were legion, but she was fiercely loyal, the least likely person he could think of to abandon a friend in need. Even one she'd only met in the past few days.

Russell shivered, and his stomach growled its need for hot food and black coffee. He walked in the same direction the retreating ambulance had taken. He must restore his strength so he would be prepared to use the injured private to end this deadly game of cat and mouse.

Chapter Thirteen

APPALLING MARINE CASUALTY.

FEARFUL EXPLOSION OF THE STEAMER SUL-
TANA SEVEN MILES ABOVE THE CITY.

TWENTY-ONE HUNDRED SOULS ON BOARD—
FORTY OF THEM LADIES.

FRIGHTFUL LOSS OF LIFE—BETWEEN TWELVE
AND FIFTEEN HUNDRED PERSONS PERISH.

ONLY THREE OR FOUR OUT OF FORTY LADIES
RESCUED FROM WATERY GRAVES.

HORROR—TOUCHING SCENES OF ANGUISH
AND SUFFERING—SHINING EXAMPLES OF
HEROISM ON THE PART OF THE ARMY AND
NAVY AND CITIZENS.

A VISIT TO THE WRECK—FULL PARTICULARS
OF THE CATASTROPHE.

FULL LISTS OF THE SOLDIERS AND OTHERS
RESCUED FROM THE BOAT AND WATER.

THE HOSPITALS FILLED WITH THEM—WHO
AND WHERE THEY ARE.

STATEMENTS OF PARTIES ON BOARD—INCI-
DENTS, ETC., ETC.
—April 28,1865, headline,
Memphis *Argus*

April 28, 1865
Memphis, Tennessee

Yvette was beginning to regret that she'd refused
the morphine she'd been offered at the hospital.
Longingly, she thought back to yesterday and the way
the drug had dulled both the pain and her senses
and hummed a melody of consolation in her ear.

But the notes that carried hope rang hollow. The
only truth she heard in the song of Morpheus
throbbed a dismal rhythm that marched on and on,
grim as a funereal procession. And she realized that
if she allowed it to bear her toward a place of comfort,
that place might well prove to be a grave.

She forced herself to picture Darien Russell laughing, finding her in a drug-induced stupor, choking
her to death, the way he had her sister. She would
be unable to defend herself, let alone force him to
pay for the crimes he had committed.

Thinking on that possibility, Yvette climbed from
the narrow bed. As one of a scant handful of female
survivors, she'd been given far more attention than
had the myriad wounded soldiers. Several of the
nurses at Gayoso Hospital, where she'd been taken,
had helped arrange for her to have use of this room

in a nearby boardinghouse. They'd collected enough clothing so she could be decently, if not stylishly, clad. And not one of them had seemed to care a whit that she was Southern. They were more concerned with practicalities.

"With so many men in need, you couldn't be provided with proper privacy in here," a plain-looking woman in her early forties explained, gesturing to the rows of soldiers lying in cots along the hall. "And as the doctor told you, you'll need nothing more than rest and a few weeks in a sling to set that arm right."

Yvette had admired the way the women bustled about, competently assisting the doctors with tasks that seemed ill suited for ladies. *Maman* and Marie had been aghast when they heard that Yankee women often worked in gruesome surgeries and wards. But these women seemed natural and confident in their role, and their steady presence had calmed Yvette's fears during her examination.

Dressing was a challenge with her painful arm. But she'd have to ignore the ache and manage on her own. She had too many things to do to allow discomfort to stop her. Her mind skirted around the edge of the hardest of those tasks, then dredged up what the surgeon at the hospital had told her.

"Your injuries are minor. You're remarkably fortunate."

Amid the severely scalded soldiers, she must have truly seemed so. And yet when Yvette had heard those words, she'd laughed—a joyless sound that made heads turn and the man shuffle his feet uncomfortably.

Fortunate indeed, she thought, her sore eyes welling with moisture. Gabriel's handsome face flashed through her mind, his touch upon her cool hand over the back of the dead mule, his soothing words amid the darkness of the river before dawn.

Fortunate indeed.

To try to make sense of what had happened, she took out the pencil and paper she had found in the desk drawer. She wanted nothing quite so badly as to speak to her lost sister. And if this was the only method that remained, so be it.

> *My dearest Marie,*
>
> *My Yankee soldier, my dear Gabriel, is gone now, and all I can do is wonder. Was he taken from me to repay in part the lives that I destroyed?*
>
> *Help me understand, Marie. Help me know where I should turn.*
>
> *I can write no more this evening lest my tears follow to wash away each line. Just as the Mississippi washed the ink from that most important letter, the one I needed to set all to rights once more.*
>
> *Yours in sorrow,*
> *Yvette*

Such sad written words seemed even more real than the thoughts trapped in her mind. So the tears spilled over, and Yvette brushed them away.

What she should do today was try to find another way to reach St. Louis, to get to Uncle André so she could seek a new way to settle with Darien Russell and clear herself of charges. But all of that would have to wait.

Because alive or dead, she had to first find Gabriel. Even if all that remained was a body as cold and waterlogged as had been Marie's.

* * *

After his night's sleep, Darien Russell awoke, his mouth dry and his heart thudding painfully against his ribs. But whatever dream provoked his discomfort quickly slipped away as consciousness reclaimed him and he remembered where he was.

As wagonload after wagonload of survivors arrived at the Soldiers' Home in the wake of the explosion, Darien realized that the best he could expect there was a cot in a common ward overflowing with naked and near-naked soldiers. His efforts to convince the staff that he deserved better had been met with disbelief and then ignored.

He'd felt a rush of gratitude at the appearance of Colonel Patterson, who had brought men to assist the overburdened staff.

Though the regular workers could scarcely be troubled to provide Darien with a decent uniform, Patterson, who hailed from Rhode Island, immediately proved himself to be a man sensible to the necessity of seeing to the comfort of a fellow officer.

The white-haired colonel had gone far beyond mere decency. Indeed, he had invited Darien, along with another stranded captain and a young lieutenant, to stay as his guest in a fine Memphis home "requisitioned" from a pair of unrepentant secessionists.

Now that he felt rested enough to take note of his surroundings, Darien saw the delicate floral wallpaper pattern and the lace-trimmed yellow quilt. As he swung his legs out of bed and reached for the shoes the colonel had found for him, his hand grazed the worn face of a bedraggled doll. Picking up the item by a fold in its soft blue skirt, he noticed that it had been constructed of some fine material before a child's fingers had rubbed the luster from it. Apparently, this had been a little girl's room. And still would be, had not her father smuggled contraband to the Confederacy long after Memphis had been captured. What a fool he'd been to lay down all he had for pride.

If he became a father, he would damned well see to it his child lived in comfort. An unpleasant twinge made him rub at one temple.

With more force than necessary, Russell tossed the doll back to its resting place beneath the bed. If he wanted to feel pity for anyone, it ought to be those men he'd seen before he'd left the Soldiers' Home.

When he had first arrived there, Darien had closed his eyes against both his exhaustion and the discomfort of looking at the damaged bodies of those men. Beneath bruise-mottled skin, ribs slashed across the half-starved former prisoners' midsections and other bones took on unnatural prominence. Pelvises jutted, vertebrae bulged, and shoulder blades looked more like stunted wings than parts of anything quite human.

Beating wings. Remembering, he shuddered. That was what had just awakened him, a dream of flapping, bone-hard wings striking at his chest and face. A legion of gaunt soldiers, attacking, all at her command.

He could see her still, Yvette Augeron at the forefront, as wild-eyed as Joan of Arc on her mad assault. A maiden warrior, insane or inspired, depending on one's view.

"Mon Dieu has charged me to destroy you," the night-

mare woman had informed him, and he saw flames wheeling around the dark hub of her pupils. Bright flames, shooting off hot embers, like the fire aboard the *Sultana*. And with one wave of her sparking fingertips, her army of winged men flew at him, laughing as their bony appendages beat an agonizing rhythm against his living flesh.

Their wings beat out her question: *"Did she tell you she was carrying your child?"*

Christ, no wonder he'd awakened cold and sweaty, his pulse roaring in his ear like the endless boom of artillery or the deafening concussion of the *Sultana* when she blew.

Darien shuddered and pulled on his shoes, unwilling to lie down once more, to risk another dream. Another man might have brushed it aside, dismissed it. He decided instead to heed it as a warning that he'd rested long enough, that if he didn't get up out of this room and enlist the colonel's help to locate her, Yvette would find a way to destroy him, just as she had threatened.

He could not afford to remain here one more minute, idly hoping that she'd drowned.

As Darien came downstairs, he glimpsed Col. Isaiah Patterson in what once had been a parlor. Apparently the room had been hastily refashioned into an office.

Patterson sat behind a scarred oak desk that looked as if it had been dragged into the home from who knew where. He appeared deep in discussion with one of the lieutenants that assisted him.

Darien decided not to interrupt, but the colonel called out, "Get some coffee and come in here. This may concern you, too."

Recalling the kitchen's location from the night

before, Darien poured himself a cup of hot black liquid, then returned to the parlor. He sat on a mahogany armchair the narrow-face lieutenant pulled up for him with his one remaining hand. His empty left sleeve had been neatly pinned, a sight that had become increasingly common as the war progressed.

As Darien took his seat, he glanced around the room, his eyes lingering a moment on the piano some-one had shoved into one corner. It reminded him uncomfortably of the Augerons' piano and the songs Yvette had sung. A relic of the former owners, an expensive-looking porcelain figure, lay broken on its dust-filmed top, and this time, Darien felt satisfied to think of the wealthy secessionists who had been banished from their home.

A plump gray-and-white cat sauntered into the par-lor as if it owned the place. Arching its back, it rubbed against Darien's lower leg. Russell winced, noticing the white hairs it left on the fabric. He might have kicked the creature away, but he hesitated, unsure as to whether it was the colonel's pet.

The colonel lit a pipe, then glanced down at the cat. "The owners left her. We toss her out a dozen times a day, but somehow she always manages to slip inside again. Especially since the lieutenant here often leaves out a saucer full of milk."

The lieutenant appeared to be wrestling to suppress a sheepish smile. None too successfully.

"Wouldn't have been so bad if she hadn't gone and given birth to half a dozen kittens in a corner of the pantry," the colonel said. "I should have had them drowned, but—"

Patterson shrugged, as if to excuse a moment of

weakness. But despite the admission and his snow-white hair, his face looked youthful and his gaze sharp. He adjusted the pipe and took several puffs. The air filled with fragrant smoke before he grunted satisfaction, and his voice turned serious. "My staff and I have been asked to help investigate this calamity. Frankly, this has all the hallmarks of some sort of boiler explosion, but since the assassination, we must be especially vigilant. Not all these secessionists are ready to give up and go home."

Darien sipped his coffee thoughtfully. Colonel Patterson, for all his kindness, seemed a shrewd man, far too astute to lie to lightly. And far too clever to allow him the opportunity to interview Yvette once she was apprehended.

Patterson continued. "You said yesterday that you were following a Rebel conspirator, a murderess. Do you have any information to make you believe that she might be involved? Could she have had collaborators aboard the *Sultana?*"

"I don't believe she came aboard with any other Rebels, but she quickly befriended one of the Andersonville prisoners. He deliberately impeded my investigation and assisted her in escaping. And I know just where he is now."

Patterson nodded. "I'll put as many men as you need at your disposal, Captain Russell. I want to question that young man, but first—alive or dead—let's find that girl."

Gabriel's mind played over one rescue, then another, a third, and then a fourth, so that all of them survived this. So that both Yvette, his future, and the three friends that summed up all the good that came out of his past could be alive still. If only for a little while more, until he was forced to face a harder truth.

No, he couldn't do that to himself now, couldn't allow himself to face that possibility. Not now, while the moans of those worse injured intruded on his dreams. If hopes could qualify as dreams, as he floated on this haze somewhere between wakefulness and sleep, somewhere he could lie, indifferent to his pain.

His thoughts began to seep down where the pain dwelt, mostly in his hands, and he thought he could feel the reddened swaths of blisters that had formed on both their tops. They were dressed now in some sort of ointment that was supposed to soothe them and prevent infection.

Recalling Andersonville, he roused enough to shudder at the idea of surgeons and attendants touching him while he remained as motionless as death.

"Never let them work on you," Jacob had advised him with a nod toward the hospital, a poorly constructed shelter inside the stockade. "That hellhole's filthier than anyplace in camp."

Rumor had it that men the Confederate surgeons vaccinated to prevent disease had died after the arms in which they'd received the shots grew putrid with infection. Opinions varied on whether the Rebel goal had been to help or kill as many Yanks as possible, but almost to a man, the prisoners avoided medical treatment until they were too sick for it to matter either way.

Although the Memphis Soldiers' Home was run by Union personnel, the habit of distrust died hard, as

did the suspicion that staying here might do more
to make him sick than heal him.

No use worrying, he thought. He was still too weak
to do a thing about it right now, anyway.

Instead, he set himself to planning how he'd search
for his friends once he felt better, how he'd embrace
Yvette once he found her. The images meandered,
pleasant but disjointed, until they beguiled him into
a deep sleep.

Darien Russell ran down leads half the day, check-
ing every rumor of a female survivor. And rumors
were what most proved to be. He'd heard early on
of a possibility from a rescuer working at the Soldiers'
Home. No one, however, could remember where the
woman had been taken. Finally, after Darien had
interrupted every worker he could find, he encoun-
tered one attendant who thought he recalled a
woman being taken to Gayoso Hospital.

Darien traveled there in a carriage driven by an
agent of the U.S. Sanitary Commission, who was working to identify both the survivors and the victims of
the steamboat explosion.

"There are, ah, a number of females among the, ah,
deceased," the agent explained. Avoiding Darien's
gaze, he fiddled with the reins, causing the chestnut
horse in harness to toss its head in irritation. "I know
you're looking for your young lady in the hospitals,
but have you considered, ah, other possibilities?"

Russell hesitated. Instinct had prompted him to
circulate the story that he was seeking his fiancée and
not a fugitive in an attempt to garner sympathy. With
so many seeking lost friends and relations, his request

seemed ordinary. As he listened to the agent's embarrassed question, the same instinct told him his dream had been true. Yvette Augeron yet lived and still sought to destroy him.

He was a man who had learned to rely upon his instincts—or dreams, or destiny, or whatever it was he chose to call that voice that had so often whispered a warning. It had proven true too often to ignore.

At length, he answered the somber-looking agent with the nervous hands. "If she is dead, it scarcely matters when I locate her . . . remains. But if she still lives, I must find her swiftly."

"God bless you in your search, then. I'm sure that seeing the face of a loved one will do her spirits the greatest good," the agent told him.

He was certain that it would. Darien suppressed a smile and wondered what effect *his* face would have.

Yvette decided to begin with the women she had met. Gayoso was close enough to reach on foot, and the nurses there could tell her where the dead of the *Sultana* had been taken.

The day had dawned a fair one, lit by the mildest of spring sunshine. Yet Yvette's feet barely lifted as she walked. For each step took her closer to finding Gabriel's dead body—if it had been recovered for her to find at all.

Inside a corridor in Gayoso Hospital, Darien Russell stopped a gangly redhead trapped somewhere between youth and manhood. His tousled hair and bleary brown eyes made it appear he'd had no sleep since news of the disaster had first reached Memphis.

"I saw a woman here. Nice-looking lady, and she did have dark hair, like you say. Can't remember the name, though. Poor thing."

Darien disguised a smile with a sweep of his hand to straighten the whiskers of his beard. "She's badly injured?"

"Oh, no sir. Mainly just exhausted. But you see, she saw her husband drown, and he was holding on to the baby."

Once again, Darien marveled at Yvette's resourcefulness. To invent such a tale would ignite a great deal of sympathy and help.

He thanked his luck that he had not yet told his "lost fiancée" story, for it clearly wouldn't hold up in the wake of Yvette's lie.

"She may be the family friend I'm seeking," Darien told the redhead. "I'd consider it a kindness if you told me where she is."

The attendant bobbed a nod. A warm smile lifted the corners of his clean-shaven mouth, making him appear even younger than Russell's earlier guess. "Nice to spread some good news for a change. Wait here and I'll ask somebody . . . What did you say your name was?"

Darien shrugged, attempting for all that he was worth to appeal to the attendant's obvious good nature. "Couldn't I just surprise her? Upset as she must be, she might not wish to see anyone, but I'm certain it will do her a world of good to encounter someone from home."

The redhead brightened. "I suppose it would at

that. Wait here for just a minute. I see just the person who might know.''

The attendant turned and walked away while Darien worked hard to ignore the moans coming from an open doorway, which made him think about the man pinned beneath debris aboard the *Sultana*. How must it have been to lie there, burning, to watch and feel death closing in? Oddly, he felt nearly as much remorse for having left that man than he had at having struck the woman for the lengths of wood. But there was no reason to feel bad, was there? In both cases, hadn't circumstance demanded that he do what was needful to survive?

He heard Grandfather's voice, deep and reassuring *". . . the finest Russell ever . . . destined for great things."* But the memory twisted deep inside him—a wormlike thread of doubt steeped in the old solace.

When he turned his back to the moaning, he saw Yvette—there to avenge the murdered. Yvette with fire swirling in those tigress eyes. His first instinct was to raise his arms to ward off the blows of bony wings.

But reality carried away the last faint traces of the nightmare. He saw her arm lying limp inside a sling, and her dress hung like a castoff. Not even anger smoldered in her eyes, only defeat and desolation.

Until she noticed him staring in her direction. Then anger sparked in her expression, followed rapidly by fear. Before he could either move toward her or shout, she spun on her heel and ran through the same door she'd just entered.

He started after her, but a firm hand gripped his arm.

"Mrs. Annis's room is this way," the orderly told him.

Darien stammered at the interruption, "Wh-what?"

"Mrs. Annis. The lady that you asked about. She's still awfully distraught about her family, but—"

"What? That isn't *her*. Not Mrs. Annis. My friend is someone else. I have to go." Darien knew the words were rushed and blunt, even rude. But he had neither the time nor the desire to invent elaborate excuses for this dolt.

Jerking free his arm, he followed Yvette out of the hospital's front door. He had to catch her before she managed to escape again.

Only moments after Yvette bolted through Gayoso Hospital's front doors, exhaustion struck a thunderous blow. It hammered at her head and elbow; it loosened both her knees. Walking along the avenue, she'd felt only slightly tired, but the jolt of anger and fear, prompted by the sight of Russell, had burned away what strength she had recovered since her ordeal on the dark river.

Still, she staggered forward, fearing at every moment the pounding of his feet on the pavement, the rasp of his breath as he drew near, the sharp jerk of her body, stopped by his restraining hands.

His hands. Those same hands that had choked Marie.

She could not outrun him. Not even terror could give her the heels of a racehorse or the wings of a swift falcon.

Turning her head, she saw he hadn't followed yet, but she knew beyond question that she had only seconds left to find some other avenue of safety: a friendly man to beg for protection, a doorway near enough to dart inside. Instead, she saw a hedge, one that ran alongside the building. Without pausing to consider, she hurried to it and hid herself as best she could behind its scratchy evergreen branches. Through the fragrant needles, she saw a plump young woman holding the hands of two young children. The older of the pair, a round little boy whose pudgy calves peeked out beneath his knee-length trousers, jabbered excitedly and gestured toward Yvette. When the mother tried to control her child, his flaxen-haired sister tottered on unsteady legs before sitting far too hard and suddenly. She gave a yowl of indignation more fitting for a steamboat whistle than a two-year-old.

Yvette felt the blood drain from her face. *Mon Dieu!* This noise would give her away for certain!

Before Yvette had the chance to reconsider her hiding place, she spied Darien Russell trotting toward the avenue. He stopped, looking this way and that, until his dark eyes came to rest upon the pointing child.

Why couldn't that woman keep her two whelps quiet? The towheaded toddler's shriek bored into his skull like nails raked across a slate board. Darien scowled disapproval at the mother, a woman whose dark brown sausage ringlets swung to and fro as she turned to tend first one child, then the other.

She chanced to look up into Russell's face, and her plump cheeks colored crimson. Darien watched the quick play of emotion transform her expression from embarrassment to irritation to out-and-out anger—apparently at *him,* for some reason. As she scooped the squalling girl-child into her arms, he hurried past, unwilling to waste time in instructing this obviously unfit mother on managing her children.

A brief search of the area yielded no trace of Yvette. Darien cursed her uncanny ability to elude him. But he saw no reason to keep looking. He had only to go back and watch the hospital, where he'd been told that her friend had been taken, and wait for her to come.

"Your hands," the surgeon told him. "My God, we'll have to take your hands."

Gabe could barely understand the man, for his voice was muffled by the folded handkerchief he kept pressed to his nose. A stench like rotted meat explained the surgeon's reasons. Gabriel had thought that Andersonville had nearly inured him to foul odors, but this one made him want to gag.

He tried to pull the sheet up to cover his nose and mouth. But nothing happened. He couldn't move his hands or even feel them. Peering down, Gabe saw them lying atop the white sheet, hideously black and swollen, the cracked and peeling skin oozing green.

"We'll amputate them both immediately," the surgeon told him.

Gabe opened his mouth to scream, but his voice was as dead as his ruined hands. The only thing that passed his lips was the reek of putrefaction, and he knew in that moment that the rot had taken hold inside as well, that no amount of cutting would be enough to save his life.

"How are you feeling?"

Gabe jerked awake at the voice, still shaking from the nightmare. He ought to thank the speaker for freeing him from the dream, but the man's voice hung heavy with menace.

Gabe opened his eyes wide, suddenly convinced this was the surgeon coming with a saw to amputate. Fresh pain rushed in at him, and he knew in an instant that his burned hands had not died. His vision blurred, he stared at the man's face for half a minute before it swam into focus.

It was not the surgeon who had come to inquire about his health. Instead, Capt. Darien Russell stood beside his cot, his expression hawklike, hopeful.

He's hoping that I'll die.

Shaking off the nightmare, Gabe took in a deep breath. "What do you want with me?" he asked.

"Only information," Russell told him. "I haven't forgotten your earlier crimes, Mr. Gabriel Davis."

He must have looked surprised, for Captain Russell's countenance turned smug.

"You told the ward master your name. Did you forget that? Now I'll know just whom to charge. Abetting a fugitive, assaulting an officer. But I'm not terribly interested in you, Private Davis. I want Yvette instead. Tell me where she is now, and you can live— or die—in peace."

"You must be insane. How should I know where she is?" True enough, but Gabe decided to embellish, anyway. It went against his grain to appear cooperative in even the slightest degree. "The last I know of her, she was on the promenade with you. You didn't see her after the explosion?"

The captain stared at him as if trying to gauge the purpose of his question. Somehow or another, Russell had conjured up a fresh uniform. Despite all the hardships he surely must have suffered, he appeared as meticulously groomed as if no cataclysm had ever inconvenienced him. But that ought not to surprise him, Gabriel thought, for one who'd clearly sold his soul so long before.

"Your loyalty is misplaced," Russell said. "I've told you, she's a criminal. A murderess, in fact. There's even talk she might have been part of a conspiracy that caused the explosion. Whatever the outcome of that investigation, she *will* hang. And if I don't catch her, you will in her stead."

"You know damned well she had nothing to do with what happened on the *Sultana*. You know where we all were, and you know what happened when the boat blew up. What makes you think she's even alive?"

A slow smirk curled the left side of the captain's mouth. "I have intelligence to that effect."

Despite the leap of hope his heart gave at the news Yvette might have survived, Gabriel forced himself to match the man's disdainful expression. "Your pardon . . . *sir,* but I sincerely doubt that. That you have intelligence, that is."

"You tread the thinnest of thin lines, boy."

"Yvette won't come back here. I'm nobody to her, just some soldier who helped her out a time or two for lack of anything better to do aboard the boat. Right now she's probably already sitting in some general's office, convincing him that you're a lying murderer. She sure as hell convinced me quick enough, and I don't normally cotton much to Southerners, not even pretty ones."

Standing near Gabe's feet, Darien Russell flinched visibly at those words. His gold-brown gaze flicked toward nearby cots, as if to check for any reaction from the men sleeping nearby. His clear discomfort felt as soothing as a balm to Gabe.

"I've known Yvette far longer than you have. She'll come back for you," Russell insisted. "And when she does, I'll be waiting."

Gabe prayed that he'd been right before, that the conversation he'd shared with Yvette had been mainly wishful thinking on his part. That Yvette had merely acquiesced out of fear and loneliness and desperation. That after having escaped the explosion and the Mississippi, she had fled for the safety of her uncle just as quickly as she could.

His hopes were swallowed by an almost overwhelming wave of bleakness, a cold black swell of utter desolation. For if Yvette were to escape with her life, it would mean that everything they'd told each other had meant nothing.

It would mean that the love that burned inside him had been based upon a lie.

Chapter Fourteen

When Johnny comes marching home again,
Hurrah! Hurrah!
We'll give him a hearty welcome then,
Hurrah! Hurrah!
The men will cheer, the boys will shout,
The ladies, they will all turn out,
And we'll all feel gay
When Johnny comes marching home.
　　　　　—Patrick Sarsfield Gilmore,
"When Johnny Comes Marching Home"

"I expect to hear of it immediately if he attempts to leave or any visitors ask for him," Darien told the ward master, a man with the unsettling name of Mr. Butcher. "I'll be at Colonel Patterson's headquarters for a few hours. Here is the address."

Darien handed him a slip of paper, and the man snatched it away.

His bald pate reddening, Butcher glowered at him, apparently offended for some reason. Like most of the hospital employees and volunteers Russell had spoken to, the man had eyes underscored by the bruised smudges of fatigue.

That must be it. Exhaustion made men as snappish as a mare in season, and there was no doubt the steamboat explosion had overtaxed the hospitals of Memphis.

"We're doing our damnedest to comfort and feed these men," the ward master responded. "I have neither the time nor a spare man to stand guard over your prisoner while you're away, and as I told you before, I will not tolerate you ordering about my staff."

"As *I* told you, Colonel Patterson is sending over a pair of guards almost immediately. However, your assistance would be most—"

"Unlikely," Butcher told him, "if not impossible."

"Do you spell Butcher with a 't,' sir?" Darien asked coolly. "I'll need to know for my report in case there are . . . complications."

"It's A-D-R-I-A-N space T period space B-U-T-C-H-E-R, Captain Russell," Butcher told him, the crimson of his scalp deepening with each letter. "And there's blood enough around here to write it in red on your report. Enjoy your visit to Memphis, *sir*. If you'll excuse me, I have patients to attend."

"Insufferable bastard," a gravelly voice grumbled.

Gabriel opened his eyes, confused. What could he have possibly done while sleeping to bother anyone? As his vision cleared, a potbellied, grizzled man came into focus. With his brawny arms, he looked as if he may have begun his working life as a blacksmith or a riverman. He still had a cigar clamped in his rear teeth—perhaps the same one that Gabe had noticed earlier, since it remained unlit.

The man was staring back at him.

"You a criminal?" the man asked bluntly.

"What?" Gabe asked, more confused than ever. "A criminal? No, I'm not. I'm a Union soldier, that's all."

The fellow grinned, but only on that side of the mouth not busy keeping the cigar in place. "Well, then, that's good enough for me. Why don't you skedaddle before that bastard captain gets a chance to send them guards he was jawin' about?"

Guards? Darien Russell's threat rushed back into Gabe's mind, eliminating any doubts as to the true identify of the "insufferable bastard" the man had been grumbling over.

Now that the effects of his last dose of morphine were wearing off, the pain of his hands began to reassert itself. Soon, he knew, the wound would throb in earnest, taxing his exhausted body. But that discomfort faded to insignificance against another threat: that Yvette would, as Russell had predicted, come to find him and be captured on the spot.

If he simply lay here, waiting for the guards and for Yvette, he could do little more than watch as she was clapped in irons. Nausea swirled inside him as he imagined her imprisoned, degraded by some of the same indignities that he had suffered so very recently. Before she died. Somehow Gabe had no doubt that Russell would find a way to guarantee she would be hanged.

Such a shameful death, and so undeserved. No, he could not allow it no matter how badly his body screamed for rest or his scalded flesh cried out for relief.

The man before him hitched his pants and adjusted the unlit cigar to the left side of his mouth. "Here." He offered a strong hand to Gabe. "I'll even help you up. Whole reason I left the army and come here is so I don't have to listen to sons a bitches like that cap'n. There's a handy window you can get outta over here."

Gabe swung his leg over the cot's side and reached out with a bandaged hand, grateful that his palms had not been scalded.

"Thanks, mister," he told the older man. "I don't know you from Adam, but you're one of the best judges of character I've met in a long time. If I get back this way, I aim to bring you a new cigar. One that you can smoke."

The man scratched his belly and grinned lopsidedly. "Butcher's scared to death I'll catch the place afire. So just don't let the ward master catch you with a lit one in the building. Otherwise, we'll both need them two guards—for protection."

As Yvette approached the river, for the first time she saw it for what it truly was, a wide brown ribbon that bound her homeland to the north, forged of sterner steel than the shackles that had once bound slave to slave.

Strange that the Mississippi, impartial as it seemed to human rivalries, would exact upon the Yankees such a costly toll. A toll that yet lined the cobblestone walkway along the riverfront, as if Mr. Lincoln's murder had not been calamity enough.

And though she'd loved it all her life, she cursed the river now for its insatiable hunger and its utter indifference to human pain. She thought back to the moment she had awakened to find that Gabriel was gone, to her certain knowledge that he would not have willingly abandoned her. The Mississippi had robbed her of even the delusion that he might have survived.

Two days later, the dead had mustered here in silent order, their number growing steadily as, by twos and tens, they were recovered from the Mississippi. These men who'd wanted only to go home. She thought about the soldier she'd seen sleeping, his emaciated body curved around the food basket she'd given him, and fresh tears filled her eyes.

Beyond the bodies, a pair of steamboats glided along, followed by faint trails of scalding steam. She shuddered at the thought of boarding any one of them again.

Yvette turned her head to gaze out over the shrouded rows. Their lines soon softened, then shimmered with the tears that filmed her eyes. She thought about the men these lifeless corpses had once been, men who had already suffered the worst that war could muster. Men not so very different from her brothers, who fought out of devotion to their homeland and would now want nothing quite so fiercely as to go back to the places and the people they had loved. Images of the starving men dawned in her memory, only to be eclipsed by Gabriel's handsome face. The longing in his blue eyes so pained her that her tears at last spilled over.

"You deserved to live," she whispered. Just as he'd deserved to love. Her mind flashed back with painful clarity to that moment she had reached across the floating mule to find him gone.

How in God's name was she going to search among these dead to find him? How could she bear to see his face set with the hideous rictus of a river death?

She began to tremble, and grief loosened both her knees. But as a pair of soldiers rushed toward her, mouthing words that went unheard beneath the roar of her own blood in her ears, Yvette shook her head in an attempt to banish the effects of shock and sorrow.

If she could not do this, Gabriel Davis's body would never be identified. Gabriel would never be sent home. No longer could she marry him, but this was something she could and must do. To let him know she truly loved him, for their time together had been so cruelly short.

"You'd better come away, miss," a thick and nasal voice insisted.

Yvette turned to face a military guard, a bearded man who squinted through watery brown eyes. His red-tinged nostrils made her want to step back before he sneezed.

"This is no place for a lady."

"But I must. I have to find him, for his family," she explained.

The second soldier grimaced. A solid-looking, pox-scarred veteran, he looked as if he'd prefer battles or even latrine duty to a woman's tears. "Hate to put you through all this. The last lady who come by here had some sort of hysterical fit and had to be carted off to the hospital herself. You checked the *Argus* yet for the list of the survivors?"

"There's a list in the newspaper?" Yvette asked, hope bubbling past her ability to tamp it down with caution. "If there's any chance, I want to know. Do you have a copy?"

"I've got one right here," someone said behind her.

Yvette spun on her heel, her eyes widening with recognition at the familiar voice. A voice she had believed that she would never hear again.

Her legs failed her utterly, but it did not matter, for Gabriel was there to catch her with hands swathed in white linen but strong and steady all the same. Gabriel—*Dieu merci! C'est fantastique!* But though her mind gushed grateful torrents, the words were dammed inside her head with the shock, the wonderful, joyous surprise of his appearance.

Gabriel appeared no less moved by her presence. Sweeping her into his embrace, he kissed her deeply, apparently oblivious to the first guard, laughing through his sneezes, and the second, who tossed his forage cap into the air.

"I'll take more of this and less of the weeping," the pox-scarred soldier commented with a grin.

Yvette heard them, but she cared nothing for what the two men must be thinking or how any other witnesses might judge her. She cared about nothing except for the flame that roared through her where their lips met and where their bodies pressed together.

Her own yelp startled her as he pressed against the sling that held her wrapped arm.

"I'm sorry. Did I hurt you?" Gabe asked.

"It doesn't matter," she whispered in reply, leaning

back into his arms. "Nothing matters except that you're alive. I thought—"

"I know. I was just as worried. We'll talk about what happened later. But first, we have to get away from here," he said quietly into her ear. "It isn't safe for us at all."

She nodded, fear opening a chasm at the feet of newfound joy. She mustn't forget Russell, and their reunion had already attracted more attention than was wise.

Only now did she notice how Gabriel, like herself, wore cast-off clothing and, worse yet, the way his shoulders slumped with exhaustion, perhaps pain. His gaze had strayed from her to the shrouded rows of corpses, and she wondered if his friends' bodies were among them.

She nodded toward the folded newspaper he had just dropped to embrace her. "Did you find your friends' names in there?"

He shook his head, still staring at the grim lines on the waterfront.

"I haven't found them yet, but I will. Every one," he swore.

He stooped to retrieve the paper. When he stood, his face had grown so pallid that she feared he might collapse. Certainly, if Russell found them here, he would not be strong enough to flee. And Yvette knew she could never bear to leave him behind to be punished as an accomplice in her crimes.

She must get him out of sight. And the only place where she might do that was her room in the boardinghouse.

Yvette thanked the two soldiers and began leading Gabriel in the direction of Gayoso Hospital and the somewhat shabby two-story town house where she had a room. As they walked, their backs toward the waterfront, she told him about the nurses' collection and the room they had arranged for her.

"We'll go there," she said. Into a little bedroom, alone and together. She shivered as her mind filled with razor-edged memories of his hands on her flesh.

He hesitated. "Could Russell find us there? He's alive, and he's convinced that you are, too. He came by the Soldiers' Home, thinking you would look for me."

"As I would have as soon as I assured myself you were not here. I swear it."

They stopped walking for a moment, and he looked into her eyes, his gaze so intense it warmed her like the Louisiana sun in late July.

She felt certain that despite his weakness, he was thinking of that bedroom, too, that he had read her mind and judged her brazen. The memory of forbidden touches aboard the *Sultana* made her body tingle with anticipation and her mind whisper warnings of what had happened to Marie.

"I know," he finally answered. "That's why I had to leave the ward, so he wouldn't catch you when you found me. Do they know you at the boardinghouse, in case anyone comes looking?"

Yvette arched an eyebrow. "I told them my name was Caroline Edwards and I was traveling with my husband, who was lost in the river after the explosion. I thought that might buy me a bit of time."

He smiled. "I should have known you'd keep your head about you . . . Mrs. Edwards, but I'm going to have to get a notebook to write down all these names of yours."

Yvette's heart thudded at the thought of what she meant to say, but the words slipped out before she had the chance to fully consider what they might signify. "Since we have the same name now, you'd best commit it to memory . . . Mr. Edwards."

Thankfully, no expression of shock or disapproval swept across his features. Perhaps after all that they had been through, strict notions of propriety meant nothing to him now. Just as they were fading in her mind.

He hooked his arm through her uninjured one, and they resumed walking. "Do I have a first name, too?"

She could barely think, yet somehow she managed to babble on as always.

"Hmmm," she told him. "Something biblical, I think. You Yankees prefer that, do you not? How about Lazarus, then, since you have come back to me from the dead?"

"Lazarus?" His smile was wan. "That might be biblical, but it doesn't sound American at all."

"Then it must be Sam, after your uncle."

"Uncle Sam?" A short burst of laughter punctuated his words. Then he shook his head and shrugged. "Sam it is, then."

His gaze once more settled on hers, so unflinching that she felt the skin prickling at her nape.

"As long as I can share a name with you, Yvette, I'm not much concerned about the details."

As Gabe walked along the avenue beside Yvette, he could not help fingering the sleeve of her gray bodice or laying his hand upon the back of her slender waist.

For if he kept in contact, the spell could not be shattered, could it? She could not fade away.

Had he hungered for her so desperately that he cast her from thin air, he wondered, the way his imagination had once manufactured meals from wishes? But those foods had had no substance, and Yvette felt warm and solid beneath his touch. So real, as if his mind had slipped the bonds of sanity.

Yet how could she be here? How could he have found her so very quickly simply by wandering the streets of a large city?

It's not so hard at all when a ghost gives one directions.

Lord. The memory of it oozed like frigid sweat along his spine. The Rebel soldier he'd seen earlier, lifting up a finger to point him toward the waterfront. The boy dressed in a uniform of butternut.

An inky tide appeared to rise up from the street, and Gabe grasped a young tree to keep from being overwhelmed. Yvette's face appeared in his vision, looking scared and mouthing incoherent words, all of them running together to join the roaring jet-black flood.

Matthew. Dear God, it had been him again, but why here, why now, why of all damned things dressed like an abomination in a Rebel uniform?

Yet he had pointed Gabriel toward Yvette. She was leaning over him, pulling at his shoulder with her one good arm. A tear trail streaked her cheek with brilliance, and slowly, her words coalesced out of the darkness.

"Gabriel, please, Gabriel, you have to come with me." The prayer that followed might have been in French, or it may have been the Latin that the Catholics preferred, but each syllable brought more light into his world.

Until the blackness all receded and his head grew clear again. Clear enough to realize that finding Yvette had been no delusion, no phantasm borne of morphine or the delirium of fever.

Finding Yvette had been a miracle of grace, even if his mind had surely conjured up the figure that had sent him straight to her.

"God damn it, what do you mean he's gone!" Darien Russell screamed at the ward master. "Why wasn't I notified? What about the guards?"

Butcher sighed, and his bald scalp reddened faster than a crab dropped in a pot of boiling water. "I told you before you left here, I hadn't a spare man to send. And as for the guards, I don't remember seeing any. You'll have to ask around to see if they ever arrived. Now if you'll excuse me—"

"I will *not,*" Darien insisted. "Not until I know how long Davis has been gone."

"I couldn't pin it down to an exact time, but I expect about two or three hours."

Across the ward, a patient began screaming as a nurse struggled to change his dressings. Butcher walked off—probably simply to escape—to assist the younger man.

Two to three hours, Darien thought, choosing to ignore the insult. Gabriel Davis could be anywhere in town by now.

Even with the use of the horse he'd borrowed from Colonel Patterson, he'd never find Yvette or Davis on his own. He'd have no choice except to ask for more men to assist him.

Darien's head ached with the strain. The more who were involved, the more likely it was that someone else would catch Yvette first, that she'd have time to talk.

But talk was all that she could do, he realized. Even if she'd had that damning stolen letter he had written in her possession aboard the *Sultana*, it surely must have been destroyed. So in the end, it would come to only her word against his. As long as he could keep her miles and miles away from Colonel Jeffers and his infernal investigation.

As long as he could prevent her from returning to New Orleans alive.

Mon Dieu, he'll never make it. Yvette glanced about, frightened that at any moment Darien Russell might appear.

"*S'il vous plaît*, stand up!" she begged Gabriel as she gave his arm another tug.

This time, Gabriel slowly rose, and she thought she detected color returning to his face. But that may have been only wishful thinking.

As they completed their walk to the boardinghouse, he never said a word. Nor did Yvette, for she feared doing anything to distract him from the task of placing one foot before the other.

As they entered the old town house, Widow Beacon looked up from the table she'd been bending over, then laid down the feather duster. A small, round woman with a thick gray chignon, she pushed glasses up her short nose. She looked from Gabriel to Yvette and back again before erupting in a smile.

"You've found your husband!" she said, clapping her hands together. "I told you he'd turn up all right, dear!"

Yvette couldn't help returning her smile. It still seemed such a miracle to have him back, where she might touch him, where they could hope.

"You did tell me," Yvette said, "and I thank you for it. But I'm afraid Mr. Edwards is rather ill and—"

"Hungry, I expect," said Mrs. Beacon. "Don't you fret, child. You just get him upstairs and into bed, and I'll bring you both a bite to eat. You'll know for certain then why we're known as the Good Samaritan City."

"Thank you so much," Yvette told her. "You've already been so kind."

The woman waved off the compliment. "Nonsense. I'm only doing what any Christian person would."

"Thank you, and thank you for taking care of her," Gabriel managed as Yvette led him to her room.

Yvette closed the bedroom door behind them, shutting them inside, and alone. *Maman*'s admonitions rose up like midnight specters, reminding her of how very far she'd strayed from her upbringing. Standing just inside the doorway, she swallowed hard.

Although the house had certainly seen better days, Widow Beacon, as people called her, whipped every speck of dust into submission. Even the baseboards glowed with recent polishing, and the bed linens and towels, though thin with age, had been bleached within an inch of their lives.

But the modest boardinghouse and its condition had little to do with her discomfort. Instead, it was the bed inside this room and the lie she'd told the older woman that smote Yvette's conscience.

Strange how, as an accused murderess, she was so bothered by a simple falsehood. She was not his wife yet, and she would do well to remember that. Though she'd promised she would marry him, they must wait until she cleared her name, until she dealt with Darien. If she didn't, if she foolishly gave way to passion, she'd do nothing but take him with her on the path to her destruction. And she refused to do that. She refused to kill him, too.

Gabriel sat on the bed's edge to remove his shoes. "Yvette?"

His voice raised the fine hairs behind her neck, and she wondered if he'd ask her to come and lie beside him. She almost hoped he wouldn't, for she knew that despite her better judgment, the memory of losing him was still too fresh. She knew she could deny him nothing.

"Yes," she told him, knowing it would be the answer to every question, even those that could cause him so much grief if she gave in.

"I'm sorry—sorry that you lost your little cat," he said.

"Ah . . . poor Lafitte." He so surprised her with that statement that her mind struggled for an appropriate response. Sorrow filled her at the memory of the little ruffian tumbling about her stateroom. Had the explosion killed him, or had the river swallowed up the basket? She shuddered at the thought of it.

"I'm sorry, too," she said. "I miss him, and I blame myself. I never should have tried to bring a kitten."

"He was from your home," Gabe said. "Sometimes it's hard to leave the past behind."

He was no longer speaking of Lafitte, she sensed, but something deeper that was troubling him greatly. And in that moment, her misgivings and her shyness disappeared. She crossed the room to sit beside him, to gently take his hand in hers, and it seemed the most natural thing she could imagine.

She heard him sigh, but instead of asking anything, she laid her head on his shoulder.

"Yvette," he whispered once more, and hearing him say her name so wistfully sent shivers rippling down her back, detonating small explosions deep inside her. Some quality in his voice felt warm and sensual, as enticing as his touch.

"Gabriel . . . I love you," she answered, and just as his voice had done for her, hers seemed to ignite the dry kindling of his soul.

He framed her face with bandaged hands and turned it until he was kissing her as fervently as the most desperate prayer. So deeply that time stopped for her, consumed inside the wonder of joined mouths and tongues that touched to spark a blaze that melted every doubt.

His fingers slipped to stroke her neck and shoulder, and a little thrill of fear convinced her that this time he would not stop.

The rap came twice before she heard it, then once again before she could force herself to answer. Outside the door, Mrs. Beacon stood balancing a tray on one broad hip. Her fist was poised as if to knock again.

"Here's a nice pot of tea and some sweet rolls, fresh out of the oven," she told Yvette as she handed her the tray. "Now I'll see you're left alone. I'm certain that your young man needs his rest."

She waved off Yvette's thanks. But as the older woman turned to go, Yvette thought she detected a sparkle in her eyes, a hidden smile as if . . .

She knew. She knew what they'd been doing. Backing into the room, feeling more uncomfortable than ever, Yvette kicked shut the door. *Mon Dieu,* did she have no restraint at all?

One look in his eyes convinced her she did not. Gabe's attention was fully focused on her, not lingering for half an instant on the food and drink.

"Aren't you hungry?" she asked, uncertain how she wanted him to answer.

Until he smiled and stood. Until he came to her and took her in his arms once more. Then she knew for certain this was what she'd wished for all along.

This time their bodies pressed together fully, and Yvette felt Gabriel's heat from her ankle to her mouth. Yet even as he seemed to lose himself inside their kiss, he avoided her left side so as not to hurt her arm.

He pulled away just long enough to tickle her ear with his words. "I'm hungrier than I've ever been, Yvette. Hungrier than any man alive."

He slipped around to mouth her neck beneath her ear, and Yvette gasped. *Mon Dieu,* how could she have guessed that this was what it was like to be devoured? Her breasts felt as if they'd come alive with aching for his well-remembered touch. Oh, please, she thought, please, soon.

As if he'd read her mind, Gabriel scooped her into his arms and carried her to the bed. Lowering her gently, he whispered, "If this isn't what you want, you need to tell me."

His eyes brimmed with such awful longing that she

wondered if they mirrored her own. Suddenly, she wanted nothing except him against her, the warmth of his bare skin, the almost painful awakening of all her senses.

So instead of answering him directly, she whispered. "I'll need your help to get out of this bodice."

Gabe's fingers trembled over every button, and he watched her carefully for any sign that she might change her mind. But all he saw was her moist lips, pink with kisses and slightly parted in anticipation. All he heard was the faint rasp of her quick breaths. Like him, she was quivering with anticipation, or nervousness, perhaps.

With her closeness, his exhaustion and pain receded like the memory of an unpleasant dream. Yet his bandaged hands were clumsy, so she helped him remove her bodice. When his fingertips next grazed the laces of her corset, her eyes closed. A faint flush colored her pale flesh, and he bowed his head to kiss away its bloom.

"I-I don't know what to do," she whispered, her shaking growing more pronounced. "I—"

"Shhh . . . It will be fine, I promise," Gabe told her. "I won't do anything that feels bad. There, you liked this, didn't you?"

He kissed her neck again and was rewarded by another gasp of pleasure. Her trembling ceased, and she seemed to hold her breath.

His mouth slipped lower until he was kissing just above her breasts.

"Oh . . ." she whispered, and her right hand strayed to the lacings.

Playfully, he nipped her fingertips, then, with her help, freed her of the constricting undergarment. When he had bared her breasts, he cupped them with his bandaged hands, then followed his fingers with gentle suckling, first at one side, then the other.

She arched her back and moaned his name aloud, arousing him so painfully that he paused to undress. He saw fear play across her features at the sight of him.

"You're not going to . . . ?" Her question trailed off into confusion.

"Nothing you don't want," he swore as he climbed back into bed with her. "Just tell me and I'll stop. As much as I would like to, we have time. Our whole lives . . . together."

"I don't want you . . ." She closed her eyes once more, and her brow wrinkled with emotion. "I don't want you to stop. I want to know this, feel this . . . the way you make me feel."

Her eyes opened, those long-lashed hazel eyes he'd grown to love. And she looked at him, her face so full of everything he felt that he had no choice but to kiss her, to run his hands along her sides and stroke her hardened nipples with his fingers.

How could it be that touching had somehow numbed his pain when all his other senses blazed to life? With a smile, he imagined her the cure for all his wounds, inside and out.

He lingered at her breasts, though he wanted more than anything to undress her lower body and to fully make her his. Instead, he forced himself to aching slowness, determined not to steal from her anything she did not wish to give.

So it was that Yvette herself removed the last scraps

of her clothing, letting them fall carelessly onto the floor. And so it was she eagerly accepted his caresses and eventually took courage to touch and explore his body on her own. So that when he finally entered her, she welcomed him, and after that first pain flashed across her features, he saw nothing but the joy that climbed and climbed until it burst upon the pinnacle into a thousand dazzling shards.

And with her release came his, so brilliant, so explosive, that he felt, for the first time since Georgia, fully free.

The bay danced and tossed her head as Darien Russell smoothed out the strap and fastened the final buckles on her harness. Colonel Patterson tightened his grip on the driving lines and patted the horse's sleek brown neck.

"Needs a bit of a run to get the tickle out of those heels," Colonel Patterson advised him. "Gabby's full of the devil, but she's young and willing. Keep her firmly in hand and she'll settle right into her work."

Darien thanked Patterson for the loan of his mare and a neat, black, two-wheeled shay. The army mount Darien had borrowed earlier had thrown a shoe and pulled up lame. But that at least gave Darien an excuse to ask the colonel what had happened to the promised guards.

"Funny you should ask that," Patterson told him. "Morrison and O'Hara left here about an hour and a half ago. Someone at the Soldiers' Home told them Private Davis had been moved to Overton. But when they got there to check, nobody knew a thing about him. I sent them back out to ask at the hospitals about the girl. Assuming that they're not successful, I'll put both men at your disposal. I'd like both Miss Augeron and Private Davis found as quickly as possible."

Patterson glanced down the street toward two soldiers walking in their direction. "There they are now," he said.

When the men saw the colonel outside watching, one quickened his pace and broke into a jog. The second hesitated, then fell into step.

"We have an address on the young woman, sir," the first and taller of the two men said. He passed a slip of paper to the colonel.

"Mrs. Beacon's on Beale Street. She's at a boardinghouse?"

"That's what one of the women at Gayoso told us," the private answered. Despite the fanged appearance given by a pair of jutting eyeteeth, the young soldier had such a look of steely-eyed intelligence that Darien was surprised by his low rank.

"Bring her in," the colonel said to Darien. "I'll want to speak to her myself."

"If this is the right one, she's going by the name of Mrs. Caroline Edwards," the gray-eyed private continued, now speaking to Darien, "and she's played on the nurses' sympathy with some tale about a missing husband."

"But the woman's description matches?" Darien asked.

The other soldier nodded in response. A thick scar split his eyebrow, and a surly expression marred his face. Something in his posture convinced Darien he'd be reluctant to respond to any question that couldn't be answered with a movement of his pointed chin. The soldier reminded him of a sullen schoolboy, but

since the colonel made no comment, Darien ignored
the impulse to correct the private.

"Perfectly, sir," the younger soldier added, as if he
felt it necessary to elaborate.

The woman was Yvette. Darien's neck tingled with
that conviction, but he tamped down his optimism
so it would not infuse his voice. He had to find a way
to be the one to capture her, and he must be certain
he did so alone.

Colonel Patterson squinted at him, then used his
hand to shield his eyes from the bright sunshine.
"How about if I ride along, Captain? It's a fair enough
day, and I'm feeling anxious to see this little murderess of yours."

Darien's mood plummeted, even as he scrambled
for some plausible excuse. He could almost hear the
sharp snap of the rope at the New Orleans gallows
as his old friend Major Stolz was hung for fraud.
Nausea roiled in his stomach as he remembered the
way the man squirmed, suspended like a silk-wrapped
fly caught in a spider's web. Darien refused to die
in such disgrace, to make lies of his grandfather's
predictions.

Yet he would if Yvette convinced the authorities
where to look for evidence. He would die, and she
would watch and, worse yet, laugh. Imagining that
moment beaded perspiration on his forehead, sweat
unrelated to the brilliant sunlight.

But the awful images convinced him that, once
again, he had no other choice. He had to find some
way to silence Yvette before Patterson could meet her.

* * *

Beside Yvette, Gabriel slept soundly, one arm draped casually across her shoulder. She watched his short gold lashes vibrate, the way the muscles of his face spasmed just beneath the skin, then saw his expression smooth out, all as if some dream had briefly troubled him, then fled.

Carefully, so as not to wake him, she stroked his blond hair, so pale and fine against her own black tresses. Noon against her midnight, North against her South. At that moment, all their differences came into sharp relief, and Yvette wondered at the enormity of what they had just done.

Had they forged an enduring link across the chasm of their varied backgrounds, cultures, and religions? Or had their lust and loneliness leapt the boundary of good sense?

He might think better of this now that he had taken what he'd desired. No, she might as well be honest with herself. Gabriel had not taken; she had given, willingly. But now that she had, would he still want her? Would he still take her with him?

Gabriel sighed contentment in his sleep and pulled her to him, spooning her body with his own. And with the closer contact, her misgivings lifted like a haze of smoke cleared by a river breeze.

This was home now, she realized as his arm tightened about her. Not the Augerons' fine town house, not the Creole quarter of New Orleans, not even the South itself; those places were nothing but a past forever lost. This place—these arms, this heart, this man—meant her future. Gabriel was her home, wherever he might take her, and she knew beyond any question that she would do anything to keep him and all they would have safe.

Even if that meant leaving him right now to send another telegram to Uncle André in St. Louis. Because now she felt more pressure than ever to clear herself of charges and implicate Darien Russell in the deaths of both her sister and Lieutenant Simonton. Because she knew without a doubt that if Russell caught her first, he'd silence not only her but Gabriel, and she could not allow that.

Nor could she allow Gabriel to come with her. For there was always the possibility that Russell would anticipate this move, that he would be watching the telegraph office with his steady raptor's gaze. She could only bear this risk if it were hers alone.

Yvette had nearly finished dressing when Gabriel awakened.

He reached out for her. "Come back here, Yvette."

That sleepy smile and the tousled hair nearly melted her resolve. Instead, she leaned over him and kissed his cheek.

"Dressing with an injured arm is not so very simple, and I suspect that if I come too close, I'll have to struggle through it all again."

His smile stretched into a lazy grin. "I may be a little tired, but I believe that I could make it worth your while."

She felt herself blushing at the images that his words conjured. *Mon Dieu*, but she would love nothing more than to taste his kisses one more time. And so much more . . .

Wistfully, she sighed. "Gabriel . . . I will count the minutes until I can return. But I have a thing that I must do right now."

He sat up and reached for his pants. "Then I'll

come with you. I don't want Russell catching you alone.''

She shook her head. Despite his eagerness to bring her back to bed, she could not forget how near to collapsing he had seemed before. "You still look exhausted. Stay here, where you can eat and rest. It will be better, anyway, if I do this thing alone.''

"What thing?''

She shook her head. "I have to send a message to the one person who might make it possible for us to stay together.''

"Your uncle?''

She nodded. "It would be better if I tell you the details later.''

She bent to kiss his forehead and fought the temptation to linger and then drop her lips to his. *Not now,* she warned herself. First she must protect him from the consequences of her past.

"Please, Gabriel, just trust me. I will come back very soon,'' she promised.

He nodded. "All right, Yvette, but please . . . be careful and be quick.''

When Patterson sighed and handed Darien the address, Russell could scarcely believe his luck.

"I'm being unrealistic,'' the colonel told him. "Much as I'd like to come along, the general will send me to the godforsaken Indian Territory if I don't attend another pressing matter this afternoon. Report back later this afternoon to apprise me of the situation. Oh, and perhaps you'll want to take this with you.''

Patterson passed him his own revolver. "It's been

fairly quiet here, but since the president's death, we're afraid there may be pockets of insurrection. Besides, this girl you're after has already shown what she can do. I suppose I don't need to remind you not to go too easy on her just because she's female. We've had our own problems with vipers in petticoats hereabouts. Not killers, perhaps, but the most treacherous spies I've ever seen. One of them was engaged to half a dozen Union officers throughout the occupation. I'm still trying to undo some of the disruptions she caused."

"Don't worry," Darien assured him. "I have no intention of proposing to Miss Augeron or of turning my back on her for a second. Have a good afternoon, sir."

Feeling jubilant, Darien saluted the officer as he hurried back inside the appropriated mansion. He then turned back toward the two soldiers and held up the address.

"This could easily be another woman passenger," he said in an almost dismissive tone. "It wouldn't do to harass an innocent survivor. I'll check with the owner of this boardinghouse. I'd like both of you to go to the rail and steamboat ticket offices. I don't want those two getting out of Memphis. Why don't you see if you can get mounts to speed this up a bit?"

"Yes, sir."

Predictably, only the younger soldier spoke. If this new order surprised him, he didn't show it.

Darien was too eager to leave the two to bother chastising the mute man. Instead, as soon as the gray-eyed man directed him toward Beale, he dismissed both men and climbed into the shay. With barely a flick of the reins, the bay mare started off at a smart trot.

As he drove, a warm breeze carried the scent of river through a host of bright spring blossoms. Darien sneezed and reached into his pocket for a handkerchief to wipe his running nose and eyes. Despite the blue sky and sunny weather, he despised this time of year.

In tribute to either the brilliant day or Memphis's thriving commerce, the streets were crowded with pedestrians, riders, carriages, and wagons loaded with merchandise. Far too crowded to allow the energetic mare a needed canter. As if to protest, she strained against the lines and threw her feet out in an animated gait. Russell smiled, enjoying the challenge of handling the spirited horse after years spent flogging half-dead army hacks into sluggish trots.

He wondered if this fine animal and the little shay, too, had been confiscated from the owners of the house Patterson had taken. For no reason in particular, he thought back to the abandoned doll beneath the bed where he had slept, then shrugged off an unexpected twinge of pity.

When he reached the Beacon residence, a short, plump woman answered the door. She wiped her floury hands on her apron.

"Yes?" she asked, eyeing his uniform with what appeared to be suspicion.

Surely she didn't imagine he'd come to requisition this hovel for military use. He only took advantage of the greed of men already rich; he had no intention of stealing from children and old ladies. Intent on getting information quickly, he managed what he hoped passed for a charming smile to put her mind at ease.

"Good afternoon, madam," he told her. "I've just learned that a dear friend of the family, Mrs. Caroline Edwards, was rescued from the river and is staying here. I would so like to speak with her and offer my assistance."

The woman's expression warmed immediately, and she returned his smile with a far more genuine version.

"You'll be so glad to know her husband's turned up safe, too," she volunteered. "Poor young man has his hands all bandaged, and he looks plenty tired, but I declare he'll be just fine. He's upstairs resting right this very minute."

Gabe Davis had found her then, and quickly, too, Darien thought. And the two of them were posing as man and wife. He smiled, thinking of this chink in Yvette's armor of Southern feminine morality. She was repaying the soldier for his help in the very coin he had imagined.

"And what of Mrs. Edwards?" he asked. "Is she resting upstairs as well?"

"Oh, no. I'm afraid that you just missed her. She left about ten minutes ago to run an errand," Widow Beacon said, pointing out the direction. "If you hurry, though, you might just catch her."

This time, his smile was genuine. "Thank you so much for your time, madam. I believe I'll do that."

Chapter Fifteen

War is at best barbarism. . . . Its glory is all moonshine. It is only those who have neither fired a shot nor heard the shrieks and groans of the wounded who cry aloud for blood, more vengeance, more desolation. War is Hell.

—William Tecumseh Sherman

Gabe ate several of the sweet rolls and drank another cup of the cool tea. If his brain hadn't been so fogged with sleep, he would have insisted upon going with Yvette.

How long had she been gone? The small room held no clock, and in this unfamiliar place, the shift of shadows offered him few clues. He peered out once more through a spotless window and glanced up toward the sun. Noon, he reckoned, or not long after. But that didn't help him, since he wasn't sure when she had left.

If only he hadn't dozed once she had gone. Then he'd have a better idea of the time. But his physical condition and contentment had conspired to chase him back to sleep, beyond the worries that now gnawed at his conscience.

As soon as she returned, he would have to go out looking for his three friends. Though he'd searched his copy of the newspaper again and again, none of their names had been listed among the known survivors in the *Argus*.

But he had seen names he knew. He was relieved to read of several men he knew from Andersonville who had been taken to various area hospitals. Several men from his Ohio unit were also listed, and though they'd turned their backs on him, Gabe was glad to think they would be going home, at least if they survived whatever injuries they'd sustained.

But Silas Deming's name appeared on the roster of men sent to Overton Hospital. It seemed painfully unfair—incomprehensible—that such a worthless bastard would come through this when Gabe's best friends were missing. Even Reuben Miller, his boyhood friend, had not yet been found.

Gabe's mind returned to the grim rows of shrouded bodies lined up along the river. Rows that would only lengthen as more corpses floated to the surface or jammed into the blades of paddle wheels. Dear God.

He mustn't think of that. Must think instead of Yvette and what had passed between them. Must put aside the guilt that he had lived to experience such joy, while Jacob, Zeke, and Seth—

No! His friends could not be dead! He pictured them, one face after the other. He heard their voices, thought of the times they'd taken turns huddling two by two in the shebang during a cold rain because all four of them could not fit inside the crude, home-made shelter at one time.

A shelter made out of three sticks and a single rubber Union army blanket, a treasure Captain Seth had been fortunate enough to smuggle inside the stockade.

Gabe stood, suddenly all nervous energy, and began to pace the little room. He noticed the corner of a paper sticking out from beneath a blotter on the desk. Curious, he pulled it out and scanned the first few lines.

My dearest Marie,
  My Yankee soldier, my dear Gabriel, is gone now, and all I can do is wonder. Was he taken from me to repay in part the lives that I destroyed?

He stopped reading, conscious only of the sharp-ness of his shock and of the many things he didn't really know about the woman he had promised he would wed. If her sister, Marie, were really dead, why would Yvette be writing her a letter? And worse yet, what did she mean by ". . . to repay in part the lives that I destroyed?"

Nausea churned deep in his belly, and cold chills sped along his spine. Dropping the letter facedown on the desk, he turned away.

Yvette. He could almost feel her, taste her tender-ness. But when he heard her voice whisper his name, it echoed with the South. The South that he had fought against. The South his friends detested. And all at once the love he felt for her welled as bitter as betrayal in his heart.

"Your loyalty is misplaced," Darien Russell had told him this morning. *". . . she's a criminal. A murderess, in fact. There's even talk she might have been part of a conspiracy that caused the explosion."*

Stupid to listen to anything that arrogant bastard said, but despite the thought, a memory crept back into Gabe's consciousness. Yvette had met him on the main deck near the boilers, though her stateroom was located on the cabin deck above.

Near the boilers, which had exploded just a few days later.

He thought, too, of Yvette's desperation to leave the *Sultana* when she'd docked in Memphis. If not for Russell's vigilance, she surely would have gone. Leaving him behind, abandoning all who were aboard the doomed vessel.

Gabe thought about what she had said to him today. Why didn't she want him to come along with her?

Please, Gabriel, just trust me. He could almost hear her words. And he wondered, Was it possible he'd trusted her too far?

Despite his appreciation for the bay mare's exuberance, she nearly caused Darien Russell to miss the very reason he had come. Only fifty yards from the telegraph office, their path was blocked by a wagon with a broken axle and a pair of lowing oxen. For whatever reason, the mare had taken exception to the scene and shied, rearing on her hind legs in fright. Darien only regained control in time to catch a fleeting glimpse of the back of Yvette Augeron as she entered a neat, white-painted building. He swore after reading the sign above the door: Memphis Telegraph Office. God damn it. Who the hell could she be contacting?

The thought sent a shudder through him, and the mare danced within her traces as if his apprehension were contagious. He settled the horse and then tied her to a hitching post a few doors down, in front of a general store.

He'd prefer to take Yvette before she sent her message but decided it would be preferable to avoid a public scene. People remembered such things all too clearly, and with what he had in mind, witnesses would cause unpleasant complications.

Instead, he decided to wait until she finished and began walking through an area less crowded. He stepped inside the general store and hurriedly looked around for the one item he would need to put an end to all his troubles.

"Excuse me," he called to a clerk, a reed-thin boy with jutting ears. "I'll need to buy a good, strong rope."

Gabriel walked along the shaded avenue, as miserable as he'd ever been inside Andersonville prison, as uncertain as he'd been his entire life. Had he betrayed his country by helping Yvette? Had he betrayed his friends by loving her as well?

Once again memories assailed him. Seth Harris told him once more, *"Think logically. Or if you can't do that, think about that beefsteak you keep dreaming on and not some girl with every reason in the world to hate you."*

Zeke had laughed, *"I hear you're courtin' trouble."*

But the words that kept coming back to him were

Jacob Fuller's: *"Do you realize you're taking this Southern girl's word against a Union officer's? She's a goddamned Rebel, Gabe. The whole idea stinks of treason. How can you be sure of anything she said?"*

And now all three of them were missing, as well as others beyond counting. Could it have anything to do with the fact that he'd helped her?

Maybe Silas Deming and his friends had been wrong about him all along, Gabe thought. Maybe what he'd been guilty of had not been cowardice but something worse instead.

Disloyalty. To his friends, to his country, and to everything he'd fought for. To everything held dear enough to take another's life.

There was no undoing what he'd done to help Yvette, and there was nothing in the world he could do to set things right. Except to see to it that she was punished if he truly believed she'd lied to him.

At the thought of Yvette, his mind leapt to the soft expression in her eyes as he had loved her, to the streak of red she'd left upon the sheets. She had trusted him enough to let him be the first, trusted him with her most precious gift outside the bonds of marriage.

Why? Why would she do such a thing if she were no more than a spy, if she were guilty of complicity in an act that had killed well over a thousand?

His mind flashed once again to Yvette down on the main deck, challenging a group of Yankee prisoners because she thought it wrong to throw a helpless man to his death in the water. For the first time, he realized the enormity of the risk that she had taken, the simple moral courage required for such an act.

And in that moment his doubts vanished, because

he knew who she was. Not a murderess, not a spy, just the scared and lonely young woman that he knew her to be. One who loved him with all her heart.

As he truly loved her.

Gabe smiled, feeling energized by the conviction and by the realization that his heart was loyal, after all.

Yvette glanced up and down the street as she left the telegraph office. Seeing no familiar faces, she began walking in the same direction she had come, her mind on anything but danger.

She felt relieved now that the telegram was on its way to Uncle André. Surely he'd reply soon, perhaps in as little as half a day, with instructions on what she should do next. He might even travel here to meet her. Then she, Uncle André, and Gabriel would soon figure out how to unknot this tangled skein of troubles. Darien would be punished, and she could marry Gabriel.

Thinking of her lover, Yvette turned her face toward the sunshine. She shivered delicately in the warm spring air as she remembered all they'd shared. And would share, from this day forth. Echoes of their kisses and forbidden touches, of their whispered words of love, lightened her steps until she felt buoyant as cork upon the water, carried toward him on a welcome tide.

So complete was her distraction that the first thing that she heard was the gun's click at her back. Something small and very hard poked painfully beneath her shoulder blade.

"Move a muscle and I'll shoot you through the heart."

She froze, not needing to turn her head to recognize the voice of the man who had used and then murdered her sister. Darien Russell's voice had so long hissed threats in her nightmares that she prayed desperately that this might number among those frightening dreams.

Around her, however, she heard the everyday sounds of voices, none very close or sounding of alarm. She smelled the ordinary odors of horse manure and damp earth laid over the familiar scent of river. Though the sun shone brightly, a cooler breeze stole through the alleyway that she was crossing and raised the fine hairs of her arms and nape. This was all too real, she reasoned, the reckoning that she had dreaded for so long.

"You found me," she whispered, resenting that it had to come at such a happy moment, when the future looked so promising.

"Simple enough," Darien told her flatly, "once your lover told me where you'd gone."

She flinched as if he'd struck her, then managed to steel herself with indignation. "Liar! Gabriel would never tell you anything!" she hissed.

He prodded her back with what must surely be a gun barrel. "Now get inside the shay, and don't think for a moment that anyone will care if I shoot a Southern spy and murderess."

Slowly, Yvette turned and began walking in the direction that he indicated.

Darien chuckled, clearly relishing this opportunity to cause her pain. "After all was said and done, Mr. Davis realized he hadn't fought and suffered only to betray the Union for a tryst. I dare say, he seemed relieved to wash his hands of the whole, sordid affair."

She wasn't going to cry, Yvette swore. Surely Russell was lying to be cruel.

But she couldn't let him think that she believed him. "I don't believe a word of it," she protested. "He—"

"*Loves* you? Is *that* what he told you? Oh, dear, Yvette. I'm shocked that with your upbringing and intelligence, you couldn't guess that he was only talking his way between your legs. After all, the man spent months in a prison camp and years before that in the field. God knows how long he's been without a woman. One can hardly blame him for—"

"Stop it!" she demanded, even as he helped her up into the shay. She noticed he'd put up the folding hood for privacy.

Despite her resolve, tears swam in her vision, then began to spill. Hating the show of weakness, she angrily swiped at them with a sleeve.

As Darien climbed inside and took up the reins, the horse started, and he had to struggle to control it. Yvette thought of running, but her limbs were shaking too hard, and the moment was too brief. Her mind spun with other explanations for Darien Russell's presence. He might have followed her or posted guards to watch the telegraphs and stations. Or perhaps he'd discerned her false identity, then tracked down Mrs. Beacon.

But the older woman hadn't known where she was going. She'd told no one else but Gabriel that bit of information. Still, she clung desperately to the conviction that he wouldn't do this, not after—

All *Maman*'s and her *grandmère*'s harshest warnings

came roaring into consciousness, thundering in horrible, discordant crescendos. *"A woman dishonored can never be a wife or mother, only a debased, pathetic creature of the streets."* And, *"No matter what he promises, you must not give in, for a man's youthful ardor is only a test of your true virtue."*

A test that she had failed, along with so many others. From the moment that she'd tried to save her sister, she'd forgotten every single thing she had been taught. Why hadn't she taken her suspicions to her father or her brothers and allowed the men to handle these matters, as any decent Creole woman would have?

Even as she thought it, she remembered how she'd tried with Papa, how he'd forbidden her to speak of it to anyone. Still, convinced of her own rightness and the danger to her sister, she had disobeyed.

And it had ended in disaster. Marie had been disgraced and murdered, and now, for all her struggles, she would suffer the same fate.

All that she had left to hope for was that she might somehow lash out at Darien Russell in these final moments that must certainly lead up to her death.

Worry quickened Gabe's steps, and a growing pressure swelled inside his chest, making it difficult for him to breathe. Perhaps, he tried to tell himself, Yvette had taken a different route. Right now she awaited him in her room, just as worried as he was. Or maybe the line at the telegraph office had been clogged with *Sultana* survivors eager to contact home with news of their escape or pleas for assistance. Yet neither of those scenarios slowed his progress, for he couldn't escape the need to see her, touch her, and reassure himself that all was well.

He wondered if his urgency was fed by guilt that he had doubted her and for the suspicion that still lay coiled in his mind, tempting him to wonder if she'd abandoned him.

"Expect little; trust less." Seth's words again returned to haunt him, and he could almost see the man's gray eyes behind the cracked lens of his glasses. How was it he'd never noticed how grim was his friend's expression? He wondered if somewhere, somehow, Seth would ever move beyond his prison walls.

Gabe hurried on, knowing he'd rather learn that he was wrong, have Yvette Augeron make a fool of him, than live without the possibility of trust, without the possibility of love. He'd be damned if he would let doubt ruin what he'd found with her.

He longed to somehow repay Yvette for his lack of faith, to show her his commitment to forever. If he could only find her.

Inside the telegraph office, he found only a man with unlined, milk-pale skin and snowy, shoulder-length hair. The clerk's eyes, framed by white lashes, peered out from thick glasses that magnified their blueness into a pair of icy lakes.

The lakes blinked several times until Gabe closed the door and shut out the afternoon's bright sunlight. The window shades were drawn, and it took several moments for his own eyes to adjust to the new dimness.

"Would you care to send a telegram?" the clerk asked.

"No, thanks. I'm looking for my wife," Gabe ventured, sticking with Yvette's story. "Have you seen her? She's a small-boned woman, about twenty, with dark hair."

The clerk nodded and gestured toward the door. "She sent her telegram and left not two minutes ago. She couldn't have gotten too far."

Gabe thanked him, although he wondered if the fellow could really see well enough to identify Yvette or anyone else. He'd never in his life seen anyone wearing thicker glasses.

Once outside, Gabe trotted up and down the street in the hopes that he might catch a glimpse of Yvette's retreating form. As he passed an alley, he was nearly overrun by a lively bay horse pulling a shay as it emerged from between two buildings. Turning his head to shout a warning at the driver, Gabe froze in horror and swallowed back his words.

Darien Russell held the driving lines in one hand. And beside him, her face nearly as pale as the albino's, sat Yvette. Russell was glaring at her, saying something, so that his gaze never settled upon Gabe. Yvette, too, gave no sign of recognition.

The horse and shay completed its turn and began to pull away. Gabe hesitated, wondering how on earth Russell had convinced Yvette to go with him without a fight.

He had to have a gun. Perhaps that would explain why only one hand held the bay's reins.

As the two-wheeled carriage began to pull away, Gabe wondered how, using only his brain and his two injured hands, he could hope to stop Captain Russell, an armed officer who would hide behind the law to break it. How in God's name could he save Yvette without costing both of them their lives?

* * *

Yvette didn't have the heart to ask where Russell was taking her. Instead, she sat in silence as they drove past building after building: churches and hotels, grand homes and lesser ones, businesses of every ilk. She barely recognized the people that they passed as human, whether soldier or civilian, man or woman, light-skinned or dark. It never occurred to her to call out to any of them or that anyone would either hear her screams or try to help.

Her mind spun like a wagon wheel seeking purchase in slick mud. Try as she might, she couldn't pull herself out of the hole in which she'd been mired.

Gabriel could not have been the one who had betrayed her. Again and again, she whispered those words to herself, then prayed desperate prayers to God. After what she and Gabriel had shared, such treachery was unimaginable, obscene.

And yet her thoughts turned time after time to Marie's example of what happened to a Creole girl when she entrusted both her heart and body to a Yankee soldier. Why in the name of all the saints had she refused to heed that lesson?

If the army caught him, Gabe doubted they would bother with a prison term. Yet as he watched the soldier tie a rangy black gelding to the telegraph-office hitching post, he wondered how much any of that mattered. After all, as far as he knew, they could only hang him once.

He forced himself to wait for what he judged half a minute, though his body tensed like a drawn bow-

string, ready to launch him in the direction that
Yvette's carriage had vanished. He glanced once more
at the storefront windows and thanked God for its
lowered shades. Praying that the soldier would stay
inside awhile, Gabe untied the horse. He scrambled
aboard its military saddle, though pain in his hands
shot up to his shoulders. More mindful of his fear
than the discomfort, he dug his heels into the animal's sides and urged it to cut between two passing
freight wagons.

As if it understood his need, Gabe's new mount
hesitated not a moment. Instead, with near-perfect
equine grace and speed, the black horse negotiated
tight spaces until their flight drew several curses from
startled teamsters. Pedestrians pointed, and a broad-
hipped woman shouted, shaking a hammy fist at this
disruption of the peace.

Yet no one cried out, "Horse thief!" At least not
anyone Gabe heard. But his relief was short-lived for
two reasons. First, he had not the slightest idea how
he might rescue Yvette from Darien. Second, and far
worse, he could not see the black shay even when he
followed the turn that he had thought Russell had
taken.

What could he do now? Surely, if he remained near,
circling the area, he would be caught and arrested
for the horse's theft. But that outcome scarcely mattered, for if he could not find—and save—Yvette, he
could not imagine living, anyway.

Yvette began to notice how thickening clouds had
dimmed the sunshine, how huge trees replaced the
buildings and undergrowth the people. Abruptly, the

dark haze of her shock lifted, and her body shook with the strain of attempting to reckon how long the bay mare had been trotting. How many miles had they come? But try as she might, she had no way of guessing where they'd gone or where Darien Russell might be driving. *No* way except to ask him, which she could not, would not, do.

Besides, their location mattered little, only the marrow-freezing fact that, just as she'd suspected, Darien had no intention of allowing her even the slim chance the courts would offer to a Southern "traitor." He could ill afford the possibility that some softhearted judge would look at her and think of his own daughter, then allow her a few words. Words that would damn Darien, if she only had the chance.

Instead, Russell meant to silence her, using the same methods as he had her sister. And she, acting like a docile little fool, was going right along with him without raising a fuss, as if she believed the threat of being shot were worse than whatever death he had in mind.

To the devil with that idea! If he meant to murder her, she was going to make the cad work for it! She'd never lived as the dutiful and lamblike woman-child, so why should she fit in that mold as she died? And if revenge against Capt. Darien Russell were not reason enough to fight him to the death, she thought of all the venom she would like to spew at Gabriel, who would repay her gift of love with this betrayal. If she had to claw and bite her way through Darien like a tigress for the chance to have her say, then so be it! It certainly wasn't as if she any longer had a genteel reputation to protect.

"Use your mind, Yvette." The voice sent a clean jolt

along the column of her spine. Marie's voice, so clear
and true that all the tiny hairs along her arms and
nape rose in recognition and her stomach leapt into
her throat.

Mon Dieu! She must be dying, to hear words spoken
by the dead! Her quivering redoubled, and she
thought that she must vomit. Yet as she bent forward,
she recalled the strange story Gabriel had told her,
about seeing his dead brother on the battlefield.
Gabriel Davis had not died that day.

Neither would she perish. Perhaps, like her lover's
brother, Marie had returned when death loomed
near, intent only on coaxing her out of its path. *"Use
your mind,"* she'd said. And suddenly Yvette could *see*
Marie's last moments, how, finally understanding, she
had fought with all her strength. And how futile, how
completely useless, that final effort had proved.

Like her sister, Yvette lacked the strength to physically overpower Darien Russell. But she'd already out-
witted him on more than one occasion.

If she tried to leap out of the carriage now or wrestle
away his weapon, he would only shoot her. Along this
empty pathway, with no one as a witness. But if her
strength could not stop a bullet, how could she manage that same feat with her mind?

Marie whispered no more words of advice. Perhaps
she hovered nearby, silently encouraging her sister.
Or maybe she had been no more than a trick of the
mind, a manifestation of the human will to live.

It scarcely mattered to Yvette, who slumped even
farther forward. Though she had no real plan yet,
she decided that feigning weakness would put Darien
off his guard. Her furious thinking halted even as the
horse did.

Russell made fast the driving lines, then gently touched her cheek, as if to offer comfort. Yvette flinched at the contact.

"I'm sorry to see you're feeling poorly," he told her. The jubilation had faded from his voice, faded into what sounded for all the world like sympathy, or even sorrow.

Was he sorry for her or for himself and what he meant to do? Did a man who had already murdered still fear earning an even hotter place in hell? Or was there something else that troubled him, something she might use?

Marie's features flashed through her mind like summer lightning, and Yvette decided on the chance that she would take.

She glanced up at Russell through lashes thickened by the droplets of her tears. "Marie comes to you, too." She spoke without the slightest hint of hesitation, surprised that her voice would not betray her mind's doubt. "She comes to you and damns you for her murder and the death of your own child."

The hand that gripped her upper arm closed tight enough to make her cry out in both pain and surprise.

"I didn't kill them. *You* did!" he accused her.

"Why not let a court decide? Why not let them hang me for all of New Orleans to see? You know that would destroy my family . . . or what's left of my family, I should say."

"You want a trial?" he raged, pausing for a moment to tighten his left hand's grip on the reins, which had come loose when the horse had started at his outburst. He braked the shay and retied the reins, then shoved the pistol's muzzle up beneath her chin. "Then by all means, let's have one!"

She leaned backward in the seat and tilted her head to escape the weapon's painful pressure. But her shifting made no difference, as he pushed even harder than before.

"*Who* in God's name tried to run me out of New Orleans with her spiteful little ditties?" he shouted. Then, answering his own question, he said, "Miss Yvette Augeron!"

Without allowing her a chance for a reply, he continued. "*Who* spied on me from dawn to dusk and stole my property?"

Twisting away, Yvette argued. "If you're speaking of that letter, you must know it was destroyed before I could prove anything. There's no need to kill—"

"*Silence!*" He punctuated that command by clubbing the side of her head with the pistol.

Yvette's world careened amid a sickening jolt of pain. Blackness threatened to drop down like a curtain, but she fought it and struggled to make sense of Russell's words.

"And who told Lieutenant Simonton about that letter and showed it to Marie—*Marie!* God, how I loved her, and yet *you*, you goddamned interfering bitch, you *made* me—"

The accusation was too much for Yvette, and with all of her remaining strength she slashed at his eyes with her nails. She felt them dig deep into the beard-coarsened flesh of his cheek, heard him shout out some obscenity, just before he grabbed her and began to shake.

And as her head struck the shay's side, her tenuous grip on consciousness melted into darkness.

Both boys bobbed their heads and peered down the road, along a pathway that cut through virgin forest. Neither pointed to indicate the answer to Gabe's question, for their arms were loaded with firewood. Dirt filmed their dark brown skin, and Gabe imagined they were contrabands, former slaves who had flocked to Union-held territory to guarantee their freedom.

"They just come along this way, white folks in a two-wheel carriage with a brown hoss," the older of the two said.

As Gabe glanced in the direction Russell and Yvette had taken, he thought he could make out a haze of dust, still airborne after the passage of the horse and shay. He thanked the boys and kicked his stolen mount into a gallop, more alarmed now than ever.

It had been bad enough when he'd imagined Russell taking Yvette to a jail cell to face trial, but with each step the two took beyond Memphis, Gabe's apprehension grew. This journey into the isolated woodlands could only mean one thing. Yvette was dangerous to Russell, too threatening to live to speak her piece. The captain intended for her only execution, not a trial.

Yvette's head throbbed in time to the pounding of her heart. She began to rouse, conscious only of the imperative to awaken, not the reason.

Her eyes slitted open just enough to see him. Darien

Russell, bending forward, his hands working at a strange knot in a long, looped rope.

Something about the knot alarmed her almost as much as the presence of her sister's killer. Something about the snakelike way it coiled about itself, completely unlike the knots she'd seen on riverboats or the ones her brothers used to tie the horses.

Russell slid his hand into the loop, then pulled against it. She watched in horror as the rope drew tight around his wrist. And then she knew for certain why this knot had filled her with such horror. The only place she'd ever seen it had been on a hangman's noose.

At the actor, William Mumford's, execution. Yvette closed her eyes, overwhelmed by the memory of the only hanging she had ever witnessed. In the hours after federal troops took New Orleans, Mumford, Southern to his soul, tore down the Yankee flag atop the U.S. Mint. Afterward, he'd been arrested, and to everyone's disbelief, General Butler had ordered his execution, earning himself the appellation "Beast" and the undying hatred of every citizen of New Orleans. At the time, she had been seventeen and naively convinced that the protests of the female populace could stop the outrage from occurring.

But she was twenty now, and she had learned that evil men had a capacity for cruelty almost beyond imagination. She had learned it in that moment a good man's weight stretched the rope.

Darien glanced up and saw her watching.

"I'm afraid you missed the conclusion of your trial, Yvette," he said casually, as if he were speaking of the weather. "This court has found you guilty of the deaths of Marie Augeron and Lt. Peter Simonton. I can see by your expression that you've already guessed the sentence.''

She tried to straighten, to defeat the quicksand of inertia that weighed down her limbs. He grasped her wrist almost before it began to rise and backhanded her into the darkling haze.

''I'm coming around to get you out of here,'' she heard him say, though the voice sounded faint and hollow, as if it spoke from far away. ''Don't try to run. I don't want to have to shoot you. The proper punishment is hanging.''

She wanted to ask what possible difference it could make, but her tongue felt as thick and clumsy as the rest of her. Besides, something had changed in Darien Russell since his days as an adulterous dissembler. Something—perhaps the murders or his own fear of punishment—had pushed him beyond the reach of rational thought, into a state as dangerous as a dog white-jawed with foam.

Before she could guess how to react, he looped the noose around her neck and snugged the knot against her throat. Without allowing her a moment to loosen the rope, he used it to roughly drag her from the shay. If he heard her strangled cries or felt her failing limbs, he gave no sign of it.

The pulling stopped abruptly, and Yvette lay face-down, tearing at the noose, in the dirt of a small clearing. She was barely conscious of the nervous whinnies of the horse as Russell unhitched it. All she knew was her body's urgent need for air. The rope loosened, but she was too exhausted to lift it from her head.

Despite her weakness, Yvette looked up at the pressure of several light tugs on the noose. Russell, holding the unhitched bay with one hand, was tossing the rope's opposite end over the stout branch of the chestnut tree that dominated the small clearing. With sickening clarity, she realized exactly what would happen. He meant to sling the rope over the branch, then tie it to the tree's base. Then he would pull her atop the horse and . . .

Black spots dotted her vision, then clotted thick as blood. *No!* She mustn't pass out now or she would never again awaken, would never have the chance to see Gabriel or touch him, would never have the chance for anything.

Suddenly, her need for revenge fell away, insubstantial as a straw house in a tempest. She would gladly leave Darien's punishment to God, would gladly turn her back on every hateful atrocity of war if she might only for a moment lie with Gabriel once more.

She knew then, beyond all doubt, that he had not betrayed her. She wondered at her foolishness for believing that he had, even for a trice. Fresh tears overflowed at the thought of the sacred vows they'd not yet taken, the ones they'd never have the chance to speak.

A burst of energy surged through her at the thought, and she once more fumbled to remove the frightful noose. Not to escape to fight the battles of her past but to forge a future for herself and Gabriel.

At the tree's thick base, Darien was struggling to tie off the rope. But the moment that he saw what she was doing, he pulled out the revolver he'd stuck in the waistband of his pants. When he cocked the weapon, its metallic clack sounded loud against the stillness.

"God damn you! Be still!" he ordered. "I don't want to have to shoot."

He didn't, did he? Why? Did he fear someone would be attracted by the sound? Or did he truly believe this execution was something nobler than an obscene mockery of justice?

If she ran, would he really shoot her? Or would that make this, in his mind, mere murder?

She removed the loop and dropped it in the dirt beside her.

"Saint Jude, pray for me," she whispered to the patron of desperate causes. Slowly, she struggled to stand, and as she did, her voice rose in both strength and volume. "That finally I may receive the consolations and the succor of heaven in all my necessities."

She kept her eyes locked onto Darien's, hoping to read hesitation in his gold-brown gaze. Dropping the rope's end, he strode toward her, still leading the bay mare.

She turned her back to him, guessing he was too proud to shoot an unarmed woman in the back and praying fervently that her guess was correct.

Her body jerked at the sound of the first gunshot. But it took only an instant to realize that she had not been hit. Her teeth chattered as if a winter storm had blasted through her veins, but somehow, after a moment's hesitation, she forced herself to walk. She didn't run. Her legs felt too unsteady, and her heart was pounding as if it might at any moment burst. Instead, she put one foot before the other and somehow managed to propel herself at the leisurely rate of a day stroller back in the French Quarter.

She took seven steps before he fired several more shots. This time, Yvette shrieked as a bullet creased the upper part of her left arm. She glanced down at the blood that bloomed against the sling, and in that moment's hesitation, Darien grabbed her.

"Turn around," he growled.

Her knees buckled, undone completely at his touch. She shook as if she were afflicted with a drunkard's thirst.

"Can't walk," she moaned, hoping desperately that he wouldn't replace the noose and simply drag her.

Instead, he picked her up as lightly as if she were made of feathers.

"Don't worry," he told her. "You'll never have to use your feet again."

Gabe could not be certain of the sound. Pulling the black horse to a stop, he paused. His heartbeat thundered in his chest as he wondered: Had he heard gunfire in the distance?

The gelding breathed heavily, tired from its gallop. Gabe strained his ears for several seconds, then decided the noise must have been his mount's hoof striking a stone.

A split second before he urged the horse to resume his gallop, a short series of shots echoed through the wood. His heart lurched, and he prayed he was mistaken. He prayed to God Yvette still lived.

"Hyah!" he shouted at the black horse.

The animal responded with a surprising burst of speed. But not even the fastest horse in all creation could outrun the sounds that Gabe had heard.

Chapter Sixteen

After all their suffering in Southern prisons, getting safely within our lines, on our route homeward, congratulating ourselves on the good news and the time we were to have at home, all this, and to have this terrible calamity, hurling so many into eternity, it makes me shudder as I write. No tongue can tell or pen describe the suffering that was on the boat on the morning of the 27th.

—survivor Arthur A. Jones,
from a letter to his brother

He hung her from a chestnut tree, inside a beam of light that slanted through the gathering clouds. After Darien hoisted her onto the horse's back, he looped the noose around Yvette's neck again. But the mare rolled its eyes toward the snakelike rope and bolted. Before Darien realized what was happening, he saw Yvette suspended, dangling in the air.

Wiping his own blood from his cheek, he watched her writhing, strangling. Like Major Stolz's executioner, he'd done a poor job positioning the knot.

Like Marie, Yvette's death would be a painfully slow process.

Thinking of Marie, Darien turned away, for watching Yvette's struggles brought back the horror of strangling the only woman he had ever truly loved. He flexed his fingers, rubbed them, and noticed the smear of Yvette's blood across the back of his left hand.

"I hereby sentence you to death," he whispered, hoping that the words would obliterate his emotions. He must be an executioner, impassive as if he'd been carved out of stone. But in spite of the officious statement, in spite of the crimes Yvette had committed and the proper method he had chosen, this felt nothing like the future his grandfather once predicted. A future bright with promise had once more been stained dark crimson.

Again he used his handkerchief to wipe away the blood; only this time it was hers, from where his bullet had torn across her upper arm. The smear was murder-bright against white linen, where it mingled with the stain from his scratch-wound.

Shoving the handkerchief into his pocket, Darien turned to find the horse. From the struggling he heard in the underbrush, he guessed its driving lines had tangled. He hoped the leather reins held the mare fast long enough for him to catch it.

Darien left the clearing. He was so eager to put this ordeal behind him that he never checked the knot at the tree's base, the same knot interrupted by Yvette's attempt to walk away.

*   *   *

"Oh, my God! Yvette!" Gabriel shouted.

The sight of her hanging from the huge tree made him want to vomit. He'd been so close behind them. How had this been done so quickly?

She hung so low that the tips of her swaying toes traced blurred patterns in the dust. As Gabe leapt from the horse's back, he caught a glimpse of her face, dark with congestion. But he turned his back to her to untie the rope from the bottom of the tree trunk.

The knot, which had already slipped considerably, yielded easily to his frantic efforts, and he fed the loosened rope upward, lowering the body to the ground.

Not a body, damn it! He couldn't think it yet. Maybe her neck had not been broken. Maybe there was still a chance she hadn't finished strangling.

He ran to her and rolled her faceup, then worked the noose free of her neck, his hands trembling so hard he could barely hold the rope. *She's not breathing, notbreathingnotbreathingnotbreathing* . . .

No! He had to stop, rein in his panic, and swallow back the sob that tried to burst free of his chest like a Minié ball in reverse. He pulled her close, both arms wrapped around her body, rocking her, while he fought to swallow back hot tears of rage and grief. He couldn't let go, not even for a moment, for that would mean that she was gone. That would—

Cold suspicion radiated through his center as his gaze fell on the shay. Still here . . . What did that mean? He couldn't imagine Russell would have left it.

Clumsily, his mind worked to fit the pieces into

place. Russell would have used the horse to hang Yvette, but where was he—and it?

Though he was still reeling with shock, Gabe knew he had to take Yvette with him on the horse. They had to get away from here before Darien Russell came back for that carriage. Ignoring the agony of his burnt hands, he hoisted her over the black gelding's withers and climbed aboard the saddle just behind her.

Along the back of Yvette's neck he could see a row of dusky bruises already blooming where the noose had bit. He ignored the impulse to lay his ear against her back to try to hear if her heart beat. God help him, he couldn't do it until they were well away from here, and even then, he wasn't certain that he wanted to. As long as he didn't know for sure, he wouldn't have to face—

Cutting short the thought, Gabe dug his heels into his tired mount's flanks. But they never left the clearing.

A gunshot cracked only an instant before the black horse staggered two steps and then fell, spilling both Yvette and Gabe out of the saddle. Gabe rolled to his feet to face Darien Russell, who had a revolver aimed toward the center of his chest.

"You killed her, you bastard!" Gabe shouted, too upset to give a damn whether or not Russell pulled the trigger. All he had to live for, all he had of hope, lay crumpled and unmoving at his feet. The only thing that he had left to wish for was the chance to pound his fists through Darien Russell's face.

"She forced me to kill them," Russell told him, and Gabe noticed that his face was ashen, as if what he had done had left him nauseated. "That made her a murderess."

Gabe stepped forward. "You sick, lying bastard, I'll send you to hell."

"You go on ahead," Darien told him, a malicious smile warming his tawny eyes, "and keep your little harlot company."

Had Russell cut her down to inflict still more torture? Yvette moaned with the pain that pounded through her head and surged through her neck into her body. How her poor lungs ached with the effort of refilling! Her soul, too, protested her return. She didn't want to leave Marie, who had embraced her warmly and then promised to take her to see François. François? *Juste ciel,* but that must mean that he had died, too. That was why the family hadn't heard from him since his unit had moved to Tennessee. She wanted to see her brother, to ask him if the Yankees—

Why had Darien taken her away from that bright place, where she could be with her sister and her brother? Why couldn't he let her die in peace?

A voice pulled her back to this world.

"You sick, lying bastard, I'll send you to hell." Gabriel's voice, so very angry.

"You go on ahead"—Darien spoke this time, and bursts of panic detonated in her stomach—"and keep your little harlot company."

He meant to hurt Gabriel! But what could she do to prevent it? It took all her strength to force open her eyes and peer through the strands of loose hair that had fallen across her face.

She heard a gun click on an empty chamber. Her vision focused just in time to see the smugness evaporate from Darien's features. An instant later, Gabe leapt at him, knocking him to the ground, hammering him again and again, long beyond the point where the captain stopped resisting.

Yvette had never seen such savage fury. In spite of what Darien had done to her today, in spite of the horrible way he'd killed her sister, she despised most of all the transformation he had wrought in Gabriel, who had loved so gently. God help her, she would not let Darien turn him into a murderer!

"No . . ." she moaned, putting all her heart into that single syllable. Even so, the word was barely audible.

Yet Gabriel froze, immobilized by the unexpected sound. His fist stopped half an inch from Russell's face, as if he'd been paralyzed by terror. He didn't turn toward her or even move his eyes, and she found herself wondering what he thought he would see if he looked toward her. Did he think the sound of her voice just another apparition, like that of his dead brother on the battlefield? Did he imagine if he turned his head, he would see her body, now beginning to cool and stiffen with the finality of death?

Instead, he kept his gaze fixed on Russell's bloodstreaked face. Even from this vantage, Yvette could see that the captain's nose was surely broken and several of his teeth had collapsed into jagged shards. Yet his breath rasped noisily through his shattered mouth. He might be unconscious, but he lived.

At least for now.

"No," she repeated, this time slightly louder. "There's been enough death . . . Gabriel."

This time, he could no more help turning toward her than the great river can help moving toward the sea. She attempted—without success—to push herself up on one elbow. Her raven tresses, which had come unbound, fell across her eyes to completely obscure her vision.

She heard his footsteps and sensed, rather than saw, Gabriel kneeling down beside her. He brushed her hair from her face with a caress so tender that she barely felt his fingertips.

"Oh, God," he whispered. "Thank God for you, Yvette."

Carefully, he pulled her into his embrace, rocking her as one might an infant. She felt moisture where their faces touched. It might have been his tears or her own or both. It didn't matter; nothing mattered except that love remained. And that they both lived to see it through.

"You stand accused of horse theft, Private," the white-haired colonel said sternly. Though he sat in one of the parlor's chairs, he had not invited Gabe to do the same.

Gabe had lost whatever patience he'd possessed for this sort of idiocy. His thoughts were with Yvette, who had been taken upstairs to be examined by a doctor. He'd explained her case first, from what had happened with her sister to her desperate flight toward safety. But Colonel Patterson had yet to comment on anything he'd said.

Outside, thunder murmured, and the first raindrops tapped at the windows.

"Are you angrier because I whipped an officer or because I dared think for myself?" Gabe demanded. "God knows, this army has done its best at every turn to punish soldiers for the slightest sign of personal initiative."

Colonel Patterson opened his mouth as if to protest, but Gabe cut him off before a single word erupted.

"I understood Russell's intentions when I saw him take Yvette—Miss Augeron," he hastily corrected. "I'm still army personnel, so I used an army mount to follow. Would you rather I allowed the captain to lynch this woman because he was an officer? Would you prefer—"

"Calm down, soldier!" the colonel interrupted. Pointing to the other chair, he ordered, "Now sit."

After taking a deep breath, Gabe complied. Shouting at this man wasn't going to help either Yvette or him out of this mess.

A pair of kittens bounded into the room. A silver tabby chased its gray-and-white littermate beneath the colonel's desk.

Patterson paid them no heed but continued speaking to Gabriel, "Fortunately for you, I received a telegram this afternoon from a Colonel Jeffers, stationed in New Orleans. He asked me to detain Captain Russell. Apparently evidence has been found to implicate him in the same crimes of which Miss Augeron had been accused."

"You *knew*? Then how could you let him—?"

"I'm not going to ask you again, Private Davis. You will remain silent until such time as I ask you a question or give you leave to speak. Is that understood? Answer me." A flash of lightning lit his stern face, and the rain came faster, harder.

Reluctantly, Gabe nodded. "Yes, sir."

"I did not receive this telegram until after Captain Russell left the premises. I sent soldiers to arrest him, but by that time, he'd disappeared. Private Davis, I am given to understand that you've become involved with this young woman. Is that true?"

"Yes, sir," Gabe admitted. He had no intention of denying it, even if he would be punished for consorting with an enemy.

"You're in love with her?"

Gabe nodded, wondering how far Patterson's line of questioning would go. He refused to reveal private details. Because, colonel or not, Gabe knew he'd pound the man who made lewd comments about the sacred act he and Yvette had shared.

Surprisingly, Patterson's expression softened. "I've seen a lot of ugliness during this war, on both sides of the Mason-Dixon line. So much that I thought I'd grown immune to horror. But when I saw the bruises on that poor girl's neck ... What Russell did deserves—"

He shook his head, and anger flicked across his features—real anger, not the annoyance he had shown at Gabe's outburst. "I'm only glad it was you that caught the bastard and not me. Otherwise, he wouldn't have lived long enough to stand trial. And long enough to experience the legal hanging he deserves."

"You think he will hang?"

"Without a question."

The colonel stood and offered Gabriel a crisp salute. "You're a brave man, Private, to steal a horse and face an armed enemy to try to prevent the murder of a Southern woman. A very brave man, and I'll see personally that you don't suffer for it."

Gabe rose and returned the salute. "Thank you, sir, but what about Miss Augeron ... Yvette?"

"We'll need to take her statement and get this sorted out, but if what you've told me can be corroborated, she has no more to fear."

Something distracted Patterson, and he peered beneath his desk. Raising his voice, he shouted, "Lieutenant Thompson, come and get these kittens out of here!"

The gray-and-white fugitive made a dash for freedom, but Gabriel scooped it up before it could escape.

"If you'd like," he offered, scarcely believing what it was that he was saying, "I'd be happy to take this little rascal off your hands."

Chapter Seventeen

Beautiful that war and all its deeds of carnage
must in time be utterly lost,
That the hands of the sisters Death and Night
incessantly softly wash again, and ever again,
this soil'd world.

—Walt Whitman,
from "Reconciliation"

April 29, 1865
Memphis, Tennessee

Yvette sat on the bed, staring numbly through the window. Mrs. Beacon had it scrubbed so clean that only the slight distortion caused by its thickness indicated she was looking through clear glass instead of air. Subtle as the glass was, she felt cut off behind it, separated from the world she had reentered.

As she glanced down at the telegram, the same sense of unreality persisted, for the words confirmed a fact she'd known already. Her brother, François, had been killed by Union soldiers in one of the final battles of the war.

The fingers of her left hand touched the line of tenderness at her neck, and her skin rippled with a chill. A Yank had done that, too, but against the odds, *her* Yankee had saved her. Her mind could reconcile what had happened, but how could she be sure of her heart?

The telegram that Mrs. Beacon had delivered swam into focus, its message somehow magnified by welling tears.

Will arrive soon to escort you New Orleans. François dead of wounds rec'd. Tenn. raid in February. Body to be returned home for interment.

André Augeron

Her brother had died in Tennessee. How far from here? she wondered. Uncle André's message indicated he felt she must return to the Quarter, just as François would be coming home this one, last time.

Yvette had thought that with Uncle André there would be some choice, that he would ask her what she wanted instead of just assuming. She'd thought he would be different, since he'd broken away from the claustrophobic expectations of New Orleans in general and of Grandmère Augeron in particular.

Will arrive soon to escort you New Orleans. Those words suggested that to his way of thinking, she was nothing but a young, unmarried woman, someone whose decisions must be made by wiser heads. He would try to do well for her. Just as they all would, but they would never think of asking her her mind. After all, her last attempts at independent thought had resulted in such tragedy, such scandal, that it was a wonder they would take her back at all. She knew beyond doubt that no one in the family would ever admit that her father's judgment of Darien Russell had been flawed. Just as no one would ever believe that Yvette, who had stepped beyond the limits of her convent schooling and her strict upbringing, had not been somehow guilty of causing this whole disgraceful episode.

And if she tried to tell them that she wished to marry Gabriel, a common Yankee soldier, they'd lock her away, convinced the strain of these past weeks had driven her out of her mind. They'd never allow her to speak to him, much less see him, again.

And yet the thought of deliberately turning her back on all of them—especially poor François— broke her heart. He'd been the brother closest to her own age, and Yvette remembered the hours they all had passed together in the nursery, under the watchful eyes of Mama Séverine, a slave whose embraces had been far warmer than their distant mother's. François had been less inclined to rowdiness than either of his brothers. His tastes ran more to reading and to music, and both his sisters loved him for it. In fact, given his gentler nature, Yvette had been surprised when he had volunteered. Even now, she wondered if he'd done it to make up for Jules's weak heart and somehow ease their brother's guilt.

And now he'd died because Jules had not been strong enough to go to war. Thinking of her brothers brought grief crashing over her like a fresh wave. Grief for Pierre's lost arm, for François's death, and for the guilt that would likely fester in Jules's soul.

Could she truly abandon all of them to run off with Gabriel?

A tap at the door interrupted her thoughts and startled the gray-and-white kitten that Gabriel had brought to try to cheer her. Chanson, as she'd been christened, puffed out her fur and hid behind Yvette's skirt.

Yvette's heart beat faster. For a moment, she'd forgotten that Darien Russell was in Officers' Hospital, under guard. She no longer had to fear that he would find her.

Nor was she certain she wished for Uncle André to come and solve her problems. Praying it would not be him, she scooped up the kitten, then cracked open the door.

"Oh, Gabriel, come in, please," she told him, feeling a bit guilty they hadn't disabused Mrs. Beacon of the fiction that they were man and wife.

Without a word of greeting or even a touch, he walked past her, his eyes so filled with pain that it could only mean one thing.

"You have found them?" Yvette asked, speaking of the friends he'd gone in search of, whose disappearance clearly haunted him.

She set Chanson down on a chair. She wanted badly to drape her uninjured arm around Gabriel, to pull him close to her. But something warned her that her touch might be unwelcome, so she hesitated, fingers trembling like marsh grasses touched by wind.

"I went from hospital to hospital to see if their names might have been left off the lists. Then I looked at body after body, and . . ."

He looked at her, and it was as if he saw her for

the first time. But instead of turning away, he stepped nearer and pulled her gently against him.

She said nothing, trusting him to tell her when he could, knowing that the contact of their bodies relayed the contents of their hearts far more perfectly than the vagaries of language.

"Colonel Patterson says they all must be presumed dead," Gabriel continued. "He says that many of the victims will never be recovered. But I can't—I won't—give up on them. They wouldn't give up on me. Those men kept me *alive!*"

Yvette nodded against him. "It is the waiting that's the hardest. Those days after Marie disappeared . . . and then my brother François. One would think that all the torment of not knowing would somehow soften the blow of finding out."

Her voice broke, and Gabriel pulled her even closer, then began to stroke her hair.

"Tell me," he whispered, and she felt the warm moisture of his breath against her crown.

The words lodged in her throat, so she pulled away to retrieve the telegram. Handing it to him, she waited solemnly while he read.

"I'm sorry," Gabriel told her. Then he hesitated, as if he feared the words he would next say. "What will you do now?"

He had asked her. Unlike Uncle André and her family, he had asked *her* what she would do. And that one question made up her mind completely.

"I will tell my uncle to go on without me. I want to stay with you while you keep looking," Yvette answered. "Everything else can wait."

And she knew she meant it. *She* would wait. Uncle André, her parents, and her grandmère wouldn't, *couldn't,* understand. But Marie would ... just as would François. They would both want her to be happy with the man she loved.

"No," he whispered, turning her face toward his. And this time, when he spoke to her, she breathed in every level of his meaning. *"Everything* cannot. That's one thing that I've learned. Nothing, nothing lasts forever, so putting off happiness is inexcusable."

With that, he closed the gap between them and took her into his arms. They kissed, neither in control, neither dominated by the other, but only by the power of a passion based on love.

When finally he pulled his mouth away, it was to tell her. "Marry me, Yvette. Please ... marry me this minute."

She took his hand and kissed it, then gently nipped the fingertips, just as he had hers before. Smiling at his gasp of pleasure, she helped him undo the top buttons of her bodice. "I will marry you today, but first ... there is one pleasure that we need not postpone."

AUTHOR'S NOTE

I hope you have enjoyed *Against the Odds*. To read Jacob Fuller's story, look for *Trust to Chance* in January of 2001. An excerpt is available online at www.gynethathlee.com.

More than 1,700 people lost their lives as a result of the destruction of the *Sultana*, making it the deadliest maritime disater in the history of the United States. But the yearly death tolls of the Civil War and Abraham Lincoln's assassination a few weeks earlier had numbed the public, so news about the steamboat accident faded, leaving few traces in most history books.

This novel is a work of fiction. However, many of the events are real, as are several minor characters, including Capt. J. Cass Mason, Capt. Frederick Speed, R. G. Taylor, Nathan Wintringer, and Major William Fidler. These characters' actions and conversations were derived from historical accounts of the final days of the *Sultana*. Their thoughts and motivations, however, are of my own construction.

To learn more about the *Sultana*, visit *www.sultana.org* on the web or explore the books mentioned in the acknowledgments of this novel.

ABOUT THE AUTHOR

Gwyneth Atlee lives in The Woodlands, Texas, with her husband, son, and a retired racing greyhound. Gwyneth is the author of *Touched by Fire, Night Winds,* and *Canyon Song* as well as the upcoming *Trust to Chance,* the story of Jacob Fuller from *Against the Odds.* She loves hearing from readers at P.O. Box 131342, The Woodlands, Texas 77393-1342 or via E-mail at *gwynethatlee@usa.net.* Learn more about her upcoming releases and sample excerpts at *http://atlee.cjb.net* on the Web.

Put a Little Romance in Your Life With
Constance O'Day-Flannery